LEXI HODGES

WAR OF HER HEART

"He's your first love. I intend to be your last."
-Klaus Mikaelson

Contents

1

Chapter 1

Violet

The rustling of the fabric of his pants being rubbed together while the servants folded them. The click of the clasp on his leather bag as the servants filled it with his clothes. The most wretched sounds I had ever heard.

I should have been the one doing those things. I should have packed his clothes and helped him ready for his trip. But I couldn't. Every task the servants accomplished—every fucking thing they packed—brought us one step closer to his inevitable departure, where he would leave to begin his engagement to another.

I didn't know what I did to the gods to deserve to have to watch the love of my life walk out the door to spend the next six months getting to know his future wife.

Actually, I did.

That was what happened when you fell in love with someone so far out of your reach that you shouldn't have had him to begin with.

Calum Evers. The Sovereign of the Mountain Realm. He was always destined to marry the daughter of another Sovereign, but I didn't know it would happen so fast.

We lived in the kingdom of Alentara. Thousands of years ago, before there was any order every type of faerie and creature lived together under pure chaos. They fought each other to survive. Fae—the most humanlike of the faeries—were among the easiest prey because they had no powers to protect themselves. They stayed hidden, constantly looking over their shoulders.

Then, a powerful witch named Evidannan came along. She summoned every fae to the center of the land. She told them of her plan to magically split the land into realms where everyone and everything was placed in the realm that they could live the most peacefully in. She painted a picture of order where instead of being hunted by creatures, fae would be given power and protection in their realms. All that the witch asked was that the center of Alentara, where she was to complete the spell, becomes her home. Eager for a place of safety, the fae were willing to do whatever it took to help her make it happen.

Of course, each realm needed someone to rule and keep order in the realm, so she held a series of games where any fae could participate. The games basically turned into a fight to the death where only the smartest and strongest survived. She then assigned each of the winners a realm and gave them a gift to help rule their realm. All that was left was to have the Sovereigns give her a vial of blood so she could complete her spell. When she spoke the spell, the earth shifted and magical borders split the land into seven realms, each with a distinct climate and landscape to meet the needs of the faeries and creatures she placed there. The seven realms became the

Mountain, Ice, Night, Forest, Flower, Ocean, and Sun Realms. While fae could move between the realms freely, other faeries and creatures became trapped in the realm Evidannan chose for them.

What the seven Sovereigns didn't know at the time was that the blood they gave for the spell linked them to Evidannan, which gave her control over them. Control of the gifts she blessed them with. She gave them their power, and she could easily take it away if she wanted to.

She became known as Queen Mother, ruling Alentara from the center of the land. The Sovereigns feared losing their gifts and their realms, so they did everything Queen Mother told them to do, without question. Whatever she wanted became law.

Queen Mother told the Sovereigns they must marry from the royal bloodlines of the seven realms in order to keep their blood pure, which is why many ended up in arranged marriages.

I thought Calum and I would have a few hundred years before we had to face this, but after everything that happened the last few years, everything changed.

When I was still a small faeling, my father became the Commander of the Mountain Realm's Guard and he moved us into the castle. It was customary for the Commander to live in the castle to ensure that the Sovereign was always protected. Commanders were raised in the Guard where they knew if they wanted the chance to become Commander, the highest title in the Guard of each realm, they must focus their entire lives on that, meaning no wife, no children. Obviously, my father never planned on having a child.

He also never planned on meeting my mother and falling in

3

love.

She ended up pregnant, and he dropped his dream of becoming Commander and married my mother. She died during childbirth, something unheard of among fae, which left my father alone with a baby that he had no idea how to take care of.

He realized almost immediately that something wasn't right with me. I guess that came with whatever curse that killed my mother. He could feel my heart stop, as if I died for a second, and then start back. He traveled to the Land of the Healers with me looking for answers. I was the only thing he had left of my mother, and he couldn't let anything happen to me. He needed to protect the only piece he had left of her at all costs.

No one knew how to cure what I had because they had never seen a faerie that had something wrong with their heart. He spent years traveling within the Land of the Healers with me, going door to door, begging for help. He finally came across a healer that came up with a solution. He developed a medicine that I had to take at the same time every day, and it pretty much cured my condition. I just couldn't ever miss a dosage because he feared that one day my heart would stop, and it wouldn't start back.

After our travels, we came back to the Mountain Realm, and my father worked as a border guard. He hired a nursemaid to take care of me since he was busy with work. Astrid took care of my every need, and when I was old enough, she began to teach me. I learned everything from basic skills a lady should know to how to communicate with any faerie I may come across—which seemed impossible given I was never allowed to leave our home.

One day while my father was working, a creature attacked

Calum's father and his Commander, and my father was the first one to arrive to help. Because he had trained his entire life to be a Commander, he was able to save both of their lives. The Commander lost his arm before my father got there, and Calum's father knew he had to get a new Commander.

He was so impressed with my father that he asked him to become the new Commander of the Mountain Realm. My father told him about me and that he couldn't leave me, and Calum's father didn't care. He told my father to bring me to the castle with him.

My father and the Sovereign, Calum's father, became very close so we spent a lot of our time with him and his family. Calum and I were in the same stage of life so we played together very well. At first, it was an innocent friendship. I mean we were only faelings. It was nothing but chasing each other around the gardens, playing hide-and-seek in the castle, and sleepovers where Calum would tell me scary stories about the Night Realm, which is the worst and most evil realm in the kingdom.

After we reached our teenage years, Calum started avoiding me and anytime we were around each other, he would ignore me and act like he couldn't stand to be around me. It hurt because he was my best friend. My only friend. Being a lady in the Mountain Realm wasn't easy. We were meant to be seen but not heard, simply pretty things to serve the men. But it was different with Calum. Since we were so close, no one dared to say anything to me when I was with the son of the Sovereign, and Calum never treated me as less than him. One day, I finally got tired of being ignored so I went to his room to confront him.

I'll never forget how he looked me up and down and said,

5

"Fuck it" before he pushed me against the wall and kissed me.

He wasn't avoiding me because he didn't like me; he was avoiding me because he had feelings for me. I had always had a crush on him, and when he kissed me it opened the floodgates of feelings.

We knew it was doomed from the beginning because he had to marry someone else chosen for him before he was even born. We would sneak around because we knew if his parents found out, they would put an end to it. He told me he loved me within a fortnight of our first kiss, and I cried because I knew that it didn't matter in the long run. He told me he could never love someone the way he loved me so I ran out of his room and avoided him for a week.

I couldn't get any deeper into the mess we made because we both knew how it would end: me, brokenhearted and married to someone my father deemed suitable, and Calum, ruling the realm with I can only imagine to be a goddess-like wife.

When it was time for our family's weekly dinner with the Sovereign and his family that week, I tried to fake a headache, but my father didn't believe me and made me go anyway. I couldn't bear the thought of looking at Calum after what had happened, but I didn't have a choice.

Of course, I had to sit in my usual seat right next to him, but I avoided looking in his direction until he said something I couldn't ignore. "Father, do you think the arranged marriage thing is something that I really have to do?"

I choked on my drink at his words. I gasped for air while everyone at the table gave me a mix of concerned and disgusted looks, then I quickly quieted myself and brought my attention to the napkin in my lap.

"Son, we've talked about this," his father said, sounding

almost remorseful. "It's a tradition that must be followed. Something like that is not up for discussion. I wasn't given a choice. I had to marry your mother."

"Wow, thanks for that," Celine said with a bite to her words.

"Oh, Celine. You know that I fell in love with you." Thank the gods I was looking down so they didn't see my eyes nearly roll in the back of my head at his response.

"But Father, what if I'm already in love?"

Fuck me, I thought. *Here it goes.*

"Calum, what are you talking about? The only person you're ever around is Vi—" He stopped mid-sentence when he looked down to see that Calum grabbed my hand and set it on the table with his covering it.

"You little bitch!" Celine screamed at me as she jumped out of her chair.

"Celine! Sit down and shut up," the Sovereign commanded his wife. He had always been a very calm and collected man, but I had never seen him look so angry.

I turned to my father to see the fear in his eyes. Fear of what would happen to me for putting myself in this position.

My father had always thought he had to protect me because of my heart condition. He called me his little bird. He'd always done everything in his power to ensure I was safe, but he knew he wouldn't be able to protect me from this.

He couldn't protect me from Celine.

She was the worst type of creature you could ever imagine. Beauty that acted as a mask for the evil that was inside of her. Her beauty was exotic in the realm filled with brown haired, brown eyed faes. She had porcelain skin with crystal-blue eyes and long hair as white as the snow that fell on the mountaintops during winter. But what made her horrible was how her insides contradicted her outsides. She was hateful, vengeful, and power hungry. She would put on a show for the Sovereign, though. If he was around, she would act like a helpless deer and always made sure she was never at fault for anything that happened.

She didn't care about her son's happiness. He was just a pawn that she could control and use to her advantage.

She had been planning his arranged marriage since the day he was born. She wanted to make sure his future wife came from whichever realm that she could gain the most from.

If I was in the picture, it would ruin everything for her.

"This ends immediately. You two may hate me for this but it's for your own good. The longer this goes on, the worse it will hurt because no matter how you feel, Calum will be marrying someone else," Calum's father said as he got up and left the room.

My father looked at me with such worry in his eyes. I know he wanted to stay—to ensure I was safe from the evil that shot daggers in my direction—but his duty was to our Sovereign, and he had to be with him. My father quickly walked after the Sovereign to catch up with him.

After Celine made sure her husband was out of hearing distance, she got up from her chair and walked straight over to me. She bent over so she was right in my face and said, "How dare you. We let you move in with the Commander as a courtesy and you repay us by doing this? Corrupting my son? I will make you pay for this, you little whore."

"Mother, stop," Calum whispered. I looked over to him to see him looking at his plate. He was strong and confident in everything he did except for anything that had to do with his mother.

8

She was in control. Always.

Celine stood up, smoothed her dress, and walked out of the room. I was hurt that Calum couldn't take up for me more than he did, but I knew my place.

The Sovereign's order didn't stop us from being together. We just continued to sneak around and spend every night together.

After a while, we got less inconspicuous about our relationship. I know that Calum's father knew we were still together, but he never said anything. He was a good man, and he knew that we were happy. If there had been a way out of an arranged marriage for Calum, he would've found it. All he ever wanted was for Calum to be happy—unlike Calum's mother who never showed her son love.

If I could've chosen which one of Calum's parents would've died fighting a Reacher, I would've pushed Celine into the Reacher's den myself.

It'd been three years since Calum's father died, but it felt like yesterday. His death tore my father to pieces. He was sworn to protect him in duty, and he was also his best friend. He couldn't have prevented what happened that day, but he still blamed himself. It didn't help that Calum's mother blamed my father too.

Calum, on the other hand, hadn't shown any emotion. Anytime I'd tried to talk to him about it, he changed the subject. It's like showing emotion would make him weak. He was immediately given the title "Sovereign," but he wasn't given the control of the realm. Instead, the Advisors of the realm were given the power to make the decisions, which would have been fine, except that his mother had snaked her way into quietly controlling the Advisors behind closed doors.

9

The Advisors had been Calum's father's Advisors during his entire rule, and they had gotten to know Celine personally. . . Well, the version that she wanted them to know.

The Queen Mother required her Sovereigns to have a group of Advisors that they chose themselves. They helped with taking care of the small tedious things like complaints from faeries in the cities to ensuring certain creatures were staying within their territories. In the event of an untimely death of a Sovereign, the Advisors made every decision for their realm until the Sovereign's eldest child came of age and was able to take over control of the realm.

One problem with that: Queen Mother never specified an age.

So over the centuries, the realms interpreted this rule differently. .

Some realms picked a specific age, like one hundred, which was right when fae stopped aging physically. It took us one hundred years to look like we were twenty-five in human years.

Some realms chose to interpret it based on the "maturity age," which to them meant the age they took their wife. Sometimes that happened when the Sovereign was eighty and sometimes, if they were stubborn enough, not until they were hundreds of years old.

Can you guess which interpretation our realm used? Calum would officially become Sovereign and get all of the power that comes with it when he married.

We never expected Calum's father's death, so we thought it would be centuries before he became Sovereign. To us, the arranged marriage thing didn't seem real because it wouldn't be required until it was time for Calum to become Sovereign.

10

You would think that his mother would want to drag it out as long as possible so she could keep her power by controlling the Advisors. She could keep pushing out an engagement for hundreds of years, which would give me and Calum a long life together, if she wanted to.

But there were two reasons she wouldn't do that:

1. She hated me.
2. She knew it would be detrimental for the Mountain Realm.

Calum being so young made our realm vulnerable and an easy target for another realm to attack.

It wouldn't be the first realm to fall from being too weak. That was the Sun Realm. It happened before I was born, but I'd read about it. They were once considered the most powerful realm because of one of the types of creatures that roamed the Sun Realm's land—phoenixes. They looked like fae, but from what I read, they could shape-shift into bird form, burst into flames, burn down entire cities, and reincarnate if they were killed.

Some of the Sovereigns feared that these creatures were too powerful and that they one day might try to take over the other realms, so they found a way to kill them, permanently. It was a complete genocide. They sent armies into the phoenixes' village within the Sun Realm and killed them all—even the babies.

The Sovereign of the Sun Realm tried to stop the armies but he wasn't enough, and they killed him too.

With the death of the Sovereign, who didn't have an heir, and the death of the Sun Realm's strongest protectors, the realm fell. The faeries and creatures of the Sun Realm seemed to disappear. It seemed like no one knew what happened to them—or where they may have gone.

Celine had spies in several other realms, and they had heard gossip about "the weak and broken Mountain Realm." She feared that another realm was going to make a move to destroy our realm.

She decided that the best option would be an alliance with another realm. She knew that it would have to be a strong alliance that the other realms would fear. And she did just that.

She managed to arrange an engagement with the worst realm of all.

The Night Realm.

2

Chapter 2

Violet

We'd been together for over two decades now and no matter how hard Calum fought his Advisors on this, he's still being forced to spend the next six months getting to know his future wife. A six-month engagement at the female's home realm was customary so the male could get to know her family before they moved back to his realm.

Calum had told me over and over again that he's not going to even give her a chance and that he was going to figure out a way out of this before it's too late. I told him I believed him but I knew that I was going to be brokenhearted in the end. I had no doubt that he loved me, but that didn't mean he still would after he spent so much time with someone that had spent her entire life preparing to be the wife of a Sovereign.

Tomorrow morning, he was leaving for the Night Realm.

"Violet, you have my heart," he said as he cradled my face in his hands.

I tried to hold back the tears, but knowing that this was

probably the last time I'd ever be with him was too much to bear.

"Please . . . tell me what you want," he said as he looked into my eyes, searching for an answer.

I want to be with you forever. I want to run away from this realm and be with you without anyone interfering in our relationship. That's what I wanted to say, but all I could choke out between the tears was, "I want you."

I grabbed his shirt, and our lips crashed together. I'd tried so hard to keep it together and have hope that he would come back to me. But in the likely chance that this was the last night I'd ever be with him, all I wanted was to feel every inch of him on me—*in me.*

I tugged at his shirt instructing him to take it off. In the second that our lips broke for him to pull his shirt off over his head, I ached for his touch. If I couldn't bear a second without him, how was I to survive six months? Or eternity?

Calum placed his hand around the back of my neck and started to push down. I knew what he wanted. And I wanted to give it to him.

I lived to please him.

He was sleeping soundly soon enough, but no matter how hard I tried to just live in this moment with him, I couldn't shut my mind off.

I lay there staring at my torn dress on the floor. Calum had literally ripped my dress in half—too impatient to take the time to correctly take it off of me. His strength had always been a turn on for me. The first Sovereign of the Mountain Realm was given the gift of strength, and every Sovereign since has inherited it. All fae were strong, but I'd seen Calum push through a brick wall . . . on accident.

14

Even with that, he had always been so careful with me. I was a lot smaller than him. He's 6'2" while I was 5'3" on a good day, and he could snap me like a twig if he wasn't careful. But I'd always felt so safe with him. I was terrified of him being gone for the next six months.

I'd been so worried about losing him forever, but I was just going to have to have faith in him and that he would find his way back to me. He'd never given me a reason not to trust him. The only way I would be able to get through the next six months was to truly believe he'd come back, without a wife.

I would be nothing without Calum. Ever since I moved into the castle, he had been my whole focus. My father had to devote all of his time to Calum's father which meant his worry for me only got worse. Since he couldn't protect me, the only way he felt I would be safe is if I never went past the castle walls. There was enough land to roam within the walls—it wasn't like I was trapped in a room—but it limited my social access. I had Calum, the only other fae around my age, and Astrid, who was my caregiver and tutor. They were the only ones I had true bonds with. Other than the time I spent with them, and seeing my father and Calum's parents for an hour at dinner once a week, I was pretty much alone.

Astrid left when I reached adulthood to care for another faeling like she had done for hundreds of years before me so all I had left was Calum. And he could be leaving me forever.

He had to come back to me.

The sun came up too quickly. I barely slept last night because I didn't want to miss a second of being with him, memorizing every one of his features. His dark brown hair that ended just above his shoulders and had the slightest wave to it. It always seemed a little messy, which made me smile given the grace and authoritative presence he had. Even closed, as they were now, I could never forget what his eyes looked like beneath his thick eyebrows. They were deep brown, and the way he looked at me with them . . . he could get anything out of me with one look.

And his body—he was pure muscle. His shoulders were broad, and his arms filled any shirt he put on.

Calum favored his father in every possible way. Looks, personality, and even the way they treated Celine—placing her on a pedestal and giving in to her every wish.

His having no features from his mother was normal, though. Heirs to the thrones of the realms always have the hair, eyes, and skin tone of the fae of their realm—another way the realms are divided. You could tell by the looks of a fae which realm they were from, and it's no different for the Sovereign of every realm. When the force of Evidannan's spell transferred all faeries and creatures to a specific realm, it took fae with them based on their appearance. Evidannan—or the spell—decided that the fae with brown hair, brown eyes, and ivory skin were now Mountain Realm fae. Even though Sovereigns marry daughters of Sovereigns from other realms, the Sovereign's features overpower their wife's features when they had faeling.

Thank the gods Calum didn't act like his mother, but I did wish he didn't have a blind eye for her just like his father had.

A slight knock on the door snapped me back to reality and told me it was time. No matter how hard it was, I wouldn't let myself cry while we said our goodbyes. I knew it was just as hard for him to leave as it was for me to watch him leave.

While we weren't secretive about our relationship, our "affair," as Celine liked to call it, could never get out because it would have caused a scandal that would ruin our realm. We knew that a few guards from the Night Realm were set to arrive at any minute to help assist in Calum's travels, so we said our goodbyes in his chambers to ensure no outsiders saw us together.

A few of our guards would be going with Calum, and while they were capable of stopping any danger within the Mountain Realm and the Ice Realm, which they also had to travel through, once they crossed the border into the Night Realm, they were as good as defenseless.

Every realm had creatures and faeries that roamed, some good and some bad. But from what I'd read in our history books and the stories Calum used to tell me to freak me out, there were no worse monsters than the ones in the Night Realm.

We were always told that evil came out at night. That the monsters in our nightmares hid in the dark. Yeah, that pretty much summed up the Night Realm.

Along with the few Mountain Realm guards, my father would be with Calum. My father's duty transferred to Calum when Calum's father died.

"I love you, Violet," Calum said, as he knew it was time for him to go. He cupped my cheeks and kissed me one last time before he transferred out of his chambers.

"I. . . love you too," I said to no one. This wasn't the last time I would see him before he left, but it was the last time he would acknowledge my existence.

When I went downstairs to tell my father goodbye, I would be nothing but the Commander's daughter. Nothing to Calum.

Calum stood in the courtyard, trying one last time to reason with the Advisors, telling them that he would be able to protect

17

the realm on his own, but they wouldn't listen.

I knew one way he could put an end to this.

Rip apart every one of those pretentious dicks, command obedience from everyone watching and *take* control of the realm. It's his birthright. One show of his power would be enough to prove he was able to protect the realm without an alliance with the Night Realm.

He wouldn't be the first to go against Queen Mother's rule, and she did nothing to the last Sovereign that took control without being "of age."

But Calum wouldn't do it. He's too good.

Again, what did I do to ever deserve him?

As I watched Calum from a respectable distance, my father walked up to stand at my side, looking ahead in his military stance with his hands behind his back. This was the only way he ever appeared when he was in public.

My father was handsome with long, light brown hair that he always kept neatly braided down his back. His brown eyes were kind, but I hadn't seen him relaxed enough to show that since Calum's father's death. Now, they were always alert, looking for possible threats of danger.

Even though, as fae, he shouldn't age, it seemed like the stress of his station had given him slight wrinkles on his forehead and around his eyes. He always seemed tense now.

"Little bird," he said as he looked ahead, "I need you to be careful while I'm gone."

"What do you mean?" I was puzzled. I may have gotten comfortable here since I was with Calum and no one would dare to do something to me in fear of angering him, but I knew my place. I was female. I must keep my head down and do as I was told.

"I mean, I need you to avoid Celine," he whispered so no one could hear us.

"Father, she hates me. What do you think I'm going to do? Ask her to tea?" I rolled my eyes as I questioned him. I was being nothing but a smart-ass, but his request warranted it.

My father whipped his head around, breaking his stance. I knew he was serious because I'd never seen him like this around others. "I mean it. Without Calum and me here, I fear what she may do to you."

I just looked at him, confused, unable to muster up words. She's horrible, yes, but would she actually hurt me?

"Stay in your room. I know it's a lot to ask, but I worry about your safety. I've already spoken to the servants. They will bring your meals and anything you ask for. Please, little bird. *Do not leave your room,*" he said as he pleaded with his eyes.

That really was a lot to ask. Six months confined to my room? No days spent outside in the sunlight? I would go insane. But I could tell how important this was to him. "I won't, Father."

Then he hugged me and walked over to Calum. I couldn't tell you the last time he hugged me. We weren't close at all. I loved him, and I knew he loved me, but he had always seen me more as something that needed protecting than someone who needed a personal relationship with him. He held his emotions in most of the time and only let them out when I did something that made him fear for my heart or my safety.

A hug from him worried me more than it comforted me.

Calum gave me a quick glance before ducking into the carriage, a glance no one would notice if they weren't looking for it. I watched their carriage until they were specks past the castle gates. I looked over to where Celine was standing; she was staring at me with such hate. I thought about what my father said and decided it was best if I got to my room as quickly as possible.

The worst part—I had to think about where my room was. I hadn't been in my room in a decade. I'd slept in Calum's bed every night since we stopped being secretive about our relationship. The servants had moved all of my things to his chambers.

I wondered if I should get my things, but no. Father said go to my room. I could send a servant to collect my things.

I walked as fast as I could, but it was a long walk. Two staircases down and six halls, I really wished I could transfer. Luckily the castle was built on a mountain, so even though my room was lower than the main floor, I still had a window. My room was right above the servants' quarters. It was the last floor before the rooms descended underground.

I reached my room, quickly closed my door, and locked it. As I looked around my room, I acknowledged how plain it was with nothing more than the necessities: a small, wood-framed bed, a desk with a small chair, an armoire with one handle missing, old wooden floors with wood paneling covering the walls and ceiling. A door on the right wall led to a small bathroom. Even though the entire castle was made of wood, my room felt different. The rooms of the castle were large with glass doors that were kept open most of the time with huge balconies overlooking the mountains and rivers. Oversized fireplaces made of black and gray stones that always had fires burning in them were the focal point of every room. Gold chandeliers and accents brought lavishness to the castle.

My room, on the other hand, felt like a suffocating box.

I had been living a fantasy with Calum. Without him, I was nothing but a servant in the Mountain Realm.

3

Chapter 3

Violet

Three weeks. It had been three weeks without Calum. Three weeks without leaving my room. I'd cried all I could cry. I'd solved every damn riddle book the servants brought me. I'd reread all of my favorite books from the library. I'd counted every star I could see out of my window.

Three weeks down. Only twenty-three weeks to go.

But I could not stand it any longer.

I *had* to go outside. I loved being outside. I used to lie in the grass for hours reading about new things while Calum attended meetings with his Advisors or traveled around the Mountain Realm making appearances, kissing faelings—or whatever he did.

Would Celine really hurt me? For all she knew, her son was in the Night Realm, falling in love with the one she picked.

That hurt to even think about.

But there was no way she's thinking about me. I could just sneak outside and go past the horse stables. She would never go over there. It's "beneath" her.

I was going to do it. If I stayed in my room any longer, I would go insane.

I held my breath as I unlocked the door and slowly pulled it open. What was I doing? Celine would never be down here.

Again, it was beneath her.

Literally.

I made my way to the staircase and began to climb, allowing my fingers to trace the banister on my way up. After reaching the main floor, I walked as quietly as I could to the nearest door. As I rounded the last corner before reaching the large double doors in the sitting room, the scariest thing that's ever happened to me occurred: I ran straight into Celine.

"I am so sorry, Celine," I said as I looked down. I was so afraid of what she was going to do. I didn't listen to my father's warning, and I did exactly what I shouldn't have done. Run into Celine.

"It's alright, Violet. Please just watch where you're going from now on," Celine said as she nodded and walked away.

You've got to be kidding me. Celine had never been anything but nasty to me but now that Calum wasn't here, she's almost . . . nice?

It must've been because she thought I was no longer a threat to her plan. She could believe all she wanted that Calum was going to marry the sister of the Sovereign of the Night Realm, but he's coming back to me.

Since I was no longer afraid of Celine, I spent every waking moment for the next seven weeks outside. I would lie in the part of the forest that was deemed castle property because it was inside the castle walls and listen to the critters run around and the birds sing their beautiful songs as they flew tree to tree. Being outside made the days go by faster, but only a little.

After almost three months, I woke up one morning to a knock on my door. With Calum gone, I had nothing to do, no one to see, so I was just living on my own schedule. So it was weird that someone was at my door, and even weirder when I opened the door to Celine standing there. I didn't think she had ever been on this low level of the castle.

"Calum's fiancée has asked that I come spend the rest of their engagement with them in the Night Realm, and you're coming with me."

My heart sank at those last four words. I hadn't left the castle walls since I moved here over fifty years ago, and now I was supposed to travel to the worst realm in the kingdom? That wasn't the worst part though. I was expecting the next time I saw Calum to be in a few months when he was back here, rid of his fiance forever. Now I had to see him with her. Even if he wasn't giving her a chance, I think it would have been better for me if I never had to see her.

"What? I . . . I don't think that's a good idea," I said as I shook my head.

"Well, I think you should go ahead and get to know the future lady of the castle. I mean you probably should befriend her if you plan to live here any longer. Once they are married, she may choose to throw you out of the castle. She may not be as nice as I am."

"I—"

"Maybe she will let you be one of her ladies in waiting." There was the Celine I knew. The snarky bitch was back. I don't know where she was for the last seven weeks, but I knew it wouldn't last forever.

"We are leaving tonight so pack your things. Make sure you

pack something nice for their wedding. It's only a few months away now."

My insides were screaming at her, but she wouldn't know from the look on my face. I gave her no emotion. She wasn't worth it. And it's not like I had any choice in the matter. I never had a choice.

I still didn't understand why I was going to the Night Realm with Celine. She didn't really give me a lot of time to process it. Her bullshit answer earlier was just because she was trying to get a response out of me.

I honestly didn't understand why she was even going to the Night Realm so early in the engagement. Family usually only attended the wedding. Calum must've been ignoring his fiancée, and she thought bringing in his mother would fix things. This was good. This *had* to be it. Calum was doing what he told me he would do, and this was their last attempt to make the engagement work.

Even though that idea gave me a little relief, I still had a bad feeling about going with Celine. If the Sovereign or his sister knew what I was to Calum, I'm sure they would have me killed the second I entered the Night Realm.

The first Night Realm Sovereign was the most vicious in Queen Mother's games. He played dirty, killed even when it wasn't necessary, and made enemies with every other victor. This trait was passed down to every Night Realm Sovereign thereafter.

But the one ruling now . . . he made the others look like angels. He was born with the gift of wielding force fields—the gift all Night Realm Sovereigns had—but he also had other extraordinary powers, and a cold heart. He had no love for anyone or anything. He became Sovereign when he was still a teenager. He murdered his father and *took* control.

From the moment he killed his father, his powers amplified. They said that you could feel the surge of power radiate throughout the entire kingdom. His power was so strong that the shadows surrendered to him. They became an extension of him, and he could do anything through his shadows. They devoured his enemies without him having to lift a finger. His abilities were not like anything the kingdom had seen, so no one dared to try to stop him, not even the Queen Mother— which may be why she did nothing when he became Sovereign before he was of age.

I shuddered at the thought of what the shadow king would do if he found out about me and Calum. I just had to trust that Celine's attempts to keep the news of our relationship within the castle walls worked. And trusting Celine was a scary thought.

It took us a few days to make it to the Night Realm. The one exciting part about going to the Night Realm was getting to see what the outside world looked like, but I was utterly disappointed. We had to travel through the Ice Realm and for as far as I could see, it was nothing but flat land covered in ice. We traveled through a part where there were no cities or villages, so we couldn't find shelter to rest at night. We had to sleep in the carriage while Celine forced the guards to stay awake to continue our journey.

When we made it to the Night Realm, I expected to see what I saw in the drawings in the books I had read, which was darkness, dead trees, and no signs of life. Instead, we traveled on a green path with large firs lining both sides of the path. Oddly enough, it looked exactly like the Mountain Realm.

Celine was just as confused as I was. She had never been to

the Night Realm before, but she knew what she saw wasn't right. She said the Sovereign must've done this to welcome his new family.

I nodded in response, but I didn't believe that could be the reason. Why would the shadow king care? He cared for no one.

Awe overcame me when we arrived at the gate of the castle. The walls were tall and made of black stone with wrought iron lining the top and battlements placed every so often, but it was nothing like I pictured. I expected spikes at the top of the walls with the heads of innocent faeries; instead, it all looked elegant and yet intimidating at the same time.

A long cobblestone road led us further into the land of the castle until we came to a stop in front of the castle itself. The castle was made from the same black stone as the walls, was taller than it was wide, and sat on a hill. Several turrets stood tall and added to the overall detailing of the castle.

I was surprised to see only what I would assume were a few servants, based on their attire, and a beautiful fae waiting for us at the castle entrance. I knew it wasn't the Sovereign's sister because this fae had long fiery red hair, whereas the sister had to have black hair, given her Night Realm blood. Where was Calum? I assumed he would at least be here for his mother's arrival if anything else.

When the carriage stopped, Celine motioned for me to get out first. As I climbed out, a cool breeze hit me. It was warm when we left the Mountain Realm and freezing in the Ice Realm, but I knew that each realm was like its own little world, each different in so many ways.

I snapped out of the daze when Celine cleared her throat. I looked back to see she was still in the carriage but had her hand out. Was she seriously waiting for me to help her out?

26

I guessed since she couldn't bring her ladies with her, she was using me as their replacement. I knew better than to object to her, so I played the part. As she stepped out of the carriage, she looked around with an offended look on her face.

"Where is my son and his fiancée?" she questioned the beautiful red head, obviously thinking the same thing I was.

The fae was taken aback by Celine's snappy tone. I hadn't even noticed it given that it seemed to be the only tone Celinehad.

"They are actually on a short holiday. They will be here tomorrow. We didn't let you know because we thought you might like to rest some before seeing them after your long trip," she said, raising an eyebrow.

"Well, where is your Sovereign?" Celine responded as she crossed her arms. I shuddered at Celine's question. "I would have expected him to be waiting to greet his future family." Celine snarked.

The servants looked at each other nervously.

The fae's eyes narrowed at Celine. "He has more important things to handle than greeting *Nathara's* new family."

Nathara. That must be the Sovereign's sister. She put an emphasis on her name insinuating that the Sovereign and his sister's affairs were completely separate.

"Please, let me show you to your chambers so you can settle in for the night." She motioned towards the castle.

Celine rolled her eyes before she began walking. I stayed back with the servants. I wasn't sure of my place because I truly had no idea why I was even here.

The female turned around and said to me, "Well, aren't you coming?"

As I opened my mouth to answer, Celine cut me off and said,

27

"Oh no. She can stay wherever you board your servants."

The fae looked confused as she looked at me and my clothes. The fabric of my dress showed I wasn't a servant, but I wasn't really sure what you would call me.

I didn't think *Calum's lover* would go over well here.

"Who are you?" the fae asked, taking a step towards me.

"I'm—"

"She's our Commander's daughter. She is fine to stay in the servants' quarters," Celine interrupted before I could answer for myself.

The fae looked at Celine with pure astonishment.

"Finnel," she motioned at one of the Night Realm servants, "please show Calum's mother to her chambers. I will escort our other guest, the Commander's daughter, to her chambers."

Celine was pissed that she was passed off to be escorted by a servant, but she knew her place. She wasn't in her realm. She was a *guest* in the most dangerous realm of all. She hesitantly followed the servant.

"Well, she's a real peach, isn't she," the fae said, bringing her glowing green eyes back to me.

I couldn't help but smile.

"I am Bronwen. I am the Advisor of the Night Realm."

My eyes widened. A *female* Advisor?

"The bitch is gone. You can speak now," she said as she began walking to the castle doors.

"Oh sorry. I'm Violet."

"No fucking way," Bronwen said as she came to a stop and looked at me with wide eyes.

"What?" I asked as I took a step back from her.

"I mean I just love that name. *So much*," she said as she began walking again. "Anyways, I was going to place you in

28

the upper floors of the west wing, in a chamber right next to, oh what's her name . . . Cindy? *Cinderella*?"

I giggled, fae are smart, and don't forget things. She was just doing this to be funny. And it was working. I played along. "Celine."

"Right! Celine! Anyways, if I were you, I'd want to be as far away from her as possible, so I'm placing you in the lower east wing. It's actually only a few doors down from my chambers. So if you need anything, please don't hesitate to ask."

"Thank you . . . for being so kind."

"I know how the Mountain Realm treats females. At least during your stay here, you'll be treated a little better."

I was so confused by the way Bronwen treated me. I'd lived in the Mountain Realm my entire life, and I was always told how much better our realm was than the other realms, especially the Night Realm. That I was *lucky* to be in the Mountain Realm, and even if I was treated more like an object than an equal, it was still better than the other realms.

But Bronwen was so nice to me. I'd never had a friendship with a female so her interaction was completely new to me.

Could we be *friends?* No. We will be back in Mountain Realm in a few months, tops. As soon as Calum got out of this engagement.

"Here's your room."

I didn't even realize we had stopped walking until Bronwen spoke. I looked around to see us standing in a long, dark hall with only the chandeliers hanging high above emitting light.

I had been so infatuated by this beautiful redheaded fae that I didn't know if I'd even be able to find my way back to the front door of the castle. I knew we made several turns to get here, but I never took my eyes off her.

29

"My room is right over there." She pointed down the hall. "There is a bell you can ring right inside your door to call a servant. They can bring you anything you need. A servant will be here at eleven in the morning to escort you to breakfast."

"Thank you," I said, giving her a soft smile.

Bronwen nodded before she turned around and walked away.

I stepped into my room quickly and locked the door. A locked door. I didn't really think that would keep any creature of the Night Realm out if they really wanted to get in here, but it still gave me a little piece of mind.

As I turned around, my heart warmed at the sight of my room. It was larger than my room back home with tall ceilings and a large four poster bed centered on the back wall. To my right, doors to the bathroom and the closet, and to the left, two large glass doors opening onto a balcony. A large desk sat at the front of the room with a sitting chair next to it.

Even with the dark stone walls and the minimal lighting, the room felt warm and inviting, and I knew it would be my safe haven for the days, or months, to come.

4

Chapter 4

Violet

I woke up early. I couldn't wait to see him. I knew I couldn't interact with him other than a cordial nod, but I needed to see him. Bronwen said Calum and Nathara were gone on holiday which didn't seem like something you'd do with someone you had no relationship with.

Calum's plan was to come here and be horrible and completely uninterested in his fiancée to the point where she would convince her brother to call off the engagement. I'm sure Nathara was trying everything she could to get Calum to pay attention to her and get him to fall for her. I hoped that was all that this holiday was, an attempt on Nathara's part.

I didn't blame her for that. Calum was perfect, and anyone would want him. It wasn't her fault that her betrothed loved someone else. I actually felt pity for her, but it didn't change the fact that Calum was mine, and we would be leaving together.

We *had* to leave together.

I sat on my bed waiting for a servant to escort me to breakfast. Breakfast at eleven. That's more of a brunch—almost lunch— but I guess the Night Realm's schedule was a little different. A later breakfast must mean they were usually up later into the night, when the faeries and creatures *thrived* here, so I'm sure it's no different for their fae.

Night Realm schedule or not, I was starving and it looked like a servant wasn't going to arrive until exactly eleven.

I was right.

There was a gentle knock on the door at eleven exactly. I nearly ran to the door. I opened the door and was taken aback by the servant standing in front of me.

The servants that were waiting at the castle entrance looked like fae, but I knew they were servants based on their attire. I thought it was weird because there are no fae servants in the Mountain Realm. Other faeries filled those roles.

The Night Realm lived by a different set of rules than any of the other realms. I guess unless you were the most important fae you were nothing but servants to the Sovereign.

I just assumed that a fae servant would escort me to breakfast.

Standing in front of me was the top half of a woman and the bottom half a gray mist. She was slightly see-through as if she was a ghost, and she had long black hair that seemed to float around her rather than rest on her shoulders. But the part that had me frozen in place was that she didn't have a mouth.

I knew what she was—a wanderer. They were benevolent creatures, but because of the way they looked, Queen Mother assigned them to the Night Realm. She must have realized that I was internally freaking out because she looked down, like she was embarrassed.

"I–I'm sorry," I said, feeling horrible, "I'm from the Mountain Realm. I've just never seen . . . I mean, you . . . I'm sorry."

She looked back up to me and nodded but still had a look of sadness in her eyes. She motioned for me to follow her.

I was almost running trying to keep up with her. She floated through the halls at a pace that was hard to keep up with. I made sure I paid attention this time to the turns we made and the stairs we took in case I needed to get somewhere on my own.

As soon as we made it to the entrance to the dining room, she motioned for me to go in. I walked past her, and as I turned around to thank her, she was gone. I couldn't believe how fast she was at leaving.

I walked into the dining room and was completely disappointed to see that Calum was nowhere to be found.

The dining room was long and narrow with the same stone walls that were in the rest of the castle. It would be very dark in the room if it wasn't for a window that covered the entire left wall.

Bronwen, a fae I'd never seen before, and unfortunately, Celine sat at the long table that could seat at least ten others.

When Bronwen saw me, she jumped up to greet me. "Good morning, Violet! I hope you rested well."

"I did, thank you," I said as I walked closer to the table.

"Please, sit." I sat at the only remaining place setting which was by the fae I didn't know. He looked at me up and down and narrowed his eyes. I knew it couldn't be the shadow king because he wasn't sitting at the head of the table. He was dressed like he was going to battle and held a stiff posture, which told me everything I needed to know. He was the

Commander, and apparently, he didn't like me.

I wished I knew what he was thinking.

"Violet, this is Adar, our Sovereign's Commander," Bronwen said, gesturing to the fae sitting next to me.

Adar was pale, ghostly pale, with long black hair tied neatly in a bun, and his eyes were black. He looked like he was dead. Exactly like fae native to the Night Realm.

"Nice to me—"

"Well, where is your Sovereign? His Commander is here, so is he joining us?" Celine interrupted me, something she was so fond of doing.

Adar gave her the same look Bronwen gave her yesterday. Bronwen giggled.

"He doesn't enjoy entertaining guests that he wishes weren't here in the first place," Adar said as he moved his food around with his fork.

"Adar!" Bronwen said as she stared at him.

"Well, she asked," he said, shrugging his shoulders and keeping his eyes on his food.

"It is customary for the Commander to be with his Sovereign at all times," Celine said while staring at Adar.

"His Sovereign doesn't need me to *protect* him. He is perfectly capable of handling himself," he said, still staring intently at the eggs on his plate.

"Then why even have a Commander?" Celine asked, pushing her luck a little too far.

Adar dropped his fork and raised his glare to meet Celine's.

"Because if my Sovereign doesn't want to get his hands dirty with tasks he deems beneath him, I will gladly step in and make the *annoyances* disappear." A chill ran down my spine when he said that. Bronwen's welcoming behavior made me forget momentarily that I was in the Night Realm surrounded by monsters and cold-blooded killers. And I was sitting next to one right now.

His response caused Celine to slide down slightly in her chair and quietly eat her breakfast.

Adar and Bronwen exchanged looks and were completely silent for at least a minute before Adar let out a huff and rolled his eyes. They had to be communicating through their minds.

It's pretty rare, but Calum was able to communicate like this with his father, and now he could with my father. Specific bonds like Sovereigns with future Sovereigns of the same realm, Sovereigns and their Commanders, and mates can communicate like this. The specific bonds they had with each other allowed them a tether into each others mind to privately communicate. Anyone else would've ignored this exchange, but I'd seen it enough with Calum that I could tell when it was happening.

Were Bronwen and Adar mates?

Bonded mates were so rare now. Ever since the realms were created, Sovereigns were seen like gods to the fae in their realms. Since Sovereigns had arranged marriages, the rest of the fae population decided they should have arranged marriages, which made the chances of completing the mating bond almost impossible. Once you're married, the only way out of it was death, so if you did had a mate and found them after you'd entered marriage, there was nothing you could do about it.

It's sad to think about.

"I do have some bad news. Calum and Nathara are running late and won't arrive until after nightfall. But don't worry! I've planned a party to welcome them home," Bronwen said, bringing my attention back to the group before me.

"We have a party practically every night, Bronwen," Adar mumbled.

"This party is different. *We have guests.*"

Adar rolled his eyes. I was starting to notice that he did that at everything Bronwen said. Nope, couldn't be mates.

"I am so ready to meet my future daughter. A party sounds like a wonderful place to meet her," Celine said.

Knots formed in my stomach at Celine's words.

"You two are welcome to explore the castle grounds today. The party will begin around eight, and I will have a servant escort you both to the ballroom." Bronwen stood up and placed her napkin on her plate. "I will see you tonight."

Bronwen left the room, and Adar wasn't far behind. I realized then that I had barely touched my plate. I was so hungry before but as soon as I was in the room with Bronwen and Adar, I was so focused on watching their mannerisms and the looks they kept giving each other that I forgot my hunger.

I started to eat when Celine let out a loud huff. I had forgotten that she was even at the table.

"A day in hell without my precious Calum. How wonderful," she said as she stared at the wall behind me.

Her favorite activity was pretending like I didn't even exist. I didn't mind because I wished she didn't exist either. She stood up and walked out of the room.

After I finished my food, I sat there for a while and looked out the large window. I still didn't understand how this was the Night Realm I'd read so many books about. It was beautiful. Even though it's the *Night* Realm, the sun still shone, but it didn't look anything like a day in the Mountain Realm. The sky was a dusty blue, the sun was out, but you could look directly at it without hurting your eyes and you could still see the stars. I guess they never went away, but other than that, it looked like a normal day. There was green grass, large shady trees, and flowers. Nothing scary or evil about the landscape.

After brunch, I wandered around the castle for a few hours. I found the library and a large sitting room. Bronwen said we could explore the castle and that's what I did. I wanted to look at the books in the library but I didn't want to touch anything without getting explicit permission first.

After I made it back to my room, I decided to go ahead and get ready for the party. I wanted to look my best for Calumeven if I had to stand in the back and pretend like he didn't mean anything to me.

All of my dresses were exactly the same but in different colors. High necklines, long sleeves, and loose fitting. Ladies in Mountain Realm fashion covered everything so only your husband could see your skin. I chose the terracotta dress because it's one of the brighter colors I had, and I thought it would help me stand out a little more so Calum would notice me.

I sat at the vanity and tied part of my dirty blonde hair back with a ribbon that matched my dress. My hair was long with the slightest wave to it, but I hated it. It had always felt so dead to me.

I saw people like Bronwen with fiery red hair or even Celine with her white hair that was so bright it almost glowed, and I just wished that I had something like that. My eyes were light brown and felt just as dull as my hair did.

After putting on my heels, I went to my nightstand and got a pill from the bottle. I had to take it at exactly nine, just like I had for my entire life. I slid it into the pocket of my dress and sat on the side of my bed while I waited to be escorted to the party.

The servant came to my room to lead me to the party. It was the same one from breakfast. As we made our way down the hall, she was going just as fast as earlier, but this time I was in heels, and I knew I wouldn't be able to keep up with her.

"I'm sorry, can you slow down? I'm having a hard time keeping your pace," I said as I came to a stop.

She turned to face me, placed a fist on her chest, and moved it in a circular motion.

"Sorry," I said as I watched her hand movement, "you know how to sign."

Her eyes widened when she realized I could communicate with her. When Astrid taught me how to read and write, she also taught me how to sign. I never understood why until this moment.

No matter how many books I read about the different faeries and creatures among the realms, I had never read of one who couldn't hear which was what I always associated with sign language. It was something messengers that visited human kingdoms learned how to do in case they came across a deaf person. But I never thought about someone who couldn't *speak.*

"What's your name?" I asked.

She began to sign a series of letters.

"Y a r a. Yara. It's nice to meet you, Yara. I'm Violet."

She nodded and began to glide down the hall again, but slower. Yara stopped once we reached the large double doors of a room and motioned for me to go inside. I wasn't sure if she was not allowed into certain places or if she simply didn't want to be seen by others.

I could hear the music and the sound of conversation coming from inside the room. I let out a sigh. I was so nervous at the thought of what I could be walking into. They had parties and events at the Mountain Realm castle, but Celine never let me attend. She was worried about others finding out about mine and Calum's relationship.

I looked at Yara and told her goodbye before I turned the handle on the door. I entered a ballroom with high ceilings made of glass so you could see the stars above. Large windows lined the room, so it felt like you were inside a snow globe. I wasn't sure if it was meant for the fae inside to feel like they were outside or for the creatures outside to be able to see inside.

On one end, there was a band in full swing with several fae dancing, and on the other end sat a large, empty throne. It was made of black iron and sat up a little higher than the rest of the room. It was made for a king. The shadow king.

But he wasn't there. A chill went down my spine when I thought of him. Even with everyone being nice so far, well besides Adar, his absence made the fear I had of him worse. Was everyone putting on a show since they had guests? Was he hiding to ensure his sister's marriage went through? I had so many questions, but I didn't want to find out the answers. I just needed to get through this and get the hell out of here with Calum.

"Violet!"

I glanced over to see Bronwen running over to me and dragging Adar with her.

"Do you like the party?" she asked as she came to a halt in front of me.

"Uh yeah . . . You did a great job," I said, looking around

39

at all of the fae that seemed to be deeply enjoying themselves between dancing and drinks.

Adar scoffed. If looks could kill, Adar would be dead from the look Bronwen gave him.

I glanced back over at the throne. I couldn't stop thinking about who the mysterious shadow king was. "Does your Sovereign not attend the parties you throw?" I said as I looked back at Bronwen.

"He does, but with his sister arriving, and the spectacle she likes to make of herself, he thought it would be best to let her have her moment, I guess you could say," Bronwen said with a bit of apprehension in her voice. It seemed like she wasn't telling the entire truth.

"He doesn't want to see her? I'm sure he misses his sister since she has been gone on holiday," I pried.

Adar started to choke on his drink when I said that. Bronwen acted like she was ignoring him but I'm sure she was mentally giving him hell.

"Well, let's say their relationship is . . . complicated." Bronwen was picking her words carefully. I knew I was already pushing my luck with the questions, and I didn't want her to take my interest the wrong way. I just liked to know things.

"Oh. I don't have any siblings, but I just assumed siblings were close," I said, shrugging my shoulders.

"Oh, some are. Some are so close that they are inside your head and don't give you a moment's peace," Adar snarked.

Bronwen opened her mouth to say something, but it seemed like she was at a loss for words. She just stared at Adar.

"Wait, are you two siblings?" I said as I looked at both of them confused.

"Yeah, you couldn't tell by our looks?" Adar looked at me,

completely serious.

Bronwen was tan with red hair and emerald-green eyes while Adar looked exactly like the rest of the Night Realm fae at this party. Just like their personalities, Bronwen and Adar's looks were completely opposite.

"I—" I tried to say something, but I just didn't understand what I had just learned.

"Adar, you ass, leave her alone," Bronwen said, elbowing him in his side.

For a second Adar slightly smiled before he was back to his annoyed look.

"Oh look, our lovely couple has arrived," Bronwen said as she raised her glass towards the large ballroom doors.

I turned around quickly to get my eyes on Calum. I couldn't wait to see him and see how his plan was coming along.

It was delusion, I guess.

The months without him were so lonely and miserable that I actually started to believe he was finding a way out of the marriage. That hope shattered into a million pieces when I saw him walk into the room with his hand on her waist. He whispered something in her ear, and she started to giggle. He looked forward, and his face went pale when his eyes met mine. He clearly had no idea that I came with his mother.

I wanted to scream and run up to him and yell at him for every promise he had broken. But I couldn't. In this moment, I knew how worthless and powerless I was. Everything Celine had always said was true.

I couldn't bear it. And I couldn't break down in front of everyone.

No one could know about us.

"E-excuse me." I looked for the closest exit so I could get

41

away from everyone. There were two large glass doors to my left that led out to the garden so that's where I went. Pushing through the crowd of fae and slinging the doors open, I made my escape. The cold night air hit me, but it wasn't enough. I felt like I couldn't breathe, and I couldn't get the image of Calum and Nathara out of my mind.

I ran into the garden. The hedges were high and cut into a maze with different paths, which were lined at the bottom with rows of violets.

A left, then a right, and another right.

I didn't really know where I was going. I just knew I needed to be far away from everyone.

I rounded the next corner and ran straight into the back of someone.

As I accepted the fact that I was going to fall on my bottom, something caught me. No—more like consumed me. It was cool, almost like a morning mist. I looked down, and my bottom half was covered in total darkness. Like shadows—*oh gods*, the shadow king. I couldn't look up. I was too scared to move. Were the shadows going to consume me? Honestly that would be a better fate than walking back into the party and having to watch Calum with *her*.

Maybe it would be painless, quick and easy. Maybe I—

He cleared his throat. "Excuse me. Are you going to let me help you up or are you too comfortable to move?"

I shifted my eyes slightly up to see he had his hand extended waiting for me to accept it.

I reluctantly placed my hand in his, which was just as cool as the shadows that were holding me. As he pulled me back to my feet, I slowly looked up a sleek, black suit to see the shadow king's face.

42

As soon as our eyes met, he let out a sigh of relief and mumbled, "Finally."

Something the rumors and horror stories failed to include was that the shadow king was the most beautiful man I had ever seen.

He had short, black hair that was perfectly placed. It looked like he ran his hand through his hair and every strand was too scared of him to shift out of place. His skin was pale, and he had a strong jawline. His eyes were dusty blue, a shade of blue that was all too familiar. It was the same blue of today's sky. Something odd—not only for that coincidence, but also because Night Realm fae should have black eyes.

I regained my balance and watched as the shadows seemed to slither like snakes back into the shadow king. Although the majority of the black mist disappeared, some lingered around his body. I watched as a trail of shadows went up to his neck and reached his ear.

It was almost like the shadows were telling him something. Whispering, even.

He towered over me, like Calum did, but he was not as wide as Calum, and while he looked as if he was tight and toned under his suit, his muscles were not as pronounced as Calum's. But he didn't need Calum's strength, because he could put down his enemies without lifting a finger.

"Are you alright? You came around the corner like you were running from something," he asked with almost a look of concern on his face.

"I-I'm sorry. I was just trying to find somewhere to be alone and get some fresh air. I was . . . getting a little hot."

He cocked his eyebrow at my response. "Hot? It's freezing . . . Are you sure you're alright?"

He was right; it was cold. When I first ran outside, the cold air hit me, yet somehow, I was now sweating. Something was wrong.

"Wait, what time is it?"

"A little after nine," he said.

"Oh fuck. I forgot to take my medicine." I stuck my hand in my pocket but couldn't find the pill. I started to look around where I was standing to see if it had fallen out when I ran into the shadow king, but it was too dark to see anything.

"Your . . . medicine?" he said, raising an eyebrow.

"Yes, my medicine. Can you tell me the quickest way back to the east wing?" In that moment, the shadow king wrapped his arm around me, and the next moment we were standing in my room.

I'd transferred a million times with Calum. It's a skill that only Sovereigns can do. Being able to move from one place to another in an instant was the gift Queen Mother blessed all Sovereigns with, along with their individual gifts. I just didn't expect the shadow king to help a complete stranger like me get to my medicine—let alone know which room was mine.

It didn't matter right now. I ran over to the nightstand to get my medicine. I'd taken it every night at exactly nine. My father always said that I couldn't miss a dose, even by a few minutes. It was too dangerous.

"You're a faerie."

I spun around, dropping the pill bottle on the floor. I fully expected him to leave after getting me to my room, not standing there watching me with such a puzzled look on his face.

"Yeah, s—" I was reaching down to pick up the bottle when it flew across the room and landed in his hand. "Excuse me. I need to take that now." I'd never been late with my medicine, and I was starting to freak out. I had no idea what would happen to me.

The shadow king was inspecting the bottle and glancing at me every few seconds with a confused look on his face. "What is this medicine for? Faeries do not take daily medication."

"Well, I do." I walked over to him and tried to snatch it out of his hand. "Now give it."

He jerked his hand back before I could get the bottle from him. He looked me up and down with a hint of amusement on his face.

"I have a heart condition, and if I don't take that medication, I could die." I was getting mad. It's not like me to get angry or have an attitude with someone, let alone someone as deadly as the shadow king. I usually sat back and submitted to anything that was asked of me.

But in that moment, I wanted to rip his beautiful head off, and I wasn't afraid of him. I was afraid of my heart stopping and then me dying.

"Faeries do not have heart conditions."

"Okay, well, hi, my name is Violet Ashwood, I am the daughter of the Mountain Realm's Commander—which, in case you didn't know, means I am a faerie—and I have a *fucking* heart condition. Congratulations, you've now met a faerie with a heart condition. Now *please* give me my medicine."

"Violet." He began to look me up and down. He shook his head and chuckled. "Of course."

I instantly regretted what I just said to him. In the past, fae had simply looked at him the wrong way and he killed them. But he just handed me the bottle.

I ran to the bathroom to take the pill and get a sip of water from the faucet. As I looked up to the mirror, I swear I saw the faintest golden glow in my eyes. I immediately shut my eyes and slowly opened them again, and they were back to brown—the plain brown eyes I'd always had. I must've been hallucinating from forgetting to take my medicine. I was scared to think what would've happened if I waited any longer. I started to feel myself cool down, and my heartbeat began to slow.

I walked back into my room to see the shadow king sitting at the end of my bed. "I-I'm sorry I spoke to you like that. I just really needed to take my medicine."

"You have quite the mouth on you, Violet," he said, allowing the most perfect smile to come across his face. It was just as sinister as it was entrancing. "It's alright. We can just pretend like it never happened."

"Thank you . . . um . . . Your Highness?"

"Your Highness? I'm a Sovereign, not a king," he said, cocking his head to the side.

"You're right. I'm sorry. I just thought that . . ." What if he doesn't know everyone calls him the shadow king? What if he took it as an insult and decided to end me right now? "Never mind," I mumbled.

"What?" He stood up and started walking slowly towards me.

I didn't realize that I was backing away until I hit the wall. I had nowhere to go to get away from the shadow king. I was trapped.

He stopped when there were only a few inches between us and allowed a smirk to form on his face.

"Being 'the shadow king' doesn't make me an actual king. You know that, right?" I was absolutely terrified and com-

46

pletely intrigued all at the same time.

He leaned in until his lips were almost touching my neck. I could feel his breath, and it was just as cool as the black mist and the hand that helped me up. Goosebumps formed all over my body.

"Please, call me Sebastian," he whispered in my ear.

And then he disappeared, leaving a faint trail of black mist where he had been standing. I stood there, unable to move, as I watched the mist fade into nothing.

I was so confused. I knew the stories I'd read, and I could feel the danger as I was standing in front of him. But at the same time, I—

My train of thought stopped when I saw Calum standing in front of me.

5

Chapter 5

Calum

The last thing I expected when I walked through those doors was to see Violet standing there in a crowd of Night Realm fae.

She wasn't supposed to be here. She was supposed to be home, where she would be safe.

Did he somehow find out about her? Did he bring her here to dangle her in front of me before he killed her? All I wanted to do was run over to her, wrap her in my arms, and transfer us out of this hell.

But I froze. I feared that one wrong move from me, and they would kill her before I could get to her.

My heart shattered when I saw the look on her face after she saw me with Nathara. I couldn't imagine what was going through her mind. The betrayal she felt.

I had to find her and explain, but I couldn't leave right after she ran out without it raising any suspicion. There was always someone watching, and I couldn't risk anyone learning what she was to me if they didn't already know.

As soon as I got the chance, I told Nathara that I wanted to rest after our travels and that I didn't want to stay at the party. Once she saw her mother, she didn't seem to care what I did. The only thing she seemed to obsess more over than me was her mother, and you would've thought the week they were apart was actually a century.

I welcomed their relationship, though. Anything to keep her off of me.

I had gotten turned around in this bloody castle trying to find her room. Transferring to her would've been the best option, but I had no idea where they placed her. I followed her scent, the only thing that kept me calm lately, but it seemed that she had already been in enough places in the castle to make this task daunting.

I had to find her soon. Every moment I spent roaming these halls raised my chances of running into someone, which would raise unwanted questions.

She was the only good part of my life. The best and worst day of my life was the day I realized I was in love with her.

I lived in a castle full of fae, but I always felt alone. Since I took my first breath, my parents' only focus was to prepare me to become Sovereign. My studies, my combat training, my sessions to perfect my gifts. Everything was to become the future Sovereign of the Mountain Realm. I never felt like I was given a chance to be a child or to enjoy life.

That was until Violet moved in.

A girl, only a few years younger than me, that I could play with. I watched how careful her father was with her, always worried that something would happen to her heart. He had spent her entire life trying to protect her, which in turn took away her chance to be around others. She was lonely, like me.

49

I knew I had to protect her if I wanted to play with her. But where her father wouldn't let her climb a tree, I would. I would just be standing under it to catch her if she fell.

We had become everything to each other in a short amount of time, because we were the only two that understood each other. Unless I was with my father touring the Realm and learning from him, I was with her. We studied together, she watched while I trained, and she read books while I practiced my gifts.

Even if my focus was on another task, she was always right next to me.

Years passed and our relationship was nothing more than a platonic friendship. What it always should have been. I never thought of her as any different than me. Meaning, I never thought of her as a female.

Until the day everything changed.

Violet and I were on the far end of the castle grounds, as far as we could possibly be from the castle, looking for some rare bird she had read about when an unexpected storm came. We started running towards the castle, but the rain was coming down so hard that we could barely see in front of us. Violet tripped on a root and twisted her ankle. Instead of trying to wait out the storm, I picked her up and continued the trek back to shelter.

About halfway back to the castle, the rain let up, and the sun shone down on us. I looked down at her in my arms. The rain glistened on her skin, and her loose-fitting dress was drenched and formed around her breasts. She looked up at me with her big brown eyes, and I realized she wasn't like me at all. She was everything I'd wanted. Everything I always dreamed of, and she had been in front of me this entire time.

It was after that incident that my father finally taught me how to transfer. Violet's father was so worried about her being in the storm that they needed a way to make sure I could get Violet back to the castle as quickly as possible if something similar ever happened again.

I knew my feelings for her would cause nothing but heartache, and I didn't want her to know how I felt. I feared the damage it would cause our friendship, and I couldn't lose her. The only way I could think of to solve this dilemma was to find her someone. She was coming to the age where she should marry, and I thought that finding her a husband that I knew would love her and take care of her the way she deserved would help my feelings go away.

Her station made it difficult to find an acceptable match. There was no one similar to her. No other Commander had had a child before, putting her in a position entirely of her own. I spent every waking moment for weeks trying to find someone worthy of her until I finally thought of the perfect person: my cousin in the Ice Realm.

His mother was my mother's younger sister, who wasn't betrothed to a future Sovereign like my mother because there were no suitable matches during her courting age. She instead married a male from the Ice Realm of higher station, and they lived in the Ice Realm castle.

My cousin, Fenrys, was set to be on the council in their realm when a position came available. He was kind, fair, and protective of the weaker fae in their realm, always finding ways to help them and ensure their needs were being heard. Exactly what Violet needed.

He came to spend a few months with us, and I pushed him to get to know Violet. He knew of my intentions, but I never told Violet. I stayed away from her, trying to push my feelings away while she got to know Fenrys.

The only time I saw her was at our weekly family dinners, but I had the servants add a seat between the two of us for Fenrys to sit in so I could do my best to ignore her.

One day, after Fenrys had been at the castle for about a month, I was walking back from the training area when I heard her laugh. Before I realized what I was doing, I followed her laugh to find her and Fenrys sitting closely under a tree deep in conversation.

Our tree. The one she used to climb in while I stood below praying to the gods that she wouldn't fall.

Jealousy overcame me, and I realized in that moment that I wouldn't be able to let her go so easily. She was mine before she even knew it.

I sent Fenrys home that night, and I know I hurt him because he hadn't spoken to me since then. He had fallen for her just like I did.

I tried to continue to avoid her until about a week later when she barged into my room to confront me about the way I had been acting.

That was one of the things I loved about her. She had fire in her that I'd never seen in another female in our realm. I didn't know if it is because she had spent most of her life in the castle with me, where she was able to be more outspoken than typically allowed or if it had to do with her being pretty much raised by her nursemaid, Astrid, who had a personality too big for her small size. No one dared to say anything to Astrid about her behavior. I think everyone had always been a little afraid of her.

It was in the middle of the night when she came into my

room, and she already had her nightgown on. It was almost sheer, and you could see the outline of her breasts.

I couldn't stop myself at that moment, and I hadn't been able to since.

This proved my worry to be true. I couldn't live without her.

I reached an unfamiliar hall, but her scent was getting stronger with every step I took. I hadn't been to this hall before, given my room was on the opposite end of the castle, and this hall seemed like it had nothing but more bedrooms.

I reached a door, and I could hear her heart beating—no, more like racing—on the other side. I had to explain and calm her down before something happened.

I placed my hand on her door and put a ward around her room, something I learned quite early in my studies. It's usually used to protect conversations from unwanted listeners, but using it now may be the most necessary time I'd ever need it.

I raised my hand to knock, but I knew she wouldn't let me in, so instead, I transferred.

6

Chapter 6

Violet

After almost dying and then being entranced by death himself, I had forgotten about my life. About Calum.

"Go away. I don't want to see you," I said as I pushed past him, trying to get to the bathroom. To get away from him.

But he didn't listen. He grabbed my wrist and pulled me towards him, and nothing could hold me back.

Before I could even comprehend what I was doing, I slapped him. I slapped my Sovereign—which would be punishable by death—but more importantly I slapped the person I loved the most.

I felt so betrayed by him.

"You lied," I said as I fought back the tears.

"Violet, I—"

"No. I am going to talk, and for once, you're going to listen to me," I said, cutting him off. "I knew from the beginning that you'd have to marry someone else. I knew you didn't have a choice, and it was your duty. We could have just spent the years we had together knowing that it would come to an end. But YOU said you wouldn't marry someone else. YOU said you would find a way out of this. You didn't have to say any of that to me, but you were adamant that it would be me and you in the end. You said it so much that you actually had me believing that it was true. And until the moment you left, you promised me that you would come back to me. But then I saw you today with her. You lied."

"Who brought you here?" he asked, completely ignoring everything I just said.

"Who do you think? Your mother. The one who would love nothing more than to see me hurt."

"Violet, I didn't know you would be here," he said while trying to grab my hand.

I took a step away from him as I said, "Are you kidding me? Is that supposed to make me feel better? What were you going to do? Marry her and have someone get rid of me before the two of you returned from your honeymoon?"

"No, I didn't mean—"

"Fuck you, Calum," I screamed before I started wailing on him. Hit after hit. He let me hit him for a while because he knew he deserved it. Then the anger turned into sadness and all I could do was cry. He wrapped his arms around me, and I didn't fight back. I was too tired. Tired from the days without him, tired from it all.

"Violet, please listen to me. It's all fake. Everything you saw was just a show," he said while resting his chin on my head.

I pushed away from him. "You expect me to believe that?"

"When I got here, I did just like I told you I would do. I was horrible. I wouldn't even look at her. I was rude to everyone. I tried everything I could for her to refuse to marry me. Then, one day, I overheard her talking to her mother. Her mother told her that she found out why I was acting the way I was. They found out that there was someone in my realm."

"How?" I asked.

"We must have a traitor in the castle. Someone has been feeding them information. Her mother then told her that once they figured out who it was that they would kill my lover. I couldn't chance anything happening to you, so I started to act like I was interested in her. I was hoping that it would prevent them from digging deeper to find out who you were."

"So, what, your plan was just to marry her to protect me?" I asked.

"No. Something is going on here. Her brother—the Sovereign—he's weak. Something is affecting his power, and I am going to figure out what it is. I'm going to use it as leverage to get out of this. But no one can find out it's you. I can't risk something happening to you."

I couldn't believe what I was hearing. He'd never lied to me before, and I could tell by the look in his eyes that he meant every word he said. He's just trying to protect me. But I couldn't get the image of her in his arms out of my head. Even though he was doing this to keep me safe, it still hurt. I didn't think I could watch them together until he figured a way out. But his plan? Crazy. I was starting to lose hope.

"What are you going to do? Save that . . . evil man . . . from whatever is taking his power and hope that in return he tells you that you don't have to marry his sister?"

"I-I don't know yet," he mumbled.

I started to walk away from him, but he grabbed my hand and pulled me back to look at him.

"Violet, please," he said as he looked at me with worry in

his eyes.

"Have you kissed her?" I asked even though I didn't know if I could handle the answer.

"Violet . . . I . . . Yes. I had to make her believe that I wanted to marry her."

I felt like I couldn't breathe.

"Did you have sex with her?" I said barely loud enough for him to hear me as I turned away from him again. I was too scared of what the answer would be.

"What?"

I whipped around and before I could stop myself, I said, "Did you fuck her, Calum?" I could feel the rage building up again. If he had sex with her, I'd be done. I'd find a way to sneak out of the Night Realm tonight, and I would never see him again.

I caught him off guard with that. I could tell by the look on his face as he said, "No. I did not fuck her. I told her we had to wait until our wedding night. I wouldn't do that to you. I love you, Violet."

"I need some time to process this. Please leave," I said, even though seeing him leave would hurt worse than him staying here to fight with me.

"Violet, please—"

"Leave, Calum."

He stood there and just stared at me as if he was contemplating doing what I had asked of him. This had been the longest we'd been apart since the day I moved into the castle.

"No. I will not leave. We've been together for sixteen years, and I've never done anything to make you lose trust in me. I know what you saw hurt you, but it's the only way I know to protect you. And now you're here, which is going to make everything harder. How am I going to keep my eyes off of you when you enter a room? I can't let anything happen to you."

"Then why are you here, in my room? You've told me that the Sovereign of the Night Realm controls shadows and knows everything that goes on in his realm. Are you not risking everything by being in my room right now?" I asked.

"I told you that he's weak. Well, weak compared to what he used to be. I was able to place a ward on every room that fae from my realm are staying in. No one can hear anything that goes on in our rooms. We are safe in your room."

"Does it keep people out, too?" I asked even though, considering a few moments ago, the shadow king was in my room, I knew the answer to that. I just wanted to see what Calum thought.

"No, if I did a ward that strong, someone would notice, and it would draw more attention than we needed. So I placed a small ward that would go unnoticed. Just one to keep noises from escaping," he responded as his eyes slowly drifted down from my eyes to my lips.

I was so hurt after seeing Calum with Nathara and learning how he'd been acting with her, but I knew he was telling the truth. He wouldn't lie to me. I had to trust him to get us through this, even if I had to sit back and watch.

But, gods, I missed him. I missed his touch. I missed the way he would make me feel with his touches. I needed to feel him.

I looked down at his body. His shirt was tight, accentuating his biceps. I opened my lips slightly, and my eyes made my way back up to his. He took that as an invitation and closed the distance between us. Calum grabbed my face in his hands and kissed me roughly. Grabbing my waist, he picked me up and lay me on the bed before climbing on top of me.

He pulled his shirt over his head while barely breaking our kiss. It was like he didn't want to miss a second of our bodies touching. Like he had missed me just as much as I missed him. He didn't even take the time to take my dress off. He just pulled it up enough where he could grab my panties and rip them off.

I didn't even notice that he had managed to pull his pants down too until I felt him thrust his length inside of me.

It was rough. Not rough wild sex like we'd done so many times before, but rough and fast like he needed to finish as fast as he could because he had somewhere else to be.

Because he did have somewhere else to be.

His fiancée was waiting for him at the party.

He finished. I didn't. He rolled over and pulled me into his arms.

"Violet, I'm sorry you had to see me with her tonight, but I'm afraid that you're going to see a lot more of it. I am trying so hard to find what or who is making the Sovereign weaker. I don't know how long it's going to take me to figure it out, so that means I don't know how long I'm going to have to pretend to be in love with Nathara."

I squeezed him a little harder when he said that. I didn't want this moment to end. All I wanted was Calum.

"But I will figure it out, and I will get out of this engagement. I promise."

"I know you will," I whispered.

Did I? Did I really believe that he would get out of this? I had to. He was all I had.

He kissed my head before getting up to put his clothes back on.

"I will be back. As soon as I get the chance, I will be back here with you. It may be a few days and it may be the middle of the night, but I'll be back."

"I know you will."

Calum transferred out of my room.

I got it. Nothing had ever been easy for me, and I shouldn't have expected anything else.

Of course, I was born with a heart condition that caused my father to treat me like an injured bird that needs to be protected at all times.

Of course, the love of my life is engaged to another.

Of course, I am going to have to watch them together for possibly the next three months.

And, like always, I had to sit back and accept it all. I had no power. I was from a realm where females were only good for one thing: lying on their backs. I'd been taught to submit to everything that was given to me.

I'd felt weird tonight, though, ever since I was late to take my medication. I felt angrier, more confident with my thoughts, and more articulate in putting those thoughts into words. I think it was from the near-death experience, but I even stood up to Calum, which I'd never done.

I'd always been able to say what I felt around him, but he always had the final say in everything. If I didn't like something, I told him my opinion and he would listen, but in the end, he made every decision.

But now . . . fuck it.

7

Chapter 7

Violet

I didn't sleep much that night. I was trying to process everything that happened yesterday: meeting the Sovereign of the Night Realm, Sebastian, and seeing Calum with Nathara. It was too much.

Then I started to think about my father. I didn't get a chance to see him last night. After seeing Calum, I couldn't focus on anyone else.

My father was bound to Calum. When a Commander was selected, they went through a ritual that tied their life to their Sovereign's life. If Calum died, my father died. That's the best way to ensure a Commander was always doing everything they could to keep their Sovereign alive. The only way out of it was if the Sovereign broke the bond that tied them together. Calum's father knew he was trapped, and there was no way out of the Reacher's den that day, and he cared for my father so much that he broke the bond. My father felt a lot of guilt from that, and it caused him to be hyper focused on Calum.

Calum came first; I came second. I didn't mind though. Calum came first for me too.

I woke to a knock on my door. I looked at the clock to see it was ten in the morning. I guess staying up so late lost in my thoughts had its advantage. I would be on the Night Realm's schedule now, so breakfast wasn't too far away.

As I started to open the door, my father pushed past me and quickly shut the door behind him. "What are you doing here in the Night Realm? It's not safe," he said.

"You said it wasn't safe to leave my room at home and I did, and I was fine." I probably should have just said I wasn't given a choice in coming here, but I'd grown so tired of him always worrying about me.

"You left your room?" he asked as he began looking at me from head to toe, even grabbing my arms and inspecting every inch of them.

"Father, I'm fine," I said while pulling my arm from him. I looked at him confused. Was he really afraid that I would be physically hurt while he was gone?

"It's still not safe for you to be here. Nathara knows about you."

"I know. Calum told me last night. But she doesn't know it's me."

"Calum came here?" he asked with a look of shock on his face. "Does he not realize how dangerous that could be for the both of you?"

"I saw him last night at the party with her. I left upset, and he came after me. He had to explain what was going on." I knew nothing I said helped to calm him, so I added, "He put a ward on my room, so no one knew he was in here."

"You need to go home," he said bluntly.

"Do you think I asked to come here? Celine made me come, and I'm not exactly in a position where I can tell her no," I said, crossing my arms.

He started to pace the room. He shook his head and stopped back in front of me. "I can't be in two places at once protecting you both."

"Father, don't worry about me," I said while placing my hand on his arm trying to calm him down. "No one is going to find out about me and Calum. I will do what I do best: stay back and not draw attention to myself. Stay with Calum. It's your duty."

"It's my duty to protect you too." He had such worry in his eyes as he placed his hand on my cheek.

"I'll be okay. I promise," I said, trying to reassure him.

He nodded like he was trying to convince himself to believe me and leaned down and kissed my forehead before walking out of my room.

I got dressed and made my way to the dining room. I wasn't sure if they had planned for us to have breakfast together again, but I figured I could peek in and figure that out for myself.

As I peeked around the door into the room, I noticed there were several more place settings this time. I guess it was time to put on a show and pretend like I didn't care about Calum.

"You again."

I spun around as I heard that voice. I thought I was alone, but he must've been lurking in the shadows.

"Sebastian! You startled me," I said as I tried to compose myself.

As my eyes focused on him, it was like I was seeing him for the first time again. He was dressed more casually today, with a loose-fitted white shirt with the top few buttons unbuttoned and black pants, which made him even more attractive, if that was even possible.

"I didn't give you a heart attack, did I?" he said in a mocking tone. I just stared at him. Did my heart condition really bother him that much? "Forgive me. I'm just not used to such a *delicate flower* being around," he added sarcastically.

He was testing me to see how I would react. I showed so many emotions last night that he probably thought I was completely crazy.

That's good. Maybe if he thought I was crazy he would leave me alone. The last thing I needed was the Sovereign of the Night Realm watching me while I attempted to hide my feelings for Calum.

With no emotion at all I said, "And yet you have a garden of violets outside."

"Violet noticed the violets? Strange coincidence maybe. They came to me in a dream," he said as he smirked at me.

"You dream about flowers? The scary Sovereign of the Night Realm dreams about flowers?" I don't know what I was doing pushing him like this, but it just came out before I even realized what I had said.

He bit his lip as he looked me up and down. "I sure do."

Oh fuck. I'd been around Sebastian twice and both times he'd made me feel things I shouldn't be feeling. I should be terrified of him. He's a killer. He's evil. He literally had shadows floating around him. But I was not scared, and I was so enticed by him that I just wanted to know more. I'd never spoken to a male the way I'd spoken to him. I knew the rules were different here—females had more freedom—but I didn't understand where this confidence was coming from.

The sound of voices coming up the hall broke the trance I

was in. Well, one voice in particular snapped me back to reality. Calum's.

"Will you be joining us for breakfast today?" I asked, trying to keep myself distracted from who would be coming up the hall soon.

"Unfortunately, yes. Being such the 'good Advisor' that Bronwen is, she *advised* me that I should," he said, even though the tone of his voice made it seem like less of advice and more of a demand.

"Do you not normally have breakfast with your sister and mother?" I asked.

Sebastian's face went cold and his eyes darkened as he said, "Lilian is not my mother."

By the look on his face, I knew I'd said the wrong thing. The shadows around him started to grow and radiate from him, making him appear even more like the shadow king I had heard about.

"I'm sorry. I didn't know," I said.

He looked ahead, avoiding eye contact with me, and started taking deep breaths. It was like he was trying to calm himself down. "Breakfast will be served soon," he said as he walked past me, and by the time I turned to follow him into the dining room, he was gone.

I heard Calum's voice and what I assumed to be Nathara's voice growing louder. I wanted to avoid an awkward moment in the hall with them, so I went into the dining room and quickly found a seat.

A few seconds later, Calum, Nathara, and my father came in and sat at the other end of the table. At least now I could avoid making eye contact with them and hopefully get through this meal as quickly as possible. If it wouldn't have looked

65

suspicious, I wouldn't have come to breakfast at all.

"Calum, aren't you going to introduce me?" Nathara asked. I looked up to see she had wrapped her hand around Calum's arm and was tracing circles with her thumb.

"Of course, this is Violet, Alastor's daughter," he said with giving me nothing more than a quick glance.

Alastor's daughter. The daughter of the Commander of the Mountain Realm. Nothing else.

"It's nice to meet you, Nathara," I said as I forced myself to smile.

Please someone else show up for breakfast.

She looked me up and down and gave me the fakest smile I'd ever seen back.

This was my hell.

Possibly the worst part of it all was Nathara's beauty. Her hair was long, black, and straight; it had a certain shine to it that I envied. Her skin was pale, like Sebastian's, but her eyes were black, like a Night Realm fae's eyes should be. She was tall, slender, and graceful with every move she made. Her lips were painted red, a strong contrast to her pale features, and it took everything in me not to picture her lips on Calum.

It felt like forever before Bronwen and Adar arrived. Their presence eased the tension, and thankfully Bronwen sat next to me. I didn't know if I could handle watching Adar roll his eyes through this meal.

She looked at the empty seat at the head of the table and let out a loud huff. "I *told* him to come to breakfast."

I guess I could be to blame for his lack of attendance.

Celine and a female I'd yet to see arrived last. They were giggling and whispering to each other. The fact that Celine was allowing this lady to be so close to her told me that she must be Lilian, Nathara's mother—but not Sebastian's.

Lilian looked exactly like Nathara except for her auburn red hair and dark blue eyes. Her features were a dead giveaway that she was from the Forest Realm.

Breakfast was horrible. Nathara was practically sitting in Calum's lap the entire meal, and he would nuzzle his nose into her neck while she giggled. I had to pretend like it didn't bother me even though I was screaming on the inside. I had to find something else to focus on before I exploded and that was Sebastian.

I struck a nerve when I thought Lilian was his mother. How could I have known she wasn't? Fae stay with their spouses until death, which meant Sebastian's mother was dead. I wanted to know what happened. Not because I cared, but because I loved knowing everything. Since my entire childhood was focused on schooling, I was always learning something new, and it was a habit that just stuck.

Breakfast went on forever. I had lost my appetite the moment Calum and Nathara walked into the room, but I couldn't leave. It was rude to leave a meal before your Sovereign. Bronwen began talking about the dinner party she was planning for tonight. I guess Adar wasn't exaggerating when he said she threw parties all the time.

Bronwen said she was an Advisor, but she seemed more like she ran everything in the castle. She planned parties, she greeted guests, and she was in charge of the servants and made sure they completed their tasks. These were all tasks the lady of the house would do. I would have expected Lilian to manage these since Sebastian wasn't married. She technically still was the lady of the house. Celine didn't skip a beat with her duties when her husband died. It made me wonder if Sebastian and

Bronwen were together. It would make sense. They were both extraordinarily beautiful.

"What do you think, Violet?" Bronwen snapped me back into reality with her question as she looked at me waiting for my answer. I had no idea what she asked me.

"About what?" I asked.

"I asked if you would like to go into the city with me to pick up a few things for tonight."

"Oh I . . ." I paused as I glanced at my father. I'd never even left our castle. Now I was in the most dangerous realm, and Bronwen wanted me to leave the protection of the castle. My father had a very concerned look on my face, and I saw out of the corner of my eye that Calum didn't seem happy about it either.

"I asked you, Violet, not your father. You're grown, and I'm pretty sure you can make your own decisions," Bronwen said without even glancing my father's way.

"She's a female from the Mountain Realm, she's *not allowed* to make her own decisions," Nathara snarked.

"Nathara, you're about to be a female in the Mountain Realm. Don't forget that," Bronwen quickly shot back. She looked like she took too much pleasure in saying that. Bronwen's response took the smug look right off of Nathara's face.

"Anyways, Violet, you're in the Night Realm, and our rules are different here. It is your decision." Bronwen stared at me as she waited for an answer.

Nathara's little remark and the disapproving way Calum was looking at me while he had his arm around Nathara angered me so much that I couldn't stop myself from saying, "Let's go."

Bronwen jumped up and said, "Great, I will have a carriage

brought to the front for us."

"Violet, I don't—" my father began to speak, but Bronwen cut him off.

"Don't worry, *Daddy*. She will be safe with me." My eyes widened at Bronwen words, while she looked my father slowly up and down before prancing out of the room.

"Come on, Violet!" she yelled from the hall.

I stood up and went after her without making eye contact with my father or Calum. I could deal with them later. I didn't want to miss the chance of seeing a city before I was stuck in the Mountain Realm's castle again.

After I made it out of the room, I heard Adar say to my father, "I will go with them. I won't let anything happen to her."

It was probably for the sake of my father, a fellow Commander, but that was the first time Adar seemed like he maybe, just maybe, was more than a heartless dick.

8

Chapter 8

Violet

I had never been allowed to do anything but stay within the castle walls, read, and learn new things. My father didn't let me leave, which never felt like a bad thing because there were plenty of places to explore within the walls. He was too scared that any little thing could cause too much excitement and cause my heart to stop.

He was also particular about the things I did within the castle walls. If he caught me running around or playing tag as a faeling, I had to stop immediately. I couldn't do anything that would get my heart rate up, which left lying outside staring at the clouds, gardening (which was hard because I seemed to kill every plant I touched), reading, and working my mind.

Don't ask me to play any type of sport but if you need a history lesson or want to learn a new language, I'm your girl.

It's funny when I thought about it, though. My father forbade anything that could elevate my heart rate, but he couldn't stop me and Calum. Calum could get me going with just one look.

Bronwen told me that I needed to change before we left because I would stand out with my Mountain Realm fashion, and she didn't want to cause any unwanted attention. She told me I could borrow some of her clothes so we went to her chambers. I'd only ever worn dresses due to the Mountain Realm's strict rules for females, and they were always simple, modest, and only in earth tones. Based on what I'd seen Bronwen wear so far, I was a little nervous about what she would pick out for me. She seemed to have no issue showing as much skin as possible.

"I'm not going to ask you to wear pants, even though that would be best. But we have to get you out of that awful brown dress," she said as she started looking through the clothes in her obscenely large closet.

"What's wrong with this dress?" I said as I looked down at my dress trying to smooth it out. "It's one of my favorites."

She immediately stopped moving hangers and turned around to look at me. She looked as if she was repulsed by what I said. "I know you're from the Mountain Realm, but what was the vision? Dirt?"

I couldn't help but laugh at her remark. She never had an issue saying exactly what she was thinking. I needed to learn from her, but I knew it wouldn't matter once we got back home. Even though I'd only been here for a few days, I'd gotten so comfortable around Bronwen.

Without overthinking my retort, I said, "And what was the vision with your leather outfit? Battle or sex dungeon?"

Bronwen's mouth fell wide open. "Oh, I like this Violet," she said as a smile grew on her face.

"I'd like to wear pants. Not leather pants. I think leather

would be a little extreme for my first pair," I said.

"You've *never* worn pants?" A look of both shock and pity replaced Bronwen's smile.

"Mountain Realm. Remember?" I said while motioning to the dress I was wearing.

"It makes me sick just thinking about that misogynistic place."

"It's not that bad," I said while thinking back to the life I had in the Mountain Realm. With Calum, I wasn't held to the same standard as any other female in the realm would be. For the most part, I could speak freely and spend my days doing what I wanted. But I knew if I wasn't with Calum, I would have had a completely different life.

I would be either betrothed to a male and spending my days preparing to become his wife, which meant learning how to care for a house, or I would already be married and doing everything possible to give my husband babies.

And honestly, neither one of those things sounded like something I wanted to do.

"Violet, it's quite possibly the *worst* of the realms."

"You're saying that while we are standing in the Night Realm. The realm where your literal nightmares come to life," I said while narrowing my eyes at her. How could anything be worse than what lurked in the darkness in the Night Realm?

"I would rather take my chances fighting demons than have to submit to a husband," Bronwen said before she turned around and began looking through her closet again. Her words had hurt in them, like this issue was personal and something might have happened.

"How about this?" She turned around and held up a pair of black pants with pockets on the sides and a black long-sleeved shirt. They still looked like I was going to battle but at least they weren't leather.

"Those are fine," I said while grabbing the clothes from her. I went to her bathroom to change. Luckily, other than the height difference—Bronwen had several inches on me—we were the same size. I folded the bottom of the pants so they wouldn't drag on the ground. I stood in front of the mirror and just stared at myself. I had never seen myself in clothes like these. They were so simple but so different. While the neckline of the shirt was high, so I wasn't revealing anything, it was skintight. Between that and the pants, you could see every curve of my body.

I wanted to throw that dirt-colored dress in the trash.

"Violet, are you okay in there? I can get you a dress if you'd rather wear that."

I opened the door, and Bronwen's face lit up. "Damn, Violet! I never would've thought you looked like that under all that fabric," Bronwen said as she moved her hands around, exaggerating the curves of my body.

Bronwen also gave me a pair of black boots to wear because she said my shoes would "ruin the look." I asked her if we could avoid seeing my father on our way to the carriage because he was already upset about me going to town, and I thought my clothes would put him over the edge. I also didn't want Calum to see me, but I couldn't tell Bronwen that. At least avoiding my father meant avoiding Calum also.

Adar was waiting for us at the carriage. He was leaning on the carriage, looking the opposite way but Bronwen must've said something to him mentally because as soon as we got down the stairs he started fussing as he turned around.

"I've been waiting out here for damn near half an hour. What took—" He stopped mid-sentence when he saw that I was in Night Realm attire. Adar closed his eyes and started rubbing his head. "You're just asking for trouble aren't you, B."

"He'll get over it," Bronwen replied as she walked past him and climbed into the carriage. I guess Adar really cared about my father. Must be some *Commander Honor Code* or something.

I quickly climbed into the carriage after Bronwen. I was too excited about going to the city to wait another minute. I sat next to Bronwen while Adar sat opposite us. He wouldn't stop staring at me, like he was trying to figure something out about me. I wished I knew what he was thinking. I tried to ignore him by looking out the window, but I couldn't help but feel self-conscious.

Bronwen must've noticed because she kicked him. "Adar, will you stop? You're creeping her out."

"If my staring is bothering her, how do you think she is going to handle the city?" he shot back. They were talking about me as if I wasn't there. I wasn't sure if they thought they were mentally communicating or just that they were so caught up in their conversation that they didn't care that I could hear them.

They continued to argue for the rest of the ride, so I just looked out the carriage window at the woods we were traveling through. The trees were very slim and looked like they were dead. There wasn't an alive plant in sight. No greenery. No flowers. A fog covered most of the space between the trees, making it hard to see further into the forest. It was odd. It looked how I pictured the Night Realm, but it was nothing like the path we traveled down to get to the castle a few days ago.

When the carriage stopped, I waited for Adar and Bronwen

to exit first. The city had a long road with buildings on either side. The outsides of the buildings were different shades of deep blues and grays. The windows and doors had wrought iron details, similar to the castle's. Faeries in conversation with each other walked past us, not even glancing our way. I guess that was why Bronwen made me change. A Mountain Realm fae in Mountain Realm attire would cause attention this deep in the Night Realm, and I'm sure they wouldn't be welcoming with open arms.

"So Violet, how do you know what a sex dungeon is?" Bronwen's break of the silence took both me and Adar by surprise.

"What?" I asked.

"I mean I wouldn't expect a modest Mountain Realm lady to know what a sex dungeon is."

Adar whipped his head around as he waited for me to answer. Why couldn't she had asked me this when we were alone?

"I . . . read a lot." I wasn't lying. I do read a lot. But I couldn't very well say the real reason I knew.

"And to think you were about to sound interesting," Adar said as he turned back around and began walking up the street.

As we walked through the city, I looked at every sign for each store and anything I could see in the windows. An apothecary, an art gallery, a cafe, and a few clothing stores. I had never seen any of these places before, and I wanted to observe every detail I could.

"I need to pick up a few dresses I had designed for me. One is for the dinner party tonight, and the others are for a few upcoming events we have."

"I'm going to the bar," Adar mumbled with the same look he'd had on his face since the first time I saw him. Like there was a stick shoved up his ass.

"I thought you came with us to watch over our delicate flower?"

Delicate flower. I'd only been called that one other time, and it was only a few hours ago by Sebastian. Had they talked about me? And if so, when did they even have the chance to talk about me? I had been with Bronwen almost the entire time since my conversation with Sebastian this morning. Was he the reason Adar came with us? Was he concerned for my safety?

"The bar is right next door to your dress shop. If danger interrupts your shopping, tell me and I'll be right there."

When Bronwen and I stopped at the entrance of the dress shop, Adar continued walking to the bar and went straight in, not even looking in our direction.

As we stepped inside the shop, I was overwhelmed by the dresses lining the walls. There were deep purples and blues on one side and the other side was full of black dresses. I went over to the black side and ran my hand down the dresses. There were so many different styles and materials, but they all had the same overall theme: fitted, revealing, and sexy. They were the complete opposite of anything I'd ever worn.

"You should get a few to wear while you're here. I know you can't wear them in the Mountain Realm, but it wouldn't hurt to play dress-up while you can," Bronwen said as she looked over my shoulder at the dress I was eyeing.

"Oh, I don't have any money," I said as I ran my hand down the beaded silhouette of the dress before me.

"It's on me, Violet."

I turned to look at her as I said, "I would love to, but I don't think my father would be okay with me wearing something like this." I didn't really think my father would care. Unless it was something that would affect my heart, he was pretty lenient. I was more worried about Calum.

"Suit yourself," Bronwen responded as she shrugged her shoulders and walked toward the back of the shop to a faerie with skeletal fingers that was busy working on a dress.

I couldn't keep my eyes off of the dresses. They were so beautiful, and I knew that in the next few months I would be back home, and I'd never have a chance to wear something like this again. My mind kept going to Calum and how he would react to seeing me in something like this. He loved when I dressed to please him, but that was always when we were alone, in the privacy of his chambers. I knew he wouldn't be thrilled about me dressing like this where others could see my body, but then I thought about his hands rubbing on Nathara's body while she wore dresses similar to these.

It may have been immature of me, but I couldn't help what I said next. "Actually, I think I would like to wear some of these dresses."

Bronwen turned around and clapped her hands. "When in the Night Realm." She winked at me.

Bronwen asked the faerie to pack up her dresses while she helped me pick a few. She then sent the faerie to the carriage with our dresses ahead of us while we slowly walked through the city.

"Are you hungry? We can go to the cafe before we go back to the castle," she asked.

"What about Adar?" I asked while we were slowly getting farther from the bar. Even if I'd rather not be around him, I was so used to having a male around to *protect* me that it made me nervous being without one.

77

"I'll tell him, and he can grace us with his presence when he feels ready."

I nodded and continued looking at the buildings around us, taking note of every little detail.

"What is it?" Bronwen asked, noticing my mind was elsewhere.

"I've just never seen anything like this before," I said while looking at the entrance to a small bookstore. I took extra time looking at the bookstore. A place where you can choose the books you want to read, unlike our library that was filled with books chosen by someone else. It had a warm, inviting feel to it, even from the outside. It was in a smaller building than the ones surrounding it with a glass door, worn wood framing, and two large windows on either side that peeked into a room filled to the brim with books.

"I'm sure this is completely different from the villages in the Mountain Realm," she said as she smiled at the beautiful architecture that surrounded us.

"I wouldn't know," I mumbled as I looked closely at a stack of books near the window I was walking past. *The Pleasant Place.* An odd title for a book here, but nevertheless intriguing.

Bronwen stopped walking and turned to face me. "Wait, you've never been to a city?"

I brought my attention back to her as I said, "I haven't stepped foot outside of the Mountain Realm's castle walls since I moved there when I was a faeling. Well, until I left to come here."

"That's . . . tragic," she said with sadness in her eyes.

"I grew up in a castle. I'd say that's far from a tragedy," I said, trying to reassure her.

"You see how many new things you've seen in the short time

we've been out today? Imagine all of the things you've missed out on. There is an entire world out there far more beautiful than the castle you spent half a century in. To me, that's a tragedy."

I had never thought of it that way. My father always told me how grateful I should be to live in such a beautiful place where servants take care of me, and I was always protected. He always said that I wasn't missing anything from the outside world. The only knowledge I had was from the books I read and the stories I heard. Reading about cities, clothing stores, and Night Realm faeries and creatures was nothing compared to experiencing it for myself.

9

Chapter 9

Violet

Once I was back in my chambers at the castle, I started to second-guess my decision to let Bronwen buy me dresses. Wearing Night Realm clothing to the city with Bronwen and Adar was completely different than attending dinner tonight in a Night Realm dress with everyone. A servant brought the dresses to my chambers and when I unzipped the garment bag, a note fell out.

Don't overthink it. Wear the dress.

-Bronwen

Don't overthink it. Every molecule inside of me wanted me to wear a Night Realm dress. They were so beautiful, and I would never have another chance like this once we got back home. I decided to wear the least Night Realm-esque dress that I picked. That way I could gauge Calum's reaction before wearing one of the riskier gowns I picked.

This gown was fitted, so it showed my figure but had long sleeves and a more conservative neckline. And by more conservative, I mean it wasn't a deep v that went all the way to my navel. It had a square neckline that showed the top of my breasts and was deep purple in color. After looking at the dress again and looking at the shoes I brought with me, I realized I had no shoes that would do the dress justice. I decided to go ask Bronwen if I could wear a pair of hers. I took the dress out of the garment bag so I could take it with me to Bronwen's chambers. I had no doubt with her massive collection that she would want to see the dress to ensure she picked the perfect pair of shoes.

When I opened the door to exit my chambers and looked down the hall towards Bronwen's chambers, I saw *him*. Sebastian had cornered someone in the hall and his shadows . . . well, his shadows were holding the fae up on the wall.

I let out a quiet gasp, and Sebastian whipped his head around. When his eyes met mine, his demeanor changed, and the shadows released the fae. The dark look he had on his face went away, and he looked as if he was shocked to see me.

Sebastian looked back at the fae and said, "I'm running out of time and so are you. Figure it out." I wasn't eavesdropping. Fae have exceptional hearing, and Sebastian, well he wasn't whispering.

"Yes, my lord." The fae nodded as he quickly left.

Sebastian transferred to stand right in front of me. "Violet."

"I'm sorry I interrupted you," I said as I looked down, afraid of what I had seen and what he might do. He was the shadow king, and I could see that now. He was threatening one of his own, but what bothered me the most was how quickly he changed his demeanor when he saw me. Like there was an internal switch that he could flip and instantly change himself.

He placed his cool hand on my chin and lifted it up so I was looking at him again. "I'm sorry you had to see that. There's just a very," he paused, "pressing matter that I need to handle, and it seems that none of my Guard are competent enough to figure it out."

"Oh, you mean whatever is making you weaker." *Why the fuck did I just say that?*

Sebastian removed his hand from my chin and took a step back. "How do you know I'm weaker?"

"I—" Fuck, I couldn't say Calum told me. "I heard some of the servants speak about it."

"My servants are smarter than that." His eyes darkened. "They know not to speak of such things when outsiders are here."

"I tend to go unnoticed."

Sebastian's eyes slowly moved down my body and I remembered that I was still in skintight Night Realm attire. "That's impossible."

I had backed myself into a corner with this one. Sebastian was staring into my eyes again, waiting for me to tell him how I knew.

"Violet, I'm going to ask you again. How do you know?" The shadows around him started to grow and began forming a circle around me like they were waiting on his command to pounce. The beautiful dusty blue-eye color that had put me in a trance last night was slowly starting to darken. I saw nothing but a cold-blooded emotionless killer standing in front of me.

"I—"

"I told her, Sebastian. Calm down."

The voice of an angel. Bronwen.

"You told her?" Sebastian asked while shifting his head to look at her.

"Yes. She probably was afraid that I wasn't supposed to tell her and wanted to protect me," Bronwen said while staring intently at him.

"Is that true?" He turned back to look at me and waited for my answer.

All I could do was nod.

He stared at me for a few seconds, his jaw clenched, before he let out a grunt and disappeared.

I stood frozen. I was so in shock by everything that took place that I was afraid to move.

"Violet, do you realize you're not wearing shoes?" Bronwen stood propped up at her door with her hand on her hip. She was completely unbothered by what Sebastian just did. I guess she was used to it.

"I was coming to ask you if I could wear some of your heels when that happened," I said as I glanced back to the spot that Sebastian once stood, towering over me, threatening me.

"Oh, of course! I have the perfect pair." She waved for me to follow her into her chambers.

I stood against the wall while she looked through her closet throwing shoes everywhere as she continued her hunt. I hadn't paid much attention to her chambers when I was in here earlier. I was too focused on Bronwen and her closet of endless options. Her room didn't match the rest of the castle. The walls were painted a deep shade of red with matching fabric draping above the bed. A large, patterned rug sprawled across the floor with a large, golden chandelier hanging high above. The gold and velvet framed bed sat in the middle with more pillows than anyone could possibly need. Her room matched her perfectly. Something that didn't match the Night Realm and yet it seemed to be perfectly placed.

83

"They've got to be here somewhere," Bronwen said as she threw another shoe over her shoulder.

"Bronwen," I said, less worried about matching heels and more worried about what had just happened in the hall.

"Ah, here they are!"

"Why did you lie to Sebastian?" I asked as I stood next to the door, still unsure of what to do with myself.

"I didn't lie to him. I told you today at the dress shop, remember?" She looked completely serious. I don't know why she did it, but I wasn't going to question her further. She saved me.

I understood why she was still lying. Sebastian could hear everything through the shadows. Even though I was free to say whatever I wanted in my room, I couldn't forget that I was always being watched in the rest of the castle. "Oh well, thank you for reminding me."

Chapter 10

Violet

Bronwen insisted that I walk to dinner with her. She was so proud of how I was dressed that she wanted to see everyone's reaction when they saw me. She also made sure we were the last to arrive so that everyone's eyes were on me. Lucky me.

When we were a few yards from the doors to the dining room, I looked down. It was a habit that I'd always done, but I started to feel very nervous about wearing this dress.

"Violet, keep your head up. If you're going to wear a Night Realm dress, you need to have Night Realm attitude," Bronwen said as she looped her arm into mine and pulled me with her to the doors.

As the doors opened, the first person I made eye contact with was Adar. He shook his head and started to rub his fingers on his temples. Calum was talking to Nathara and stopped mid-sentence to stare at me. Nathara and her mother both looked to see what he was staring at, and they began to glare at me. I quickly shifted my eyes away from him. I couldn't get caught up with him right now. Especially after what happened earlier with Sebastian.

Sebastian. That's who I saw next. He was sitting at the head of the table leaning back and staring out the window, looking completely uninterested in his guests. The silence that had overtaken the room caught his attention because he turned his head back towards everyone, and he locked eyes with me. His dusty-blue eyes were back with no trace of the darkness I had seen before. He shifted up in his seat and sat a little taller as if he was finally interested in the dinner party.

Bronwen pulled me over to sit next to her and after I sat down, I realized everyone was still looking at me.

"So, I take the silence means everyone is at a loss for words at Violet's new look?" Bronwen asked while looking around the room proudly as if she was a little girl showing off her new toy. I guess I was a dress-up doll for her. I didn't care, though. After saving me earlier, she could dress me up all she wanted.

No one spoke. Calum did everything but look at me, but I didn't know what I expected. He couldn't show any interest or disinterest because anything would be suspicious. He had to be indifferent. Nathara ignored Bronwen, which seemed like that was normal around here, and Adar was rubbing his head still as if he had a headache. I wasn't sure if that was because of me or Bronwen or both.

"You look beautiful, Violet." My father finally broke the silence. Between Calum and Sebastian, I had forgotten my father was even there and that he might have an opinion on how I was dressed. I gave him a small smile before a few servants came in with trays of food, taking the attention off of me.

Everyone slowly picked back up on their conversations that

our entrance interrupted and that's when I looked back at Sebastian, who was still looking at me with no hint of emotion on his face. He was tapping his finger on the table and seemed to be contemplating something. I just hoped he wasn't still thinking about earlier. I didn't want to revisit that again.

I honestly didn't want to have a conversation with him ever again. It was a good thing that I saw who he truly was because the way he acted last night made me feel like he wasn't evil. That maybe he was just misunderstood. But he proved that to be wrong today. I saw the shadow king.

As much as I loved getting dressed up for Bronwen's dinner party, I really hoped this wasn't something that happened every night. Being forced into a room with Calum, Nathara, Celine, and Sebastian may have been my worst nightmare, and I couldn't put on a fake smile every day. I needed space to breathe and be alone. And sulk in the misery that was my life.

Nathara had too much to drink and was a giggling mess, falling over into Calum's lap. Calum took her to her chambers, and of course, my father followed them out.

"Well, since the lovebirds are gone, there is no reason for the two of you to still be in my presence." Sebastian glared at Lilian and Celine and while Celine cowered, Lilian held his glare.

"Celine, why don't I show you where I plan to have the ceremony?" Without breaking eye contact with Sebastian, Lilian left the dining room with Celine following closely behind her.

There was a deep-rooted hatred between Sebastian and Lilian.

"Bronwen, let's stop with this charade of the meals. I may go mad if I have to have one more meal with Lilian and Nathara,"

Sebastian said.

Bronwen let out an overexaggerated huff. "Fine, but don't you dare try to cancel any of the parties I have planned," she replied.

"Oh, I wouldn't dare," Sebastian said as he cut his eyes at her and started discussing a "border issue," as he called it, with Adar, even though Adar never said anything back. Bronwen poured herself another glass of wine. I wanted to leave but I didn't want to interrupt their conversation, and I felt like I may have missed my chance.

A tingling sensation in the palm of my hand caused me to look down to see a balled-up piece of paper appear under my hand. I carefully opened the paper, trying to not make a sound, to see what it said.

Excuse yourself.

~C

That was enough to make me forget all of my manners, and I jumped up and said, "I'm not feeling well, if you'll excuse me."

I didn't wait for permission as I turned around and made my way to the doors.

"Violet." My name from Sebastian's lips made me stop, but I couldn't turn around. "Can I have a word with you, alone?" he asked. I could feel his eyes boring holes in the back of my head as I kept my attention on the door—to the escape in front of me.

"No," was all I said before I left the dining room. I couldn't think too much about telling the Sovereign of the Night Realm no, but I also wasn't willing to hear what he had to say. I didn't know if he was going to attempt to apologize for earlier, when he almost killed me, or question me more about what I knew.

Either way I didn't want to ever be put in a position where I was alone with him again.

No matter the way he acted when I first met him, or the way he made me feel, I was afraid of him now. And it was best if it stayed that way. Even if no one can know for now, I was with Calum. Calum was the love of my life, and nothing could ever change that. I knew when I opened the door to my room, Calum would be there, and I knew what to expect with him. He has been the same Calum for the entire time I've known him, and Sebastian . . . well, I'd met two different Sebastiansin the past two days. One entrancing and one terrifying. Either way I couldn't give him any more of my time.

I quickly shut my door after me because Calum was standing in front of my bed waiting for me, and I didn't want anyone to see from the hall. As soon as the lock on my door clicked, he closed the distance between us and kissed me.

"I love you," he said while resting his forehead on mine.

"I love you, Calum."

"I'm sorry for breakfast and dinner today," he whispered as he gently placed kisses all over my face.

"I know. But you're protecting me," I said. I'm not sure if it was more to reassure him or myself.

"I will always protect you."

I gave him a knowing smile, but I didn't want to talk about the things we couldn't change when I knew we didn't have a lot of time to be together. "What do you think of my dress?" I asked as I spun around to give him a full view of the dress.

"It's very . . . Night Realm," he said as his eyes looked down at the dress.

I crossed my arms as I responded to him. "It *is* a Night Realm dress."

Calum brought his hand back to my face and cupped my cheek. "You look beautiful in it. You look beautiful in anything you wear, but it's not you. It's not my Violet."

"It is different, but it's not like I've ever been given a choice in what I could wear."

He looked dissatisfied by my response but quickly shook the look off of his face and asked, "Well besides buying dresses, what else did you do in the city?"

"We went to a cafe, but we mostly just walked around looking at the buildings. Calum, it was so beautiful, and there were so many different faeries and creatures. I can't believe everything I've missed out on."

"Your father has just worried so much about your heart."

"Well today proved that I can leave the castle. I mean, I spent the entire day in an unfamiliar place with faeries and creatures I have never seen before. I don't think anything back home could surprise me now."

"You're right. I'll talk to him once we are home."

I jumped in his arms and wrapped my arms around his neck. My hug from excitement turned into kissing passionately which then turned into me being on my knees.

Like I said, I knew what to expect with Calum. I knew what he loved and what to do to satisfy him.

I plunged his length deep into my throat while keeping my eyes locked on his.

"Gods, I've missed you, Violet," he said while he grabbed a fist full of my hair and began pumping into me.

Tears began to run down my face and just when I thought I couldn't take anymore, he picked me up and threw me on the bed. He ripped my dress off and threw it on the floor. It was something he'd done more times than I could count, but this time my heart sank when I saw the beautiful dress I had just gotten in shreds on the floor.

Calum flipped me onto my stomach and inserted himself. He put his hand under me where he could rub me while he began thrusting. He had made everything else disappear from my mind and all I could think about was him.

"Yes, Calum! Yes," I screamed as I felt my climax coming.

He finished shortly after me and rolled over onto my bed so he could pull me into his arms.

"Do you have to leave now?" I whispered while I lay with my head on his chest.

"Soon," he mumbled while he ran his fingers through my tangled hair.

My heart sank, but I had to get used to it. This would be the new normal for a while. "Have you found out anything about what is causing Sebastian to weaken?"

His hand stilled, and I felt his chest tighten beneath me. "Sebastian? How do you know his name?"

Fuck. I couldn't very well tell him the truth. "Bronwen and Adar were talking about him today, and I heard them call him Sebastian," I said while I traced circles on his stomach.

He relaxed and said, "Oh. No, not really. I've been talking with a scholar from back home, and he says there must be an object that is drawing his power from him. Someone within the castle must have introduced the object because it has to be somewhere near Sebastian to be effective. But the object could be virtually anything from a pillow in the sitting room to silverware in the kitchen, so it doesn't really narrow it down."

"Oh," I said quietly.

If Sebastian couldn't figure it out with his shadows that hear everything, it seemed almost impossible that Calum would be able to figure it out.

He stayed with me until the early hours in the morning. I slept better that night than I had in weeks. I had grown so used to having someone else in the bed with me every night that the time without him made me realize how lonely the nights without him were.

"I need to go now, Violet," he said, waking me up as he kissed my forehead and got up from the bed. "I'll see you at breakfast in a few hours."

"Before I left dinner last night, Sebastian told Bronwen to stop with the 'family meals,'" I said as I sat up on the bed, pulling the sheet up to my chest.

"Well, then, I'll be back here as quick as I can," he said, giving me a soft smile.

"Okay," I said as I fought back the tears.

We said our goodbyes, and Calum transferred out of my room.

11

Chapter 11

Violet

I had spent my entire life around the same few people and now I had been pushed into a place where I'd experienced more in the past few days than I ever had.

I had become so used to spending so much time alone that I now was exhausted by the things that had happened in the past few days. I was restless after Calum left so early, but I decided to spend the rest of the day in my room. Bronwen came about midday because a servant told her I didn't come around breakfast time looking for food.

"The past few days have just been . . . a lot," I said as I sat at the foot of my bed.

"I understand that all of this might be a lot to take in, but you can't just stay in your room and skip meals. I'll have a servant bring you some food," Bronwen said as she jumped on my bed, making herself comfortable. My day of alone time had come to an end.

"Can it be Yara?"

"Yara?" she asked as she sat up a little straighter, waiting for my answer.

"You know . . . the wanderer." I paused. "The one without a . . . a mouth."

"I know which one is Yara. She just wasn't assigned to you, so I'm not sure how you've come across her."

"She has escorted me to a few meals. Maybe there was a mix-up with assignments?" I asked. I hoped Yara wouldn't be in trouble because of this.

She looked at me as if she was offended by what I had said to her. "I don't have *mix-ups*."

"Please don't send a different one. I like her," I begged. Something about her—even with her disturbing appearance—gave me comfort.

Bronwen let out a sigh before she said, "I won't, but how do you know her name?"

"I know how to sign. Being stuck in a castle every day with a nursemaid that believed knowledge was power meant I had to learn everything I could."

"Knowledge. I'm not sure how well that would hold up in a battle against physical power." Bronwen giggled as if she was picturing it in her head.

"Well, I don't think my father would ever let me near a battle, so I think I'm good."

"Oh right, because of your 'heart condition.'" Bronwen had the same mocking tone that Sebastian had.

"He told you about it?" I asked.

"Are you talking about your father?" Her eyes narrowed.

"You know who I'm talking about." After she protected me from him yesterday, I felt comfortable enough with her to not hide what I was thinking or feeling. But I didn't want to say his name. Saying his name would make him more real. I'd rather him stay the evil presence that I was going to attempt to avoid for the remainder of the time that I was here.

"Yes, he did. He asked if I had ever heard of a faerie with a heart condition," she said as she picked at a loose string on her top.

"Why is he so concerned?" I asked. I shouldn't even be on his radar.

"I feel like I can't answer that," she said, bringing her attention back to me.

I rolled my eyes at her response. She probably didn't feel right about calling her Sovereign a nosy ass. "Well, have you ever heard of it before?"

"No, but I've seen enough things that anything could be possible. Unlikely, but not impossible."

"Are you and *him* together?" I couldn't stop myself from asking. I have been wondering about this since I first saw them together.

"Gods, Violet!" She looked at me as if I had said the most horrible thing anyone had ever said to her. "No. Sebastian is . . . not my type."

"Oh, I just wasn't sure because you do so many things that the lady of the house normally does."

"Is he your type?" She was so blunt with everything.

"Are you really asking me if the shadow king that almost killed me yesterday is my type?"

"He has his flaws," she said, shrugging her shoulders.

"I'm pretty sure that's a big one," I said as I crossed my arms.

"Violet, if you were put through everything Sebastian has been through, you'd understand. But don't take the way he acted yesterday as a sign that he is incapable of emotion. He is just very careful about who he shows it to."

I didn't know what to say to Bronwen. Was she so delusional that she saw *good* in Sebastian? There couldn't be good in him. *There couldn't be.*

Bronwen had a few things to take care of around the castle, so she left me, and shortly after, Yara was at my door with a plate of food and something even better than that: a stack of books. She brought the tray in and sat it on the desk. I thanked her and watched as she faded into nothing, which made me realize how she always left so quickly. She didn't fly away, she simply disappeared.

All I wanted to do was look through the stack of books, but the ache in my stomach told me I needed to eat first.

There was an assortment of fruits and cheeses on the plate. It wasn't a mealtime, so I'm sure the kitchen staff threw something together as quickly as they could at Bronwen's request. I didn't care. I was starving.

I opened the first book to see a piece of paper tucked between the first few pages.

Strengthen your power.

The friendship I had formed with Bronwen in the short time I had been here was something I had always wanted. I hoped somehow we would be able to stay in touch once I returned home.

The first book was called *Book of Healers.* It told the history of the healers, their findings, and the methods of curing things from curses to deadly bites from nymphs. I had no doubt that Bronwen sent this book for a reason.

I flipped through the pages to see if there was anything on heart conditions. I trusted my father, and there had never been a reason to doubt him about my condition. I wasn't looking to find answers. If anything, I was looking to prove that it was possible just to stop the remarks.

There was nothing in the book about heart conditions, but it was only the first volume. Maybe I could find information in a later volume.

I had told myself that I wouldn't go to the library without explicit permission, but Bronwen bringing me these books was too tempting. I had read every book in the library in our castle and yet the three books Bronwen brought me were ones I had never seen. I had to see what else they had.

I didn't want to see anyone else today. My visit with Bronwen was enough, but the curiosity about what other books I could find was eating me alive.

The halls were empty, other than a few servants busy carrying boxes. I'm not sure if they were bringing things in or taking things out, but it wasn't any of my business.

Even though I found the library the other day, I somehow got turned around in the winding halls, and eventually I stopped a servant to ask them to point me in the right direction. He looked at me as if I was stupid before quickly changing his expression and motioning me to follow him. I understood why when we walked to the end of the hall, turned left, and were standing at the large double doors that opened into the two-story library.

Warmth rose on my cheeks as I thanked him before he left me to return to the large painting he had been trying to remove from the wall—the task I had interrupted.

Luckily, the library was empty, so I started on the left wall to see how the books were organized.

After seeing the first few sections were maps, biographies

of the first seven Sovereigns, and spell books, I knew finding the next volume of the *Book of Healers* wasn't going to be easy. Clearly whoever organized this library didn't create a system that made sense. If only I could fix this mess.

A small section tucked in the corner of the left and back walls had me stop and take a closer look. The book were of various sizes, all terribly taken care of. Some had water stains, some looked like they were thrown in the dirt and stepped on, and some were so faded that you couldn't read the title. But the part that had me unable to move on: they were books from a human kingdom.

I had only seen a few in my lifetime because Alentara had little contact with other kingdoms. The one way to travel to human kingdoms was through the Sea of Mavrola, which was nearly impossible between the waves, wind, and creatures that lurked below the surface. Human items were rare in the Mountain Realm but because Calum knew how much I loved to read, he was able to find a few human books on his travels throughout the years and brought them back to me.

I could recognize those colorful book covers anywhere. Even though I wanted to look through every one of those human books, I needed to find what I was looking for first.

"Violet."

12

Chapter 12

Violet

I didn't have to turn around to know that it was Sebastian. I could see the shadows lingering out of the corner of my eye.

"I was just leaving," I said as I tried to walk around him without having to look at him.

"Violet, stop," he said and grabbed my wrist. I froze at the realization of how close he was behind me. I had forgotten how cool his touch was, and it made the hair on the back of my neck stand.

I knew by the tone in his voice that he was serious. I stood there facing the door. I didn't want to look into his eyes. I didn't want any reason to forgive what happened yesterday. To get pulled back into the trance his dusty-blue eyes seemed to put me in.

"Turn around, *please*," Sebastian pleaded with a strain in his voice. Like he needed so badly for me to turn around.

I turned around but kept my eyes on the ground.

"You're going to make this difficult, aren't you?" he said,

letting out a sigh.

"You were going to kill me," I said quietly.

"You knew something that no one should know about me." There was a bite to those words that had me turning around, trying to make my escape again.

But to no avail, he was in front of me again.

"Bronwen told you she told me," I said as I focused on a small crack in the stone floor beneath my feet, which proved to be no use as the shadows crept into sight.

"Look me in my eyes and tell me that, *love*."

A mix of butterflies from the choice of his words and the urge to vomit from the fact that he knew I was lying formed in my stomach. I couldn't avoid him. I was trapped. In his library. In his castle. In his realm.

I looked up, meeting his enchanting gaze as I said, "I don't know who or what is doing this to you. Is that enough?"

He studied me for a moment, but I never broke my stare. I wanted to make sure he knew I was telling the truth, but I also didn't want to look away. His eyes were the most beautiful eyes I had ever seen.

"I wasn't going to hurt you," Sebastian said, breaking the daze I was in. His eyebrows had furrowed, and his eyes pleaded as if he was trying hard to make me believe him.

"Really? I'm pretty sure your shadows were waiting for your command to consume me," I said.

"Consume you?" Sebastian looked at me, confused by my choice of word, before a smirk formed on his lips. "My shadows don't *eat* people. You read too many *Mountain Realm history books*."

I disregarded the "Mountain Realm history books" part of his response. I was too concerned with knowing. Knowing what the shadow king was. "Then what do they do?" I asked.

"They're an extension of me. My sight. My ears. *My touch.*" As he said those last two words, I felt something rub from my shoulder to my neck. But Sebastian's hands were in his pockets.

Dear gods. This is why I didn't want to be around him again. This feeling. This bad-but-feels-so-good feeling.

"I-I need to go back to my room now," I said as I pushed past him.

No matter the feeling Sebastian was giving me, my mind told me to stop talking to him. I couldn't let it go any further.

I quickly made my way back to my room. I knew I shouldn't have left my room in the first place but the thought of what I would find in the library was too intriguing. And what I ended up finding had made me feel a way a book never had.

I took a few turns down some halls before I realized I had no idea where I was again. I needed to pay more attention to where I was going.

"Fuck," I mumbled quietly. I feared that if I stayed still too long that Sebastian would be back in front of me to play his little game again. That must be a part of his evilness: saying things to make others uncomfortable. Saying inappropriate things to me to watch me squirm.

An idea popped into my head. It probably wouldn't work and would leave me feeling stupid, but I had no other choice than to try it.

"Yara?" I called.

A cool breeze rustled my hair, and I turned around to see the ghostly faerie standing behind me.

I couldn't believe that worked.

"Can you take me back to my room?" I asked.

She nodded and started walking the opposite way I had been heading. I blindly followed her, not paying attention to the specific turns and steps she was taking because my mind was still in the library. Still imagining Sebastian and his shadows touching me.

I thanked her once we reached the familiar hall, and she disappeared before my eyes.

As I closed the door to my room and turned around to rest my back on the door, Calum was suddenly standing in front of me. I'm not sure why he was here in the middle of the day, but I didn't care.

"Where—" Calum began to speak but stopped when I immediately pushed him on the bed.

I needed him. I needed a release of everything I was feeling.

"Violet, what—" He stopped mid-sentence when he saw my dress fall to the floor. I climbed on top of him and pulled his shirt off.

"Violet, I can't stay long. I just needed to tell you something," he said as his eyes looked down at my naked body.

"This won't take long," I said as I unbuttoned his pants.

He nodded and lay back to let me continue what I had started. I didn't even attempt to take my panties off. Instead, I moved them to the side before grabbing and inserting his length in me. I didn't even give myself a chance to adjust to his size before I rode him. Hard. All I could see in my head was Sebastian. I tried so hard to focus on Calum, as I didn't want to see Sebastian, but it was like I had no control over my thoughts.

And with the picture of Sebastian in my head, and the thought of how one touch from his shadows could make me feel, it didn't take long for me to finish.

I fell over in exhaustion after my release, and Calum flipped us over so he was on top of me. I watched as he pumped into release. My eyes were on him, but my mind was still somewhere else.

"What has gotten into you, Violet?" Calum said while putting his clothes back on.

Sebastian. Sebastian had gotten into my head. If I didn't know any better, I would think he had broken through the walls in my mind and was controlling my thoughts. That seemed better than the truth.

"Just trying to make up for lost time," I said as I reached down to pick up my dress off of the floor.

"Well, I came to tell you that I will be gone for a few days."

"Again? Weren't the two of you just on a trip together?" I asked as I pulled my dress over my shoulders.

"Nathara wants to visit possible honeymoon spots," he said while fumbling with the button on his pants.

I just looked at him. I didn't know what to say to that.

"Please be careful while I'm gone. It feels like I'm leaving you in hell with no one to protect you," he said as he walked to me and grabbed my hands in his.

"I'll be fine. I don't think anyone here has intentions to hurt me."

Someone seemed to have *other* intentions, but it was proba-bly best that Calum didn't know that.

"I don't think you understand the evil that is here. Every fae you've been around has killed more than you can imagine. They have no rules. They have no morals. I don't think they would hurt you because they don't want to risk the engagement, but I wouldn't do anything to provoke them."

"What do you want me to do? Stay in my room until you return?" I asked. Honestly staying in my room might be best for everyone.

"No, I wouldn't ask you to do that." He brought my hands to his lips and gently kissed them. "Just be careful."

13

Chapter 13

Violet

I spent the next day in my chambers. Most of the day, I stayed on the small balcony that was connected to my room. The cool breeze seemed to help clear my mind which had been running wild since the moment I arrived here. Yara had brought me breakfast that morning, and I asked her if she could get me the second volume of the healer book. I would've gone and gotten it myself, but I didn't want to chance running into Sebastian again.

I skimmed through the pages, but again, nothing about faeries with any type of health problem.

The next morning, I was still lying in bed when my door flung open and Bronwen came walking in. "Alright. I let you hide in your room all day yesterday, but that's enough."

"Did you forget how to knock?" I said to Bronwen as I sat up on my bed.

"I know you're used to being locked in a tower, but while you're here, you're experiencing life. You're going out with me," Bronwen said as she jumped on my bed and lay next to me.

"*Out?*"

"Yes, out. And I'm not taking no for an answer. So you can either be a willing participant and pick out your outfit, or I will force you, and I promise the outfit I pick will leave little to the imagination," she said as she looked at her nails that seemed to be freshly painted a blood red to match her hair.

Even though I was so used to being stuck in a castle, that little taste of the outside world I got when we went to the city only made me want to see more. And I knew Bronwen wouldn't take no for an answer.

"Will Adar come with us?" I asked as I got up from my bed. Even if his mere presence made me uncomfortable, I felt a little safer with a male with us.

She scrunched her nose at my question. "No, we are having a girls day. It will be fun, I promise."

Her response didn't ease my worry, but I had to trust that Bronwen wouldn't put me in danger.

"Fine," I mumbled before following her out of my room.

Thank the gods I didn't fight her on going out. She showed me the outfit she wanted me to wear, and it, in fact, did not cover anything except what was necessary.

I wore something similar to what I wore the last time she took me to the city except the top was low-cut and the pants had a little shine to them. Not leather, but close enough that Bronwen giggled when I chose them. Even though I wore her clothes to not draw attention, I liked dressing in Night Realm clothing. They made me feel beautiful even if they were simple, casual clothes.

She dragged me all through the city, in and out of various

shops. She had no problem buying anything that caught her eye. It was the same routine in every store. The owner would greet Bronwen as soon as she walked in the door, they would show her the newest additions after which Bronwen would have them send someone to put them in the carriage, and Bronwen would beg me to pick something out.

The last store we visited was the small bookstore that I had noticed the last time we were in the city. I began perusing the books while Bronwen followed me. She never looked at the books herself, so I knew she brought me here just so I could shop.

I looked through a few books before I realized what Bronwen was doing. Every time I touched a new book, she would nod and the store owner would write something on a piece of paper. She was making a list of books to pack up and take to the carriage.

For me.

I knew better than to object to Bronwen about anything so I just stopped touching books and turned to her. "How do you pay for all of this?"

"What do you mean?" she asked.

"Every store we've been in, they never told you an amount, and you never gave them any money."

"Oh, they send a bill, and Sebastian pays it," she said as if it was the most normal thing possible.

"Sebastian? He just pays for your shopping sprees?" With all that he was, I would've never imagined he would be willing to just pay the bill of a manic shopper.

She shrugged. "With everything I have to put up with in the castle, it's the least he can do."

I laughed at her response. Knowing Sebastian was footing the bill made me worry less about Bronwen buying me things.

107

Sovereigns have more money than they know what do to with.

A few books wouldn't hurt him.

"Will we be heading back soon?" I asked as we walked down the street. I'm pretty sure we visited every store in the city today.

Her eyes narrowed. "You act like you have somewhere to be," she said.

"No, it's just getting dark," I said as I looked up at the sky. The dusty blue was growing darker by the minute, and I was worried about being out in the city after dark. Bad things came out at night here.

"Violet, nothing is going to happen to you," Bronwen said as if she could read my thoughts. My father taught me from a young age how to build walls around my mind or I'd be worried that she really was in my head.

"Are you saying that evil things don't come out at night here?" I asked even though I knew the answer.

"They most definitely do, but I am perfectly capable of protecting us if it came down to it."

"Really?" I asked. Adar came with us the last time we left the castle, so I never thought about Bronwen's capabilities.

"There is a lot you don't know about me," she said, still walking down the street like we had somewhere to be.

"I don't know much of anything about you actually," I mumbled.

"Well, you know I am the Advisor of the Night Realm."

"And that Adar is your brother," I said, trying to keep up with her pace.

She let out a small sigh before she said, "I thought you may have forgotten Adar's little comment."

"No. I've thought about it quite often. I just wasn't sure

how to bring it up." Even though they seemed to be opposites, the idea of them as siblings was so fascinating. I had no siblings, and neither did Calum, so this was something that was completely new to me.

"He's my twin actually."

I stopped walking. It took her a moment, but Bronwen stopped a few paces ahead of me and turned around smiling.

I shook my head. "That's impossible. You two look nothing alike."

"Maybe we look exactly alike," she took a step closer and whispered, "but you're only seeing one version of us."

I looked at her confused before it clicked. The reason they were able to speak through their minds without being mates. "You're not fae, are you?"

Bronwen looked at the ground and then looked back up at me, slightly opening her mouth before looking away again. It's like she wanted to tell me something but was afraid to. I'm not sure if she was afraid of how I would react or if she was afraid that she would say something she wasn't supposed to. "I will tell you everything I can one day, but not yet. Some of it isn't for me to tell."

I wanted to know. I wanted to know everything that she was holding back, but I didn't want to overstep. I thought about Calum's warning about the fae of the Night Realm. I liked Bronwen, and I didn't want her to change on me.

"One day, but I will be gone in a few months," I said as I thought about returning home. I wanted my life with Calumback, but I knew I would miss my freedom here. And more importantly, I'd miss my friendship with Bronwen.

She studied me for a moment. "Do you think we can't be friends once you return home?" she asked.

"I'd like to."

Bronwen smiled before she looped her arm in mine as we continued walking down the street.

"So where are we going now?" I asked as I looked around trying to figure out what store we may have missed earlier.

"Do you remember that bar Adar went to while we went dress shopping?"

"Yes . . ." I said reluctantly.

"Get ready, Violet. I'm taking you to your first bar."

14

Chapter 14

Violet

I had only gotten drunk once in my life, and I hadn't had wine since. It was only a few years into mine and Calum's relationship.

Calum's parents had gone on an anniversary trip to Sartova, a small town on the north end of the Mountain Realm. Calum's father gifted Celine a home in Sartova in the early years of their marriage. Since Celine was native to the Ice Realm and had to leave her home for an arranged marriage, he wanted her to have a place where she felt comfortable. Sartova was the perfect place for that because it sits on the top of a mountain that was always covered in snow and looks out into the Ice Realm.

Celine never deserved him.

Since Calum's parents and my father were gone, Calum thought it would be a good time to let me try wine. He knew my father wouldn't approve because of my heart, but he wanted me to experience it. It was a good time—until it wasn't. We both got drunk, trashed the dining room, and passed out in the sitting room.

An unexpected storm ruined Calum's parents' anniversary trip so they came home early . . . and found us in the sitting room.

Having to sit and listen to our parents yell at us while nursing a throbbing headache from a hangover was enough for me to never want to drink again.

To make it even worse, my father brought it up for weeks after the incident saying it was too dangerous with my heart condition and that I had to be more careful—which was exactly why I tried it when he wasn't home.

Be careful. The words I had always had to live my life by.

I'm glad I had put a pill in my pocket before we left the castle today. I didn't know we would be out so late, but I knew better than to go somewhere without a pill. Just in case.

I took the pill as we walked towards the door at the bar. I tried to be as inconspicuous as possible because I didn't want to hear any comment about it from Bronwen.

Going to a bar with Bronwen seemed like a bad idea from the start, but it got even worse when we walked in and I realized it wasn't just a night out for the two of us.

Sebastian and Adar were standing at the bar top.

"Bronwen," I said as I stopped at the door. Sebastian was staring at me, like he sensed it the second I walked through the door, and based on our last encounter, there was no way this would end well.

Other than a few females gawking at Sebastian, no one seemed to make a big deal of the fact that their Sovereign was in the bar with them. Even with his casual clothes—a long-sleeved black top with pants to match—nothing could diminish his striking blue eyes and the shadows creeping up his neck like tattoos.

Despite his female admirers trying to get his attention, he never took his eyes off of me.

"Oh yeah, I forgot to mention that Sebastian and Adar were meeting us here," she said as a smile grew on her face.

"You *forgot*?" I looked at her with a knowing look.

"No, but I knew you'd object if I told you earlier. Just live a little, Violet," she said as she pulled me towards the bar.

Live a little.

She was right. My time here in the Night Realm where I had the freedom to do whatever I pleased was limited. I needed to enjoy myself. And what would happen if I just had one drink? I could ignore Sebastian.

Doubtful. But I could try.

One glass of wine turned into two, which turned into more, but I needed them. I couldn't live my entire existence around being careful because of my heart condition. What was the point of living if I just feared death the entire time? And it felt so good to make decisions for myself, even if it was something as simple as telling Bronwen I would have another drink.

The bar was small; the bar top was on the back wall with a few stools and a couple tables on both sides. Most of the room was open for dancing, which seemed to be what everyone came here for given the crowd of fae enjoying themselves and dancing to the angelic voice of a dark-skinned faerie with small weblike wings on her back and the drums of the two males with her, both with silver skin, black holes for eyes, and tails swaying to the music. It was dark, with only the candles on the walls lighting the room.

We sat around a table in the corner, and Bronwen talked the

entire time—something she seemed to always do. She either just didn't like silence or really liked to hear herself talk.

Adar found a lonely fae pretty quickly and left us to dance with her. This was the first time I ever saw Adar act normal. Like he was actually enjoying himself.

"Sebastian, I know you said no more family meals, but I'm growing bored of the mundane tasks I do around the castle. I need something else to focus on," Bronwen said as she stretched her arms across the table to add a little drama.

"If you continue putting me in a room with Nathara and Lilian multiple times a day, someone will end up dead," Sebastian said while ignoring the spectacle she was making of herself.

"So . . . not multiple times a day," Bronwen said, skipping the part where he threatened to kill someone. She sat up and began tapping her finger on the stone table as she ran those words through her head. "Then it's settled! We will just have dinners."

"Why can't it just be us?" he asked Bronwen, but he didn't take his eyes off of me. He hadn't taken his eyes off of me since I walked into the bar.

"You want your sister out of the realm. Excluding her and her new family from group dinners may look bad. They want an arranged marriage with her because they want an alliance with the Night Realm. *With you.* They could back out of the engagement if they learn she means nothing to you and that you don't intend to keep an alliance with them."

I couldn't believe they were talking about this in front of me. If this got out, it could jeopardize the engagement which was obviously something Sebastian wanted to happen. And yet they were saying it in front of the daughter of the Commander of the Mountain Realm.

"I've seen the way Calum is with Nathara. He's in love. He will marry her with or without an alliance with me," Sebastian said.

My heart sank when I heard those words. I grabbed my glass and drank what was left.

Sebastian's eyes narrowed at my reaction to what he said.

"Well, I disagree. You can perform your duty for the greater good and handle dinner with them for a few months," she said, doubling down.

Sebastian glanced at Bronwen and gave her a nod.

"And on that note," Bronwen continued as she looked down at my empty glass, "I will go get us some more wine." She grabbed my glass and walked to the bar.

"Did you enjoy yourself today?" Sebastian asked as he continued to study me.

"Yes, not as much as Bronwen did though."

"Do I even want to know how much she bought today?" he asked as he rubbed his forehead.

I giggled. The wine I drank was taking away the little willpower I had to ignore Sebastian.

"Probably not. But why do you buy everything she wants anyways?" I asked. I knew Bronwen's reason, but I wondered if there was more to it. Bronwen said there was nothing going on between the two of them, but they were so close. And the way she talked to him without any fear, there had to be something going on.

"She deals with Nathara and Lilian so I don't have to. I'd buy her the world if I could for that."

I didn't know if it was all the wine I had, but this was the first time I actually felt comfortable around Sebastian. I wanted to know more about his relationship with his sister and why he couldn't stand to be around her, but I didn't want to risk upsetting him and him turning back to the cold Sebastian I'd seen before.

"Oh, I love this song! Come dance with me!" Bronwen said as she ran back over to the table and grabbed me and Sebastian and pulled us to the dance floor.

The wine was in full effect as I felt the music run through my body. I danced with Bronwen, forgetting everything around me until a cool hand grabbed me and spun me around.

Every ounce of better judgment left my body when my eyes met his. There was such hunger and wanting looking down at me.

He wanted me, and I liked it.

I danced with him. Our bodies were closer than they had ever been, and they moved in rhythm with the music.

My heart was racing, and every part of my body was begging me to get closer to him as if the centimeter between us was too far apart. The hand he had wrapped around my waist felt too good, and I wanted to feel every part of him. And the crooked smile he gave me as he looked at me, like he could devour me— my gods, it warmed me deep in my belly. But as soon as I felt myself giving in, Calum popped into my mind. I couldn't do it. I couldn't do this to Calum. I needed air.

I pushed myself off of Sebastian, broke through the crowd of drunk, dancing fae, and went out the door.

As I stood there on the street trying to calm down, a pale-skinned, dark-haired fae walked out of the shadows.

"What are you doing out here all alone?" he asked as he looked at me, tracing the curves of my body with his eyes. I knew this wasn't good. The look in his eyes told me I wasn't safe, and every instinct in my body told me to get away from him.

I turned to go back inside but he grabbed me by the back of my head and pulled me away from the door. I started to scream but nothing came out. It was like he had taken away my voice. No matter how hard I tried, I couldn't make a sound.

He took me to the side of the building and slammed me against the wall. He bit my neck while he attempted to pull my pants down. I pushed him away, but it only made him madder.

He grabbed me by the throat, hitting my head against the wall again as he said, "Don't try to stop me. It will only make it worse."

Tears started to run down my face when all of a sudden something ripped him off of me and threw him against the stone wall of the building in front of me.

Sebastian walked over to him, and his shadows grabbed the fae and pinned him to the wall.

I stood there, frozen in place, as Sebastian looked at the fae and said, "She's mine," before plunging his hand in the fae's chest and ripping his heart out. He turned around to look at me. His eyes were dark, and he was still holding the fae's heart in his hand.

He killed someone right in front of me, and my mind was telling me to run before I was next. But I couldn't.

Because deep down, I didn't care what he had done.

He protected me. He *saved* me.

Even as he walked towards me, blood dripping from the once-beating heart in his hand, blood splattered across his face, and a sinister look in his . . . *black* eyes, I couldn't move. I didn't want to move.

He stopped as Bronwen and Adar came running into the

small alley where we were standing.

"What the hell did you do, Sebastian?" Bronwen asked as she looked at the lifeless body on the ground.

"Take her home." His words sliced through the air as I still stood there, unable to move my eyes from his.

The ride back to the castle with Bronwen was silent.

I couldn't stop thinking about what Sebastian did. I knew he was capable of it as he'd done it so many times before, even to his own father. But to see it firsthand . . . I'd never seen someone kill. And Sebastian didn't hesitate.

The part that scared me the most was that in that moment, I wasn't afraid of him. As he stood there with evil in his eyes and a bloody heart in his hand, I felt safe. Because he did it to protect me.

S*he's mine.*

Those words would forever be engraved in my mind.

15

Chapter 15

Violet

"So what did you do while I was gone?" Calum asked as I lay in his arms. He returned two days after the incident at the bar and woke me up in the middle of the night. Apparently, that was the first chance he was able to get away from Nathara.

"I stayed in my room most of the time." Which was true. The next morning after the night at the bar—when I thought more about what happened and what I felt—I refused to leave my room. I didn't want to take the chance of running into Sebastian and allowing any feelings to come back up.

I shouldn't have let myself be in a position like that in the first place. I shouldn't have drunk so much and let my guard down. Sebastian just did something to me that I couldn't explain, but I knew it was wrong. I loved Calum. I wanted to spend eternity with him, and I couldn't let a moment of weakness and bad judgment do anything to jeopardize that.

I'd spent the last two days reminding myself how evil Sebastian was, picturing him standing there with that fae's heart in his hand. He could've just made the fae leave. He was his Sovereign, and he would've listened to him.

But that fae was going to hurt me. He was going to do the unthinkable. Anyone who could do something like that deserved to die.

So no matter how hard I tried to make myself believe that Sebastian was evil, I ended up contradicting myself. Because he saved me.

Yara had come by both nights asking to escort me to dinner. I guess Bronwen didn't hesitate to plan dinners as soon as she got the OK from Sebastian, but I told her that I wasn't feeling well both times and asked her to bring food to my room.

I was surprised Bronwen didn't try to make me attend the dinners, but she must've been trying to give me some space. She was silent the entire carriage ride from the bar, which I think must have been the first time in her life. I didn't know if it was because of what Sebastian did or if something else was bothering her.

"Most of the time? So what else did you do?" Calum asked.

"Bronwen took me to a bar in the city," I said nonchalantly. Maybe if I acted like it wasn't a big deal, he wouldn't ask any more questions. I couldn't tell him everything that happened.

"A bar? Please tell me Adar went also." I could hear the concern in his voice.

"He did."

"Thank the gods." I knew the relief in his voice wasn't going to last long.

"Sebastian was there too," I said quietly. I didn't want to chance him finding out from someone else. That would be worse than him hearing it from me.

"Sebastian?" I could feel his head move to where he was

looking down at me, but I didn't want to look at him.

I nodded.

"I don't want you around him," he said.

"I don't want to be around him either. I didn't know he would be there," I mumbled.

"He's evil, Violet."

Was he though? If he was so evil, why would he kill someone that was trying to hurt me? Someone truly evil would allow something like that to happen.

See, all I did was contradict myself.

"I know."

I hated this. I hated keeping things from him. But what I'd done and how I'd felt was wrong. He didn't deserve this.

"I know you say you know, but I don't think you realize how evil he really is. Nathara has told me some things that have happened over the years."

I pushed myself off of him and sat up to look at him. Did he really just bring Nathara into this conversation? "Oh, Nathara told you some things, did she?"

"I am with her constantly. What did you think we did? Sit and stare at each other?" He looked at me like he thought I was being ridiculous.

"Well, I have tried to not picture you two together, but now I am. Just sitting around, talking about your lives, finding things that you have in common. How nice," I said, rolling my eyes.

"Violet, it's just talking. It's not like I'm fucking her."

"What did you tell her you like to do in your free time? Because the only hobby I know of you having is fucking your Commander's daughter."

His eyes widened at that, even though he knew it was the

truth. "Violet."

I was fuming, and I didn't even know why. I knew him having to fake a relationship with her would entail talking, of course. It wasn't like he shouldn't be talking to her, but for him to bring her into our conversation because of "some things" she had said about Sebastian—like we should take everything she said as the truth—just ticked me off.

"I would prefer if you never bring up anything the two of you have talked about—or done—again," I said through gritted teeth.

"You're right, I'm sorry. I just worry about you, and I can't protect you here," he said as he pulled me back to lay with him.

I didn't say anything. I understood his worry, but I couldn't very well tell him how safe I felt here.

We lay in silence for a while before I finally looked up to see he had fallen asleep. Obviously our conversation didn't bother him as much as it bothered me since he had no trouble going to sleep. I rolled over to the edge of the bed to kick my leg out from under the covers. Calum and I both ran hot while we slept, and I always ended up drenched in sweat before the night was over.

A cool breeze from the balcony door that I had left open hit my leg, bringing instant relief from the heater that was only a few inches away from me now.

I stared out of the opening at the night sky that was lit with more stars than I could count.

The Night Realm had done nothing but surprise me since the moment I arrived. I expected creatures of the night around every corner. The servants in the castle should be creatures that send chills down my spine, but other than Yara, they were all fae, which made no sense in itself. Nothing in my history books mentioned fae servants here. Sebastian did mention "Mountain Realm history books" with a negative undertone.

If they got things like this wrong, what other lies were written in our books, forcing us to believe them true?

I rolled back over to look at Calum, but as soon as my eyes were back on him, all I could picture was him at the dinner table with Nathara hanging all over him. If she did that around others, what does she do when they were alone?

I gritted my teeth as my imagination ran wild. I had to stop sulking and dwelling on this. I had to keep my trust in Calum because I knew he wouldn't hurt me.

Morning came too early after I spent most of the night consumed in my thoughts. I didn't know what time Calum left because he didn't wake me to tell me goodbye. I wasn't mad though. I didn't get enough sleep as it was. My heart felt a little lighter when I rolled out of bed. A step towards peace maybe. Peace about my situation.

I gave it until dinner tonight. As soon as I saw them together again that peace would fly out of the window.

My stomach growled, reminding me that I barely ate the dinner Yara brought me last night. It was a dish that I wasn't familiar with, a type of red meat, with a grayish sauce served over rice. Yara signed that it was "heart of traitor," at least that's what I think she signed. But I'm not completely fluent in sign language so I was hoping I was wrong.

But even the thought of it made me lose my appetite. The only thing I ate was the side of vegetables that was in a separate bowl far away from the traitor's heart.

I thought about ringing the bell and asking Yara to bring me breakfast, but I felt a little guilty having her run—well, fly—

123

around bringing me food again when I was perfectly capable of getting it myself.

I was better than this constant hiding in my room afraid of simple conversations with others. I used to dream about being outside of our castle, and yet here I was completely free to go where I chose, and I'd chosen to lock myself in my room.

I quickly threw a dress on and loosely tied my hair back with a ribbon before slipping into my shoes. I slung open my door but before I couldn't take a step out into the hall, Yara was standing there with a tray of food and another book.

Okay, one more day in my room wouldn't hurt.

16

Chapter 16

Violet

Here's what I'd learned after being in Night Realm for a little over a week:

1. You can't believe everything you're told. You have to learn for yourself.
2. Having to smile while watching Nathara practically hump Calum at dinner every night would eventually make me go insane.
3. I could spend the rest of my existence reading, and I would be okay with that.
4. Sebastian Kieran (I learned his last name in a book I read yesterday) would be the death of me.

It had been a couple of days since Calum and Nathara arrived back from searching for a place to honeymoon. They chose a small island in the Ocean Realm because of its seclusion. Like I wanted to know that.

The only time I had left my chambers was to attend dinners to show my face. I know I said I wasn't going to spend my days in my chambers any longer, but Sebastian ruined that. Well technically, he didn't. My dreams were actually to blame.

The moment I closed my eyes, all I could see was him. All I could feel were his shadows creeping up my body. And all I could hear was him saying, "She's mine." Over and over and over again.

So in fear of this getting any worse—if that was even possible—I didn't want to chance running into him while I was alone. So I stayed in my room, reading anything Yara chose to bring me.

Knocking on my door woke me from dreaming of Sebastian. Half asleep, I opened my door to see who could possibly want to see me at this hour of the night.

"Calum?" I pulled him into my room and checked the hall to make sure no one was around. "Is everything okay? Someone could have seen you."

I was so confused. He always transferred to my room and yet he was standing in the hall like he wasn't afraid of someone seeing us.

"Don't worry. Everyone is asleep. I have something to show you."

"What is it?"

"It's outside," he said as he grabbed my hand and tried to pull me towards the door with him.

"Are you sure no one will see us? What about the shadows?" Maybe Calum walking though the hall in the middle of the night didn't look suspicious, but I knew me and Calum in the hall together would set off alarms in Sebastian.

He may not care about an alliance with the Mountain Realm,

but he definitely didn't want anything to risk Nathara leaving.

It terrified me to think of what he would do if he found out about me and Calum. He may have protected me the other night, but if I interfered with his plans, I might be his next kill.

"You're right. Meet me past the garden in ten minutes." Calum left using the door. It's not like he didn't ever use doors, but he'd only ever transferred in and out of my room to make sure no one saw him. He was getting way too comfortable.

I put on my coat, waited a few minutes, and left my room quietly.

The castle halls were eerily empty. Faeries in the Night Realm stayed up later into the night, but it was so late that no one was up. There could only be one reason Calum would risk us being together outside of my room. He must have found the object that was draining Sebastian of his powers.

I didn't know what he had been doing from the time he left my room early this morning until now, but he really meant it when he said he was doing everything he could to find the object.

I walked through the gardens, finding it using only the light of the moon and stars in the night sky. Any other time, I would be terrified of being out in the dark by myself, but the idea that Calum had potentially found our way out of here kept me going further into the darkness.

We had to leave sooner rather than later. I had to get away from Sebastian. He had taken over every thought I had and all I could hope was that those thoughts would leave once I was out of his realm.

When I got past the gardens, I saw Calum facing the other direction, looking into the woods.

He must have heard me approaching because he said, "There

you are. Come here."

As I walked towards him, I watched as he turned to me and transformed into a tall, skinny black figure. A paramic. The thing Calum used to tell me about to scare me when we were faelings. A creature that shape shifted into someone familiar to lure their victims. Something straight from my nightmares.

I stood, frozen to my spot, while the creature closed the distance between us.

I turned to run but the paramic was standing in front of me again. I let out a partial scream before its long, skeletal fingers wrapped around my mouth stopping any further noise from escaping.

"Shhhh. We don't want to wake anyone. This will be over soon enough," it said as an evil smile came over its face. Its voice sent a chill down my spine.

I closed my eyes as I waited for it to take me away when all of a sudden its grip on me disappeared.

I opened my eyes to see someone had slammed it onto the ground and had their hands on its neck.

It was so dark that I couldn't make out their face. It wasn't until I felt something cool caress my hand that I knew who it was. I looked down to see shadows floating all around me.

Something that terrified me a week ago now made me feel safe. They weren't going to eat me. They were protecting me.

Sebastian was protecting me. He was always protecting me.

I took a step closer so I could see and watched as Sebastian placed his hand on the paramic's head. The creature let out a scream that pierced through my ears before it faded into a black mist and was gone.

Sebastian stood up, ran his fingers through his hair, and walked towards me. He was shirtless and wore a pair of loose-fitting black pants which made me assume he was asleep before he came to my rescue.

"Violet, are you alright?" he said as he looked all over my body.

"I–I'm fine," I said as I stared at the spot where the paramic faded into nothing, trying to figure out how he could do something like that. But then I remembered one of his gifts. A gift that no other fae had ever possessed. Something so hard to explain that the scholars simply called it the "touch of death."

And I just saw it firsthand.

Sebastian gently grabbed my chin and turned my face, forcing me to look at him. "I know you're from a different realm, but you know more than most anybody about, well, everything. You know better than to go out into the darkness of the Night Realm," he said.

"You're right. I don't know what I was thinking," I said as I turned to go back to the castle. I knew it was useless, but I was attempting to make an escape before he started asking questions, which was something he always seemed to do.

"Who could it have possibly been to have you follow it into the woods in the middle of the night?" And there it was.

I turned around to look at him. "It . . . it was my father," I said. Maybe looking into his eyes would make him believe me for once.

"Oh bullshit," he snapped, causing me to take a step back. "I've seen you and your father say all of two words the entire time you've been here. I don't think you'd leave your room for him, lct alone come outside."

Nope. Looking into his eyes didn't work.

He stopped searching for answers in my eyes and instead a look of understanding took over his face. "It was Calum, wasn't it?"

"What? Of course not," I said, trying so hard to stay strong. How could he possibly have any idea about me and Calum? I'd been in the Night Realm for just over a week, and I'd only been in the same room as him, excluding my room which presumably no one knew about, at dinners with everyone else.

"He put a ward on your room. I knew as soon as he did it, but I just assumed that it was so your father wouldn't worry about you. But I've seen the glances you give each other when you think no one is paying attention." He paused as his eyes began to darken, shifting closer to black than their normal blue. "You're fucking him, aren't you?"

Tears started rolling down my face. There was no way out of this. He'd known every time I'd lied to him, and I was backed into a corner now.

He put his hand on his face, turned around, and started to pace away from me. He stopped and looked up at the sky. After a moment, he came back to me and said, "You should know by now that I won't hurt you. And I'm telling you now, as if these past two encounters haven't already proven this, I won't let anything happen to you, but you have to tell me what's going on."

His eyes were normal again, and he looked at me, pleading with me to tell him the truth for once. And he was right. No matter how hard I'd tried to convince myself otherwise, deep down I knew he would protect me. I didn't know why, but he would.

"We're together. We've been together for about sixteen years now," I blurted out. I probably shouldn't have been so specific, but I had nothing to lose anymore.

"Bloody hell." Sebastian threw his arms up as he walked

away from me again.

I stood there waiting for more of a response, but he didn't look at me again. He was tapping his finger on his side as he looked up to the sky. "Violet, I think you should go back to your chambers now. We can talk about this later."

I couldn't say anything. I wanted to be back in the safety of my chambers, where I should never have left in the first place.

17

Chapter 17

Sebastian

I listened to her footsteps as she ran back to the castle and then to her room, which seemed to be the only place she wanted to be anymore.

And now I knew why.

I could feel the anger and darkness building up inside of me at the thought of what her confession meant.

But it made sense.

For the life of me, I couldn't figure out why she tried so hard to stay away from me. I knew she felt the pull, even if her side was suppressed from those stupid pills she'd been taking.

I may be the bad guy in every story she'd heard, but that shouldn't have been enough for her to fight her feelings so adamantly. But another male, one she'd been attached to for almost two decades, would do it.

If it was just for a fuck, which was all it should've been on his side given the rules of the Sovereigns, I could have handled it a lot better.

But a relationship? A relationship that had lasted for so long? All I wanted to do was go to Calum's room and rip his head off.

He was here preparing to wed my sister and yet he was still with Violet. He should have broken it off the moment he left to come to the Night Realm. She didn't deserve the life of a Sovereign's mistress.

As if I didn't have enough to deal with already, now I had this too.

Something was taking my power from me. It felt like there was a leak through which my powers were slowly draining, and I was not generating any more power to replace what I was losing. I was trying to conserve my power until I could find the object or person who was behind it.

My shadows once roamed the entire Night Realm. They were my eyes and ears to ensure nothing happened in my realm without me knowing. Once I felt myself losing my powers, I brought them in to watch over just within the castle walls. I felt Calum place a ward on Violet's room, but I thought it was to give his Commander peace of mind. Even though I wanted to know what she was doing at all times, I felt like breaking through the ward wasn't a necessary use of my dwindling power because I knew she was safe and that's all that mattered.

Idiot.

I now only used my touch of death, something I once used without giving it a second thought, when absolutely necessary. The disgusting fae that touched *my* Violet was an easy kill without any power, but with the paramic, I had to use my power. The only other way to kill a paramic was with a silver dagger, which I didn't just keep on me, and nothing mattered in that moment other than killing the thing that she was afraid

133

of.

I had always kept a force field around the castle, only allowing who I wanted to enter and exit, and that was something I knew I couldn't let go of easily. It was the only thing keeping the monsters of the night away.

I was growing weaker by the day, and somehow this paramic was able to push its way through my force field and creep through the castle without me knowing. I only knew it was here because of Violet's little scream. Nothing could keep me from hearing her.

Violet couldn't have come into my life at a worse time. All I could think about was being with her—protecting her—but now I was at my weakest, and I had yet to find a way to stop it.

The next issue had to do with those bloody pills Violet took.

She had haunted my dreams for almost a century. I should have been able to picture her, but I couldn't because something was suppressing the connection.

Instead of seeing her face, I saw damn flowers in my dreams. Violets.

Even if I couldn't see her, I knew what the obsessive dreams meant. I had a mate.

Violets consumed every thought I had. The castle garden that once was nothing but a few tall hedges was now covered in violets.

Dreaming of violets took me to the Flower Realm. I spent every free moment I had searching for her. I thought the violets in my dreams meant she was in the Flower Realm. It never once crossed my mind that it was her damn name.

Nothing seemed to bring me closer to finding her. I had almost given up hope. I thought it was some type of punishment for everything that I'd done. I had a mate but could never find her.

Then one night, while I was staring at the violets in my garden, like I did every night, it hit me.

Well, she hit me.

I knew from the moment our eyes met that the search was over. I looked into her big brown eyes, eyes that made me forget to breathe in that moment, eyes that made everything around me fade away.

I had found my mate.

The pull I felt made me want to fall to my knees and never let go of her.

But I could tell she didn't feel what I felt. By the way she looked back at me, I could feel her fear.

And then came the pills. A faerie with a heart condition? Bullshit.

When I wasn't searching the castle for the object that was slowly killing me, I was contacting every healer and scholar I knew to figure out what those pills were.

Violet said she had a heart condition, and she was telling the truth when she said that. At least the truth to her. I could tell when she was lying. She rubbed the palm of her hand on the side of her thigh, and she didn't do that with the heart condition.

She believed she had a heart condition, but I knew she didn't. It was impossible and yet everyone around her believed the bullshit. Either that or they all were in on it.

I wanted to just take her pills and force her to stop taking them. To prove to her that she was fine, for her to feel what I feel, and for us to figure out why she was given the pills in the first place, but I couldn't do that. If it was anyone else, I would. But not her.

She had spent her entire life being a submissive Mountain Realm lady. Not anymore.

She had to make the decision herself. I just had to do enough research to prove to her that I was right. One thing I'd learned in the short time she'd been here was that she loved to read and learn. She liked to know things. Maybe if I came to her with facts she would listen and stop taking the pills.

What did she tell Bronwen? *Knowledge is power.*

I'd like to show her what real power was.

But on top of all of that, I now had to deal with her being in love with someone else.

It hurt. I hadn't felt hurt like this in three centuries.

She was mine.

But she needed to realize it herself. I would not force her.

Since she didn't realize I was her mate, Bronwen had been working so hard to make her comfortable here. To make her not want to leave after the wedding so she could choose to be here, close to me.

But a relationship with Calum just complicated it all.

A week ago, I wouldn't have had a problem killing whoever stood in the way of me getting what I wanted.

But now I cared more about her and her happiness than I did myself. If she wanted him, I wouldn't stand in the way. I wouldn't force her to choose me.

I would spend eternity in misery if it meant she was happy. But how could she be happy? Calum was to marry the daughter of a Sovereign. If not Nathara, it would be one from another realm. He was a rule follower and that was one of the rules Queen Mother created. He would never put her first.

I was assuming he planned to keep her as his mistress, which never ended well. I'd seen it happen firsthand. Her needs would always be second to his wife's needs.

But with me, I'd let the world burn before I put someone above her.

I'd like to see Queen Mother try to stop me.

All I wanted to do was go to Violet and make sure she was okay. But as long as I knew she was safe in her room, I had to focus on finding the object that was draining me.

It started nearly a year ago. At first it was a small feeling that I was missing something. I disregarded it and assumed it would go away, that it was more mental rather than a physical loss of something.

After a few weeks and a few incidents of having to deal with some rather large and powerful creatures that needed to be reminded who they submitted to, I realized that my power wasn't replenishing after being used.

I traveled to the Land of the Healers where I learned of a rare black opal found in the bottom of the Druan Swamp that has the ability to absorb power. When mixed with a few other things, a witch can place a spell on it to have its absorption ability directed towards one thing.

And someone chose me for this. It didn't surprise me. Being the most powerful Sovereign makes for an endless number of enemies who would love to see me fall.

The problem was that when creating the spell, the black opal is turned into liquid which can be used to forge any object, which makes finding the object virtually impossible.

I knew the object was in my castle. When I was outside of the castle walls, my power stopped draining. I was still unable to replenish what I was missing, but I seemed to be too far out of reach from the object for it to continue to absorb my power. Since I had no leads in finding the object, I was going to leave

137

my castle while Bronwen and Adar continued the search. I was getting ready to leave when Violet showed up.

I couldn't leave her.

I'd rather lose all of my powers than spend a second where I couldn't feel her presence.

So now I was slowly replacing every object in the castle until the object was destroyed.

We should take Violet dress shopping with us.

Anytime someone said her name, my shadows brought the conversation to the front of my mind. I wanted to know anything and everything that happened with her. *Why would we do that?* Nathara asked Celine.

I wanted to know why they would want to take her with them. Celine had to know about Calum and Violet's relationship, so why would she want Violet anywhere near Nathara?

Well, I don't see her ever leaving the castle, so it might be good for you to get to know her. She could become one of your ladies in waiting. She should have to earn her stay now that she is no longer a faeling. We don't want her to think she can do as she pleases.

I knew Celine was a snake. She brought Violet here when there seemed to be no reason to do so, and now she was pushing to have Nathara around her. It was like she wanted Nathara to learn of Violet and Calum's relationship. Like she wanted Violet to get hurt.

If only she knew the fire she was playing with. If she knew what Violet was to me, she would never put her in harm's way.

But if she even tried to hurt her, I would become her worst nightmare.

I had to warn Violet of what I had overheard. She needed to be prepared before she was forced into the lion's den.

I transferred to her room before I even thought about what I was doing. She was in the middle of taking a sip of water when I appeared in front of her.

Every bit of water in her mouth ended up on my face. I definitely should've used the door.

The shock on her face immediately turned into fear after she realized she had spit all over me.

The last thing I wanted was for her to be afraid of me, and yet I kept doing things that scared her over and over again: threatening her with my shadows in the hall, killing a fae right in front of her, forcing the truth out of her about Calum and then reacting the way I did. And now transferring unannounced, unwelcomed, into her room. Well, the last thing may have shocked her more than anything. I think she feared more about how I would react.

"I-I'm so sorry," she said as she waited for my reaction.

"No, I'm sorry. I shouldn't have come into your room like that," I said as I wiped my hand over my face.

She looked at me, still scared, but also confused by my apology.

"We need to talk about last night."

"Look, I know you are upset because you want Nathara out of the Night Realm, and I seem to be standing in the way of that but please don't tell her of our relationship."

Dread settled in my chest at what she said. Did she really think I acted the way I did because of . . . Nathara?

Was she truly that blinded by her pills that she couldn't see the way I looked at her? The way I was unable to do anything but look at her when she was in the same room as me?

I knew I had to tell her something to help her understand why I was so bothered by her confession. I had to keep part of the truth hidden because I didn't want to tell her we were mates. I didn't want her to feel like she *had* to be with me. I wanted her to want me the way I wanted her.

"I was upset because I know what your future entails if you keep a relationship with Calum once he is married."

"I don't understand," she said with a confused look on her face.

"How much do you know about me?" I asked.

"What do you mean?" she asked nervously.

"I know you like learning things. That's why you were in my library. You spend your time reading, so what all have you read about me?" I was trying to approach this in the best way I could, by playing into her interests.

"Considering your reaction to what I said about your shadows, I don't know if my information is correct."

"Well, tell me what you know, and I'll correct you if you're wrong."

She looked at me for a moment with apprehension on her face before she crossed her arms and began, "You became the Sovereign of the Night Realm when you were still a faeling, making you the youngest Sovereign in the history of Alentara. You were born with the gift of wielding force fields, which every Night Realm Sovereign has, but you also have other gifts."

"Do you know all of my other gifts?" I knew I should get to the point, but I knew the quicker we made it to why I was here, the quicker I would have to leave her. And I also wanted to see how she acted when she talked about my powers, to learn whether she was truly terrified of me and what I could do. I'd gotten mixed signals from her every time I'd been around her.

I knew it was because she was fighting the pull. Sometimes she let it bring her to me, like the night she let herself dance so closely to me, and sometimes she pushed me away. When she wanted to push me away, she must have thought of all the things I'd done and what I was capable of.

My gods, that night. It had played on repeat in my mind the past few days. Feeling her body on mine, how she melted into my touch, the things I wanted to do to her.

"The shadows, mind reading, and," she paused as she glanced down to her feet, "the touch of death, like what you did last night." Every time she looked away from me, I did everything I could to get her to look back at me. So I could see her beautiful brown eyes again.

"What you saw was only a glimpse of what I can do, love."

"What do you mean?" she said as she looked back into my eyes. "You touched the paramic and it just misted into nothing."

"My 'touch of death,' a name the scholars have come up with since they have never found another faerie with this gift, can kill any creature that I touch. But do you remember how I told you my shadows were an extension of me and my senses?"

"Yes," she said, waiting for my response.

"I have learned how to use my touch of death through my shadows," I paused for a moment as I listened for her heartbeat. I wanted to see how she reacted to the darkest parts of me. "Meaning, I can kill anything or anyone I want no matter how far away they are."

I waited for her heart rate to jump or for the fear to come over her face again, but instead she said, "So I was right."

"Excuse me?" I asked, taken aback by her response.

"Your shadows can consume others."

I thought about what she said. My shadows do not *eat*, but from an outsider's perspective, shadows circling a creature and then the creature disappearing may look like the shadows consumed them.

"I guess they do," I said, smirking. She was so focused on learning everything she could that she wasn't fighting the pull. She wasn't forcing herself to think about how evil I was. Instead, she was hanging on every word I said, and I didn't think she realized that she was slowly moving closer to me.

"What do you know of my parents?" I asked. I didn't want to give her a chance to think about what she was doing.

"I thought Lilian was your mother, so anything I've read is probably wrong."

I took a deep breath. I couldn't let my hatred for Lilian ruin this conversation with Violet. I needed to stay around her for as long as I possibly could. To test how close she would get to me before either her relationship with Calum or her pills would pull her away from me.

"What did you read?" I asked.

"Why don't you tell me the truth, and I'll tell you if the *Mountain Realm history books* have it right," she said.

I smiled at the attitude she had given me. Without even realizing it, she was getting more comfortable with me.

"I killed my father," I said as I held my breath.

"Maybe he deserved it."

There was the pull. The bond that would make her believe anything I did was done for a good reason. I watched as her face immediately changed as if she was shocked that she said that. The pills seemed to fight the bond every time it tried to show itself to her. I knew the pills weren't to suppress our bond. No one could have known we were mates when she was a baby. The suppression of our bond was just collateral damage to the pills suppressing something else inside of her.

But that was something I could deal with at another time. Right now, I needed her to trust me.

"Why don't I tell you everything and then you tell me if my father deserved it?"

18

Chapter 18

Violet

I couldn't believe those words came out of my mouth. Why would I try to justify Sebastian's actions after everything I knew about him? Just because he'd saved me twice?

He grinned at my response, as if he had been waiting for me to say something so absurd, like a father deserved to die at the hands of his own son.

"Why don't I tell you everything and then you tell me if my father deserved it?" he asked, seeing the regret on my face for what I had said. As much as I wanted him to leave, I wanted to know more. I *needed* to know more, and he was going to use that to his advantage. To stay with me as long as he could.

"My parents were mates. They found each other when they were very young and completed the bond immediately. My grandfather was still alive, so the last thing on my father's mind was becoming Sovereign. My grandfather wouldn't allow my mother to live in the castle because their bond was a betrayal. My father was betrothed to a daughter of another

Sovereign, and with the mating bond completed, he couldn't wed another.

"My father chose to stay with my mother, so my parents lived in a small village where my mother was from. She was an achluo. They had me pretty quickly, and we were happy.

"My father was an only child, meaning there was no one for the line of succession to go to and with him breaking Queen Mother's rules, my grandfather knew he had to father another child to be the next Sovereign. My grandparents spent decades trying to conceive another heir but to no avail. A healer told my grandfather of a plant deep in the woods of the Night Realm that could help them conceive so my grandfather sent soldiers from his Guard to retrieve the plant. But each time he sent them, they never returned.

"My grandfather was desperate, so he and his Commander went to get it themselves. His Commander died, and my grandfather was bitten by a Naga, meaning his death was imminent. Since he had run out of options and knew the realm would be vulnerable without a Sovereign, he sent some of his soldiers to bring my father back to the castle.

"My father refused to leave me and my mother behind, so we came with him. What my father didn't know was that my grandfather was waiting with a witch at the castle. Guards at the castle held my parents down, and the witch stripped the mating bond away so my father could wed and become Sovereign.

"I was only a faeling and watched as my parents lay on the ground, screaming from excruciating pain, as the bond between them was ripped away.

"He wed Lilian the next day.

"Even with the bond gone, my mother still loved my father,

and you would think he would've loved her back after all of the years they had spent together. But that witch . . . she did something else when she broke the bond. She took away the love my father had for us.

"Even though it seemed as if a switch had flipped, my father wouldn't let us leave. He wanted to keep us under his control. So my mother became his mistress.

"She had to watch my father be with Lilian, watch her be the lady of the house and have control of everyone in it, including us. She watched her mate fall in love with another. We even had to be at the party where he announced he and Lilian were pregnant with the heir to the throne. The next Sovereign of the Night Realm."

"But he had you. His firstborn. The next Sovereign, right?" I asked as confusion came over me.

"I am a bastard, love. I was never meant to be Sovereign of the Night Realm."

"So you killed your father to become Sovereign?"

Sebastian's eyes darkened. "No. I killed my father because I had to spend two decades watching the light leave my mother until one day it was too much for her, and she took her own life.

"After finding my mother's lifeless body in the garden, I found my father on the training field outside the castle walls. With me being so young, no one tried to stop me when I threw myself onto my father. But they should have. Because as I had him pinned to the ground, with my hands wrapped around his throat, I wished death on him, and he just . . . misted into nothing. That's how I discovered my gift of death.

"But that's not all that happened. I had known of my shadow gift, but they stayed within a few feet of me. When I killed my father, it's like it released something inside of me that had been waiting to come out. My shadows exploded from me with such force that you could feel the earth shake in all of Alentara.

"My eyes turned as black as the sky that always covered the Night Realm. Killing my father awoke a part of me that had been lying dormant. A part of me that could control the entire realm without lifting a finger. A part of me that," he paused for a moment, "enjoyed death.

"His entire Guard watched me come into my gifts. Due to the fear of what I had become, they knelt before me and swore to serve me. I became Sovereign because I have so much power that no one dares to object. It's not my birthright. It's Nathara's. She was meant to become Sovereign of the Night Realm.

"Now, love, I'll ask you. Did my father deserve to die?"

I paused for a moment while I thought about everything he had told me. I knew I couldn't lie because somehow he always knew. I had to tell him the truth no matter how he might react.

"No. It wasn't his fault that a witch changed his feelings," I said. I looked at him, waiting to see if what I had said angered him.

"You're right. He didn't deserve to die, but I don't regret it. I would do it a thousand times over to get my power and my throne. The feeling I felt when I came into my powers, nothing has ever felt so good. And now, because of a fucking object that I can't find, I feel my powers slowly drifting away."

He had just admitted to me everything I thought true. He was evil. So sick and twisted that he even enjoyed killing. And yet—I was completely unfazed by it.

Which made me just as bad as he was.

"Are you afraid of me again?" he asked with a look of

concern. He must've taken my silence as fear.

"No. You won't hurt me," I said with complete confidence. He'd protected me twice, and now he had found something out that had the potential to ruin his plan to be rid of his sister. The easiest thing for him to do would be to kill me to ensure Nathara left his realm. But instead, he chose to come to my room and explain to me the kind of life I was in for.

"You're right, I won't. And I've told you enough times that I won't let anyone else hurt you either. Your secret is safe with me. I just . . ." Sebastain paused for a moment like he was searching for the right words. "You don't deserve to be the mistress of a Sovereign. It's a miserable life."

He had more concern for me than I did for myself. But why? He barely knew me.

If only he knew that I never planned on being a mistress. And Calum didn't plan to marry Nathara. His concern for my safety would probably disappear if he found out what I was keeping from him.

"Telling you all of that wasn't the only reason I came to your room. Nathara is going to ask you to go dress shopping with her tomorrow."

"What?" I asked with complete shock. Why the hell would she want me to go with her? I'd barely spoken to her, and it was clear to me that she saw me as less than her due to my rank.

"It was Celine's idea," Sebastian responded.

"Of course it was," I said, rolling my eyes.

"I take it she doesn't like you?"

"How did your grandfather feel about your mother? The one who was standing in between your father and the throne?" I asked.

Sebastian shook his head. "He hated her."

"There's your answer," I said, shrugging my shoulders.

"Why do you think she wants you to go with them?" He scrunched his eyebrows.

"When she is bored, she loves nothing more than to see others suffer. Especially me."

"Tell them no. That you won't go with them," he said.

"I can't. If I don't do what Celine says, it'll be so much worse."

His eyes darkened at what I said. "She won't do anything to you here."

I looked at Sebastian, seeing his unwavering need to protect me. "She's patient. She'll do something once we return home."

"Calum will allow that?"

"He has a weak spot for his mother." I shrugged my shoulders. "I don't know why. She has never been a good mother, but he submits to her and pretends like he doesn't see what she does."

His jaw clenched. For the life of me I couldn't understand why Sebastian got so bothered by things that happened to me.

But what was worse was that I liked that it bothered him. I liked seeing his eyes darken, and the shadows radiating from him.

And the feeling I started to get deep down, that's when I knew I'd been around him long enough and that he needed to go.

"It's my time to go, love."

"What?" I responded but he had already transferred out of my room, and immediately there was a knock at my door.

Oh, that's why.

149

19

Chapter 19

Violet

I waited for a moment hoping she would just leave because I knew who it had to be and what she was going to ask, and I knew I couldn't say no.

Another knock.

I might as well get this over with.

I opened the door to Nathara standing with her arms crossed and an aggravated look on her face.

"We are going dress shopping tomorrow, and Celine said I should invite you."

"Why did she say that?" I asked even though I had no doubt as to why she would bring me into this—to watch me be tortured.

"She said I should get to know you before you become one of my ladies," she said as she peeked around me into my room.

It took everything in me not to slam the door in her face. Celine had already made a remark about this to me when she told me I had to come with her to the Night Realm. I had thought it was her just trying to get a reaction out of me, but hearing Nathara say it made it so much worse.

But I couldn't refuse. I had to play the part until Calum got us out of this.

"What time should I be ready?" I said as I tried to muster up a smile.

"Noon," Nathara said before looking me up and down and continuing. "Please tell me you'll look better than you do right now after you get ready."

Gods help me.

"I'll try to fix myself up tomorrow for you."

Without responding, she turned around and walked back down the hall.

Bitch.

After clearing the air with Sebastian and actually feeling like we were in a good place, a place of understanding each other a little better, I didn't dread dinner as much as I usually did.

Nathara had gotten in my head with her remark earlier, so I took my time getting ready for dinner. I wanted to be as beautiful as Bronwen, and as much as I hated to even think about her, *Celine*. Their eyes practically glowed with the vibrancy of their shades of blues and greens while my eyes were dim and dull. Their hair was both so different, yet both so alluring. I envied their distinct looks as I had nothing to compete with them.

It shouldn't have bothered me. There was nothing to compete for as I had the one I wanted, and he had never made me feel less than beautiful. But a part of me wanted others to think I was beautiful.

I removed the ribbon that I always used to tie my hair up. It was a habit I had formed ever since Astrid used to fix my hair when I was a faeling. It gave off a look of innocence, which never bothered me before, but being here—surrounded by goddess-like ladies—I wanted to look like them.

As a few strands of hair fell in my face, I ran my fingers through them and tucked the right side behind my ear.

I shuffled through the drawer in the desk where I had placed a few of my personal items in until I found the small bag of makeup I had. It was nothing more than a few eyeshadows and lip stains that my father had brought back from his travels with Calum's father over the years.

No one had ever taught me how to correctly use makeup, so I taught myself. A little eyeshadow to bring out my eyes—if that was even possible—and a soft pink on my lips.

I looked through the dresses in my closet but none of them compared to the ones in the garment bag I had hung in the back of the closet.

And I had never felt as beautiful and sexy as I did in the purple dress at the last dinner I attended. Bronwen had helped me choose a few more at the seamstress's shop that day. The purple dress, a couple black, and a dusty blue that seemed to be eerily the same shade as Sebastian's eyes. The seamstress must have chosen the color as a nod to the sky as I'm sure she wasn't thinking of her Sovereign when making the dress.

The black dress I had chosen for tonight was sleek, revealing, and no doubt would put everyone's eyes on me. I just hoped I got the reaction I was wanting.

Yara knocked on my door at the same time she had done every night before dinner. When I opened the door dressed the way I was, her eyes widened with shock. I was sure she had expected me to be dressed as I usually was.

She shook off the look and gestured for me to follow her.

I'm not sure why I was always escorted. I knew the way to the dining room, and I knew the time they liked to have dinner—right after nightfall.

I didn't mind Yara's company, though. Even with the silence, her presence was comforting.

She didn't lead me like she had always done. Instead, she kept my pace and stayed right beside me.

You look beautiful, Yara signed as she floated down the hall.

She thought I was beautiful. Yara's reaction was exactly what I had been wanting. And I felt my heart warm at her comment. If no one reacted to my attire at dinner, I wouldn't mind, as Yara's compliment was enough.

As I walked into the dining room, I began to regret wearing such a revealing dress because I was the second to arrive, coming in after only Sebastian.

He was standing at the window, staring out into the garden, but turned around when he sensed a presence was in the room with him. His eyes were looking on the ground but began to shift up slowly while his mouth hooked into a half smile.

Sebastian was taking his time, soaking in every detail of the dress . . . of my body. All the insecurity I had went away when his eyes met mine because the look he was giving me told me how badly he wanted me. How beautiful—how sexy—he thought I was.

He opened his lips slightly as if he was going to say something to me before he closed them and returned to his crooked grin.

Was he . . . speechless?

I felt my heart rate heighten at the thoughts I imagined running through his mind. He began walking towards me before he came to a halt a foot or so away from me, and I

153

watched as his smile left and he clenched his jaw.

Sebastian closed his eyes and inhaled deeply before meeting my eyes again as he said, "Your *lover* will be here in a few moments."

He had no hint of emotion on his face. He was preparing for a dinner with his "guests" where he put on a facade of being one thing when I had already seen so much more.

He was so much more than a cold, emotionless, evil killer like he preferred everyone to believe he was. Though I learned of what he did to his father, and how he enjoyed it, I also learned of the side that cared for his mother more than anyone. The side that would put my safety above his own needs.

"Was that who this dress was for?" he asked.

I scrunched my eyebrows at his question. I couldn't answer him because I didn't know how to answer him. Was it for Calum? Was it for me? Was it to show Nathara I was more than the plain Mountain girl she thought I was? Or was it to get a reaction out of Sebastian?

I didn't know.

I turned around as I heard Calum and Nathara enter the dining room. Calum looked between me and Sebastian before looking down at my dress. His eyes widened for a moment before he caught himself and quickly changed his expression. He looked away and pulled Nathara to the table.

As they took their seats, I made eye contact with Nathara who was glaring at me. I bit my lip to hold back a smile. Her reaction told me everything I needed to know. I did better than what I was attempting.

But it's her fault. If she hadn't made that little comment earlier, Mountain Realm Violet would be at the table right now.

My father came a pace behind them, and by the look he gave

me, I could see his utter shock at the way I was dressed.

"Hello, Father," I said as I realized that this was the first time I had talked to him in almost a week. Unless he was gone with Calum, I used to see my father every day. I guess that was because he wasn't ever far from Calum, and if Calum was home, he was with me.

My father quickly glanced at Sebastian, who was standing so closely behind me, before he said, "I see you have another new dress, little bird."

"Bronwen purchased several for me when we went shopping," I replied as I nervously smoothed out my dress, even though there was no need. It was so fitted to my body that there was nothing out of place.

"I will have to pay her back for those," my father replied.

Just as I opened my mouth to respond, Sebastian interrupted and said, "No need, they're on me. They suit *our* little bird."

I watched as my father glanced at Calum in fear of a reaction to Sebastian's statement. I followed his eyes to see what he saw. Calum didn't look away from Nathara, but I knew he was listening because his jaw flexed and his hand gripped part of the tablecloth so tightly that his knuckles were white.

Luckily, Nathara was too entranced to notice. I turned around to look at Sebastian, but he had transferred to his seat at the head of the table and was looking out the window, which seemed to be his favorite thing to do during dinners.

My father and I followed suit and sat at the table, but my eyes never left Sebastian. If I had the power to wish death on someone, he would be dead right now. He knew what he was doing when he said that. He wanted a reaction out of Calum. Now that he knew our secret, he was going to have fun with it.

As if he knew what I was thinking as I glared at him, he

quirked a real smile before going back to his emotionless facade.

"Whew! You could cut the tension in here with a knife!" Bronwen said as she waltzed into the room, breaking my stare from Sebastian. She came in with her arm looped in Adar's, who looked like he was being forced to be a part of her entrance.

I felt for him. Only a little. Because I knew how it felt to be paraded around by Bronwen. But better him than me.

"Hot damn, Vi, if I would've known I'd be competing with you for attention tonight, I would've worn a little less," she said as she sat in the chair next to me.

"Dear gods, please no," Adar said at Bronwen's remark while walking to the other side of the table to sit next to Sebastian.

I looked at the dress Bronwen had chosen for dinner and wondered how she could possibly get away with wearing less.

Her breasts were barely covered by thin pieces of deep blue fabric and a slit came up all the way to her hip on her left leg.

She would have to wear lingerie to wear less.

As I studied her dress and exposed skin, I noticed two small scars on her thigh. It was odd as it was so rare for a fae to have scars. Our healing abilities were so advanced that an injury healed with no proof that there was ever an injury in the first place, unless the injury was absolutely brutal. But I remembered that she wasn't fae. She was only in the form of a fae right now. Even so, if she chose a fae body, why would she have a scar?

I knew from our past conversations that I really knew so little about her, but I wanted to know more. I *needed* to know more.

She must have noticed that I was focused on her scar because she moved her hand to cover it. When I looked back up, I realized she was watching me.

"A story for another time," she said as she winked at me.

"Your bride asked me to go dress shopping with her tomorrow," I said to Calum as we lay in my bed.

He came to my room not long after dinner, which was the first time I had been around him alone since the paramic incident.

I thought about telling him what happened, but I knew no good would come of it. His learning of that would lead to the questions of why Sebastian saves me which was something I couldn't even answer for myself. Not to mention the fact that Calum didn't need to know about Sebastian learning our secret.

He had enough to deal with right now. I could handle Sebastian.

I think.

Calum sat up from the bed and looked at me as he said, "What?"

"It was your mother's idea," I said as I rolled my eyes. Her involvement in anything just angered me. More than it used to. I wasn't sure why, though. Before we came here, I would just ignore her digs or attempts to make my life more difficult.

I remember one time, after she learned of Calum and me, she brought a nun from Our Lady's Keep to try to convince my father that I would be safer, which everyone seemed to notice pretty quickly that was all he cared about, if I left the castle and went to become a nun.

Even after my father declined, she had the nun stay for months, following me around, to *teach* me, which just made it harder to see Calum.

157

I guess that was good practice for us having to sneak around now.

"And what did you say?" Calum asked. That seemed like such a stupid question.

"I told her to fuck off," I bit out.

"Violet."

I sat up from the bed to meet his gaze and glared at him. I don't know why it had aggravated me so much. Maybe it was thinking about Celine and the things she'd done, adding dress shopping with my lover's fiancée to the list, or maybe it was Calum asking me what I said to Nathara. Like I don't know better than to submit to her.

I mean it really was a stupid question. He knew I couldn't do anything but comply. "What do you think I said? I asked her what time I should be ready. You know, after she told me that she was expecting me to become one of her ladies in waiting."

He rubbed his hands over his face at my response. "Well, you know that's not going to happen. Just humor her until I get out of this."

Humor her. Seriously?

"Since you aren't going to marry Nathara, what do you think the council will do? I'm sure they won't just allow you to officially be Sovereign when you come home without a wife."

Until my conversation with Sebastian earlier today, I hadn't really put much thought into what would happen once we returned home to the Mountain Realm. Specifically whether Calum would be given control of the realm after not doing what was expected of him.

I'd just been so worried about being with him that I hadn't really thought of the logistics of it all.

"I think that when I come home with an alliance with the

most powerful and feared Sovereign, they won't have any trouble giving me control," he said while positioning himself so he could rest his back on the headboard of my bed.

"And what's your plan for us after we go back home?"

"What do you mean?" he asked as he raised an eyebrow.

"You will have to marry eventually so you can make the next heir to rule the Mountain Realm. When that time comes, will we just end things, and I will have to find somewhere else to go?" I asked, even though I wasn't sure if I wanted to know the answer.

"I don't think I could let you go. My duty as Sovereign may be to another fae one day, but my heart will always be with you."

"So you would expect me to stay and be your mistress? Watch you have a family with another and stay back waiting for any chance you get the time to see me?"

Calum scrunched his eyebrows. It may have been because of my choice of the word mistress, as we had never used that word when talking about me. I had never really thought of myself that way until Sebastian said it. It wasn't something that was normal. Once you marry, you are meant to forsake all others, even if your spouse wasn't of your choosing.

Or his confusion could have been from the fact that this was the first time I had ever asked questions about our future.

"My duty to another would be nothing more than creating heirs," Calum said.

"It takes years to successfully get pregnant. Years of rituals, blessings, bonding, and sex." Unless you had a mate, the one that was created specifically for you, it was not easy to procreate. I continued, "You don't think all of that wouldn't cause feelings to develop? I mean if that's the case, you might as well marry Nathara and go ahead and get started."

I didn't mean it. But I was hurt by what he said. He expected me to become his mistress even if he didn't explicitly say it. Bound to him forever as less than his wife and never having a chance for a life of my own. I didn't want to ever lose him, but I think watching him with another—forever—would be far worse.

And after everything Sebastian told me about his mother, being a mistress sounded like hell.

I had been living in delusion my entire life. Being in a castle with Calum as my sole focus made me really believe that no matter what happened, I would be okay with whatever little bit of him I could get. But leaving the Mountain Realm, seeing the outside world, and learning that there was so much more than I knew, I was no longer sure I could live bound to Calum when he could never put me first.

"No one could ever cause me to lose sight of you, and I will not marry Nathara. She already wanted to kill my lover before we were even married. I'm not going to put you at risk by having her at the castle with us. And I will not let this happen any sooner than it has to. We could still have a few hundred years together before a wife has to come into the picture," he continued as he grabbed my face, cupping it in his hands. "Violet, please don't push me away."

That look. The look he had always given me that caused me to fold every time.

And it was no different now.

Even though I knew time was running out, whether that was only a few months, if Calum didn't find the object, or a few hundred years, I didn't want to think about it anymore.

It just reminded me how powerless I truly was. And I didn't

like that feeling.

20

Chapter 20

Violet

Calum spent the night and woke me up before he left. It was always before daylight before anyone else would be up.

I usually had no problem going back to sleep, but I couldn't today. I lay there for a few hours tossing and turning, dreading what the day entailed. Having to put on a facade of the meek, less than Violet that I was supposed to be.

Not the one that was fucking the groom.

Please tell me you'll look better.

I couldn't get her out of my mind. I knew what she wanted. I knew she wanted me to look more like someone she would be out with. A female from the Night Realm. Someone *worthy* of being with her.

At first, I felt pity for her being forced to marry someone that loved another. Sitting in my room alone for weeks after Calum left to come to the Night Realm allowed my mind to run wild with thoughts. I had thought about her more than I'd like to admit. I thought about how she was probably trying everything she could to make Calum fall for her. How she probably went to bed every night wondering why she wasn't enough for him. Or why she couldn't have been betrothed to someone who loved her.

Then after arriving at the Night Realm and finding out what happened, the pity disappeared and was replaced with jealousy. Even if the attention she was getting was just a show. But to know she'd felt his lips, his touch. I felt nothing but hate towards her. And on top of it, she was a bitch. So the hatred seemed to run deeper.

I didn't have many clothing options to wear today. I had my dresses I brought with me and the dresses I got with Bronwen, which were far too fancy for daytime shopping. My only other options were Bronwen's outfits I had borrowed and worn.

Part of me wanted to just put on one of my dresses, tie my hair back in a ribbon, and throw on a pair of slippers, which was definitely what Nathara wouldn't want, but I knew I should try to blend in and draw less attention to myself by looking like I belonged here.

After contemplating my options for far too long, I went with the outfit I wore on my first day in the city.

We took two carriages to the city. Lilian and Celine said they had some things they needed to do after shopping while Nathara wanted to return to the castle immediately. She said she wanted to be back with Calum as soon as she could.

When it came time to board the carriages, I debated which carriage would be the lesser of two evils.

Celine seemed like the better choice. The evil I knew. But throwing Lilian in the mix just gave me a bad feeling.

Nathara, whom I should consider my biggest enemy, didn't scare me as much. She was horrid, but I had what she wanted so badly, which made me feel superior, even if she didn't know it.

"I like your necklace," I said, gesturing to the small pendant around Nathara's neck. It was a small gray stone set in gold that hung right above her breast line. We had ridden in silence the majority of the time, but I could feel her staring at me.

I knew leaving her alone with her thoughts could be far worse than making small talk with her about something I didn't even care about.

"It was a gift from Celine," she said as she grabbed the pendant between her fingers. "She had it sent right after her husband's death as sort of a start to the engagement."

Of course she had this engagement in motion the moment she saw the opportunity.

"That's nice of her," I said as I gritted my teeth.

The bridal shop was right above the shop where Bronwen got her custom dresses. I hadn't even noticed there was a second floor in the building until now. We went up a small staircase that was tucked in the back right corner of the shop that had nothing to indicate we were going to a separate part of the seamstress's shop.

On the left wall of the second floor were floor-to-ceiling mirrors and a small podium for the bride-to-be to stand on to get a full view of the dress. Small, cushioned chairs sat in a half circle around the podium so the bride's entourage could sit and gawk at the bride as she showed off the dress.

Bridal gowns lined the wall opposite of the staircase. The room was busting at the seams with white dresses. Probably because most ladies of the Night Realm chose to wear dark colors, even on their wedding days.

Dresses also lined the right wall, but there was also a small opening that seemed to lead to a separate room.

I followed Nathara to the podium and sunk deep into my chair, wishing it would swallow me whole.

Other than the glances Celine gave me every now and then, just to rub it in, they had all but forgotten I was even with them.

I blocked out their voices as soon as Nathara brought up picking out lingerie for her wedding night.

I kept glancing at the doorway that was tucked between two rods which were overflowing with dresses. I felt like my eyes were playing tricks on me because I thought I could see a dress similar to the one I almost put on this morning, which was tan. I knew I had to be mistaken because there was no way a Night Realm seamstress would make a dress like that, let alone have it in her shop to sell.

The curiosity at what could be in that room was eating me alive. I quietly got up from my chair and walked towards the door. No one even looked my way as they were too concerned with watching Nathara twirl in a sparkly ball gown-style dress with a sweetheart neckline.

I stopped as soon as I stepped through the doorway to take in the sight before me.

To the left of the doorway were dresses made of shades of deep greens, reds, and browns which then flowed into a section of pastels and florals, to various hues of blues.

As my gaze continued around the room going from blues to reds and yellows. I understood why this floor wasn't on display. These dresses weren't like the Night Realm dresses that filled the room below. They weren't Night Realm dresses at all.

These dresses represented each of the other realms.

To see all of the realms coming together, even in something as simple as the dresses in a room, was enchanting. Each section was so different and yet they complemented the others so beautifully.

I started on the left side, which seemed to be dresses inspired by Forest Realm fashion, and made my way around.

I stopped at the Sun Realm dresses because I had never seen a dress like the ones before me.

Even though I was never allowed at Celine's parties and balls, I would sometimes sneak into them and hide between the tall curtains, just to observe the different fae in attendance.

While most of the time, it was only fae from our realm, some of the bigger celebrations brought in guests from the outside.

I had seen dresses from every other realm except for the Sun Realm. When the Sun Realm fell and the fae fled to other realms, they assimilated and took on the persona of a fae from that realm. They left behind any trace of their old lives, including the fashion.

It was such a pity, as there was a certain fire in these designs that I didn't see in the other dresses.

Bright, bold colors with sleeveless tops and high slits on the leg. Some were covered in orange and yellow jewels that looked like flames of a fire when the light hit them. I knew the fae who wore dresses like these had personalities that fit the fashion.

Kind of like Bron—

"Calum already can't keep his hands off of me. Just imagine how he will be after he sees me in this dress!" Nathara's voice echoed into the room I was in, and I shot my eyes to the doorway to see what she had chosen.

"Be careful, Vi, your face looks like you could kill her. She might begin to suspect something."

I jumped at her voice, not realizing anyone was behind me, as I was lost in the details of the dresses before me.

"What are you doing here?" I asked.

Bronwen was the last person I expected to run into while shopping with this forced company. Well, Adar would be the very last, but she was a close second.

"I'm just," she paused as she ran her fingers down the fabric of a Mountain Realm dress before turning up her nose at it, "shopping."

I gave her a knowing look. It was no coincidence that she just happened to be here while I was here . . . *without protection.*

A few guards came with us, but I know who they were here for, and who would be the last fae they'd protect if danger came near.

"Did you really think he would let you come alone?" she asked as she walked past me to pick up an Ocean Realm dress.

"Why does he care, Bronwen?" She didn't have to say his name for me to know who she was talking about.

"Ask him," she mumbled as she held the dress to her body and looked down at herself.

Yeah. That's not happening.

After the initial shock of seeing her faded I thought about her words.

She might begin to suspect something.

That . . . that bastard said he wouldn't tell anyone.

I wanted to say something to her. But I couldn't with the three in the next room. Even though they were probably too focused on Nathara picking her dress, they could still hear us if they wanted to.

"Would you like to return to the castle with me? I'm sure

167

your company wouldn't mind."

I looked back at the doorway to see Celine and Lilian standing around Nathara as the seamstress placed a veil on her head.

I simply nodded in response.

"He told you about me and Calum?" I asked as I crossed my arms. We were already out of the city and riding down the long path that took us back to the castle when I finally interrupted Bronwen's nonstop talking about how ugly Nathara's dress was.

She scrunched her eyebrows at my question before a look of horror came across her face. "No. But you just did."

"But you said—"

Bronwen cut me off. "I said that more as a joke." She let out a sigh. "But I'm not surprised."

"What do you mean?"

"Imagine having someone that looks like you locked away in your home, with no contact with the outside world, just available at your beck and call. I don't know of a male who wouldn't jump on you and keep you all to themselves."

"It's not like that," I said, taken aback by her words.

"Isn't it though?" She leaned forward. "Have you been given the chance to be with another? To even see what else is out there? You don't have to answer because I already know."

"He loves me."

"I'm sure he tells you that."

Bronwen's words hurt me. I knew I didn't have to explain our relationship to anyone, but she was the only friend I had ever made.

I didn't know what to say after she said that because one thing I had learned was that Bronwen had her opinions, and no one could change them.

21

Chapter 21

Sebastian

"What did you say to her?"

I transferred into Bronwen's room after I saw her and Violet arrive. Violet was clearly bothered by something. She was trying her hardest not to show it on her face, but I could feel her.

She was upset, and I knew who to blame: Bronwen and her big ass mouth.

"I just told her the truth," she said, shrugging her shoulders.

My eyes widened at her response. I was ready to . . . to consume her, like Violet said.

"Not *that*," she said as she shook her head. "She told me about her and Calum, and I pretty much told her she's delusional. I mean, I don't understand why you haven't already told her that." Bronwen walked into her bathroom, and I followed. She touched up her lipstick before she added, "Speaking of, when did you find out she was fucking him, and how did you manage not to destroy the entire castle at that information? I'm proud of you."

I ignored her added questions because even *I* didn't under-stand how I managed to keep my composure. The smallest thing used to send me into a darkness where I would destroy anything that got into my way.

But now, I didn't want to do anything that would scare her.

I was constantly trying to hide a part of myself because I feared that the darkest parts of me would be too bad for her to accept.

I was surprised that the things I told her about when I killed my father didn't scare her off. But that was just the tip of the iceberg. It was nothing compared to other things I'd done.

"I am just getting to the point where I feel like she is starting to trust me. I'm not risking ruining that by telling her something she'll figure out eventually," I said.

"So you're, what, just going to be patient? Yeah, I give that two days." Bronwen pushed past me and walked back into her bedroom.

"Just stay out of it. Okay?" I turned to her. "I appreciate you trying to push her to me, but I want her to come herself."

"Yes, my lord," she said as every bit of emotion left her face.

"Bronwen—"

She cut me off. "No. You told me to get close to her and now you want me to back off? I like her, and I don't want you and your 'patience' to cause us to lose her. If you would just tell her the truth, or better yet, take those fucking pills so she can see for herself, we wouldn't have to do this tiptoeing around her."

She was right, but I would never admit that to her.

"I'm not going to do that to her," I said, trying to keep my composure.

"Why? The Sebastian I know wouldn't have hesitated to take what he wanted. And you know once she feels the pull, she won't care about what happened before. It's got to be more than that." She paused while she studied me. She was always so good at reading me. "Does your apprehension have something to do with you losing your powers?"

I walked away from her, running my hands through my hair. No one could get under my skin more than Bronwen.

"We have to be on the same page," she said as she approached me and laid her hand on my shoulder.

I knew Bronwen well enough to know that she wouldn't let up until I told her.

"I will not force this on her. But also, I fear that once others find out about our bond, I will not be able to protect her. Not in the way she needs to be protected. Not until we find the black opal," I said as I turned back to her. "I have a lot of enemies. And she would have a target on her back."

"Some honesty. Finally," she said.

I rolled my eyes.

"We will find the object. And we will all protect her. No one would stand a chance against all of us," she said, trying to reassure me.

"And Adar? He didn't speak to me for days after I made him go with the two of you to the city."

"His duty is to you. He will do as you command, even if he doesn't want to."

She was right. He would do whatever I said, but not without giving me the silent treatment—his favorite weapon of choice.

I didn't know why he seemed to have a problem with Violet, but every time she was around, he closed himself off.

Another dinner planned by Bronwen. I hated having to look

at Lilian and Nathara. Every time I saw them, I was reminded of my mother and what their presence took from me all those years ago.

I hadn't been around them this often in centuries. Even though they lived in my castle, they'd kept to the area that I designated for them after I became Sovereign. I didn't want to see them, but I also couldn't let them leave.

The only reason I'd agreed to these dinners was to see her. Bronwen had valid points that I needed to keep up appearances in front of our Mountain Realm guests to ensure the marriage went through, but I wasn't really worried about that.

Their fear of me was enough to ensure that the marriage went through.

But getting to be around Violet made their presence bearable. I knew she saw me looking at her. She would glance at me every so often, and her heart rate would heighten. If only I could get into her mind to know exactly what she was thinking, without her knowing.

She had walls that I would have to tear through. I could do it, but I didn't want to hurt her. Most did not have the knowledge to build walls around their minds to keep fae like me out, but her father—or Calum—had taught her well.

"Lulenacht is in a week, Sebastian," Bronwen said while taking a sip of her wine.

"The ball of the bachelorettes, where I get my pick from Sebastian's rejects," Adar said as a faint smile came across his face before he returned to his mask of anguish.

"What is that?" Violet whispered faintly to Bronwen, hoping no one could hear.

"Oh, well it's a uh," Bronwen said, glancing at me. It was amusing seeing her at a loss for words.

172

Bronwen first started this ball when I told her I could feel that I had a mate. Since I hadn't had any luck finding her myself, she thought this would be a way to better my chances. We didn't want anyone to know I had a mate out there because it seemed more like a weakness. Something that would cause others to search for her to use as leverage against me.

So we instead said the ball was for all eligible ladies to come and have their chance to become my wife. A ball for the ladies to take their swing at me.

I hated it. I hated every minute of it. But in the off chance that my mate would show up one year, I never stopped doing it.

After a few decades of me sitting on the throne, bored the entire time, and never giving anyone attention, fewer ladies started to come every year.

Bronwen had the idea for me to choose my "favorite" of the night to dance with, which seemed to bring in more females. I usually just picked the one that looked like she'd be the most fun to spend the night with.

And I'd never been wrong about that thus far.

Even when it became obvious that I had no intention to take a wife, the ladies kept coming with the hopes of being the favorite.

"It's a ball held every year for ladies to come to see if I have enough interest in one of them to wed them," I answered for Bronwen, closely watching to see Violet's reaction.

This may have been wrong of me to do, but I wanted to see how far she could be pushed. How much that stupid pill could suppress her instincts. Something that she shouldn't be able to control.

She glanced up at me, wide-eyed, and she almost seemed

concerned about the ball before looking back down at her food.

I probably should have canceled the ball since my search was over.

But the part that got me was seeing her jaw clench as she moved a few berries around her plate with her fork. And that made me want to do it anyway. To push her as far as I could until she cracked.

If she wouldn't stop taking those pills, I'd give her enough of a show that the bond would push through the suppressants.

22

Chapter 22

Violet

A few days had passed since Nathara's dress shopping excursion, and other than the dinners, I remained a recluse in my room. I knew I said I was going to do better and stop hiding away in my room, but I couldn't help that my room had become my safe space. Away from the talking, away from the facade I had to put on, and most importantly, away from Sebastian.

Calum had only come to see me once in the past few days, and it was nothing more than sex. He said he had a few things he needed to take care of, but it seemed more like we had nothing to talk about, and he wanted to avoid it becoming awkward.

Or maybe it was that he feared that I had more questions for our future. Which I did.

Bronwen came by and visited for a few hours yesterday and she was overly nice. More than usual, that is. I think she may have been trying to make up for what she said in the carriage. I was over it, though.

She didn't know our relationship. I may worry for our future, but I had no doubt that Calum loved me. But from an outsider's perspective, they may be weary of that.

She told me more about Lulenacht and the things to expect from it. I didn't expect to be invited but she said everyone would be there and I should take the night to enjoy myself.

She also explained that at the end of the night, after hours of ladies flaunting themselves in front of Sebastian, he picked the one that stood out the most to share a dance and spend the night with.

"Why hasn't he taken a wife?" I asked.

Sebastian was well older than me, centuries older, and with him being Sovereign, I was sure he knew he needed to produce an heir for the line of succession to continue.

If he didn't, the throne would inevitably go to Nathara—or her future children—and I knew he wouldn't want that.

"He's never been interested in the fae he's met," she said, shrugging her shoulders.

"Really? After all these years he hasn't found someone to keep him company?" I looked down at the thread I had absentmindedly managed to pull from my dress. "That seems . . . lonely."

Her nose scrunched. "Oh, he's had plenty of *company*. I have spent countless nights awake because of the things he does to keep himself . . . entertained."

My stomach fluttered at what she insinuated. Was that why he was interested in me? A new female to keep him entertained?

I shook away my thoughts and knew I had to steer the conversation away from him. Even the thought of him felt wrong.

And I was not something for him to toy around with.

"The gardens," I blurted out to get my mind away from him.

"What?" Bronwen was clearly confused by my outburst.

"Is it safe past the gardens? I spend a lot of time outside at home. But I like to find somewhere I can be alone. Would it be alright if I went past the gardens?"

"Oh. Well, yes. Anywhere within the castle walls is safe. It may feel and look unsafe, which is natural given we are in the Night Realm, but Sebastian keeps unwanted creatures out."

I guess he didn't tell her about the paramic.

Shortly after Bronwen's visit, it was time for dinner. It was different than usual, though. Sebastian and Adar weren't there, and Lilian and Celine took that as an opportunity to be loud and force everyone to listen to them.

They spoke of wedding plans, their home realms and how much better they were than the realms that were forced to move to, and how cute their future grandfaes will be.

I lost count of the drinks that Bronwen had. She was a giggling mess, and I knew it wouldn't be long before she excused herself from this hell.

I kept my head down and focused on my food, counting down the minutes until dinner was over.

The next morning, I rang for Yara and asked her to bring my breakfast packed in a satchel so I could spend as much time as I could outside. I went for a walk in the gardens. I needed fresh air and to gather my thoughts.

I knelt down and studied the violets that lined the walkways between the hedges. They were so out of place here. In the Mountain Realm, we had native wildflowers, and everything else was imported from the Flower Realm. They were hard to maintain in our realm's climate. Celine usually brought them in for her parties and events and they died shortly after.

A waste.

But these flowers were so delicate and yet they looked strong and healthy. They were thriving in a realm that they didn't belong in.

A flower that needed sunlight and yet here it was in the Night Realm where the sun seemed more like a painting hung in the sky than a blazing star.

I continued my walk past the gardens to find the spot where I almost died. I knelt down at the spot where the paramic disappeared into nothing only a few days before. You would never have known something had happened here. There wasn't a blade of grass out of place.

"Please tell me you aren't paying your respects to a paramic."

I wasn't startled at his voice. He saw everything through his shadows, and I knew he would be watching me.

Maybe I came out here to see if he'd follow. Maybe I wanted to see him.

"It was one of your subjects. Something you are meant to protect. Just like the fae at the bar. You killed it for someone from the Mountain Realm. I'm pretty sure that breaks every oath a Sovereign is supposed to live by."

He shouldn't have any regard for me or my safety. I was an outsider, and yet he seemed to put me first. Every fucking time.

"Do you really think I abide by the rules? The bastard that took the throne?" he asked as he walked around until he stood in front of me.

"No, because you're evil and . . . and cruel," I answered, keeping my eyes on the ground.

"Really? You didn't seem to feel that way when I told you

about my father. It's almost like you're trying to convince yourself I'm bad."

"You are," I said as I laid my hand on the ground before me, where that creature lay before disappearing into nothing. I was doing everything I could to not look at him.

"You're right. I am. But do we not all have a little darkness in us?"

"No," I mumbled.

"You mean to tell me you've never had . . . bad thoughts?" he asked.

I had. When something upset me and I couldn't show how I felt, it would build inside of me. I would run scenarios in my head of what I wish I had said or did. And it would fester and grow darker and darker the longer I thought about it.

Usually those thoughts were about Celine. Or, during the times I'd hidden behind the curtains and watched Calum at his mother's parties, about the beautiful females that would fawn over him, begging for his attention. I wanted them all to die.

"I thought so," he said as if he could hear what I was thinking. I knew I didn't say it out loud, but he must have taken my moment of silence as confirmation.

"It is still wrong," I said as I stood up and crossed my arms, locking eyes with him.

"Why, though? Because someone said it is? That we should fight against our true nature because someone tells us to?" He took a step closer to me, but I didn't back away. I kept my head high, holding my ground. "I have darkness in me. The darkness from my mother and power from my father made me who I am. Should I not use the gifts I was given to get what I want?"

179

He was right. If I was given even an ounce of the power he had, I would use it. But I said nothing. Instead, I kept his glare as he continued to inch closer to me.

"Tell me, love, if you had my gifts, would you not use them to get rid of the ones standing between you and your Sovereign? Or . . ." He grabbed my neck and pulled my face until it was only inches from his before he said, "The other things you feel deep inside?"

My eyes widened at what he had done for a moment before I quickly changed my expression, knowing I was giving him what he wanted. "I'd let them burn," I whispered.

"Just say the word," he said as a wicked grin came across his face.

I rolled my eyes and pushed him away. "I came out here to be alone, not to be followed by you."

"You spend all day alone in your room," he said.

"I wanted a change of scenery."

Sebastian bowed as he said, "As you wish, love," and disappeared before my eyes.

He was such an ass.

Even so, I couldn't help but smile.

23

Chapter 23

Calum

"Are you even listening to me?"

No. I wasn't. I zoned out of the conversation the second I saw Violet walking through the garden and into the woods. Where was she going?

All I wanted to do was to follow her. To protect her.

But I couldn't.

Nathara and I had been on the balcony for what seemed like hours looking at flowers.

She had a florist brought in from the Flower Realm to show us every type of red flower possible for our wedding ceremony.

Because red roses weren't enough. No, they weren't the right *shade* of red.

Neither were tulips, daisies, or peonies.

I had expressed to her time and time again that I didn't care about any of the details. That she should do all of this herself, but she refused. I spent every waking moment being pulled around by her, making wedding plans.

The only relief I got from her was after she went to bed. She'd tried multiple times to stay in my room, but I'd been adamant that we needed to save one thing until we were married.

And the moment I got away from her, I used to go straight to Violet. Lately though, her questions had been keeping me away.

I'd never been good at expressing my emotions, and everything I seemed to say to her lately just made it worse. Maybe it was the change of realms or something in the air, but Violet had never questioned me the way she was now.

I didn't have all of the answers that she wanted. I wasn't sure what our future would look like, but I knew one thing for sure: I couldn't lose her.

Have you seen anything? I asked Alastor through the tether that linked me to him.

He shook his head slightly, giving me the answer I didn't want.

Because Nathara was so clingy, it had become more difficult to find time myself to search for the object that was weakening the shadow king's power. While I was busy playing the doting fiancé, helping Nathara plan the wedding, Alastor would slip out and roam the castle, watching for anyone acting oddly.

I dreaded dinners, and they always came too quickly, just like this dinner did tonight. It was one thing to have to pretend like I didn't care about Violet when she wasn't around. I could play the part of the loving fiancé to Nathara, and if Violet crossed my mind, that was okay because I had a stone wall built around my thoughts. I could look at Nathara, hold her in my arms, kiss her when I had to, and the entire time I could think about Violet and no one would know.

But to be in the same room with her, where I had to act like she didn't exist, where I couldn't look at her for more than a second without worrying it would raise suspicion, it was hell.

I could smell her. I could hear her breathing. And yet I couldn't touch her.

I knew every time Nathara caressed my neck or placed her hand on my thigh, Violet was watching. It hurt her, but it was necessary.

While the servants began placing plates in front of us, Sebastian caught my eye.

I didn't like the way he looked at her. I could only imagine the vile things that monster was thinking of doing to my Violet.

Before Violet got here, he would spend meals staring out the window and not saying a word unless Bronwen or Adar said something to him first. And he would only give them one-word answers, still with his eyes locked on the window.

Now, he looked at her. He said little things about her that a stranger shouldn't say. I knew Violet had been around him that night at the bar, but that was the only time, I thought.

I glanced over to Violet to see she was holding his stare, not in an affectionate or even fearful way, but almost like a challenge. A challenge to see who was going to look away first. I looked back at Sebastian to see a smile stretch across his face.

I had never seen him smile.

He realized what he did because he broke her stare and went back to staring at the window.

I'd never seen Violet be this way in front of others. She'd always been confident and outgoing around me. But with others, she would shut down and become everything a Mountain Realm lady should be. I liked it that way. That way only I saw a different side of her and others saw how she was supposed to act.

But this side of her was something completely in and of itself, and I didn't know where it had come from. I knew she had been spending a lot of time with Bronwen, and she had probably rubbed off on her. Bronwen had enough confidence and personality for a thousand ladies. But for her to be that way to him. To the shadow king . . .

Something was up.

My avoiding her might have pushed her further into the mess she may have gotten herself into.

When I was finally able to get away from Nathara that night after hours of telling her I was ready for bed, I transferred into Violet's room. She was already fast asleep.

So beautiful. So peaceful.

She had kicked the blanket off of her. She ran so hot at night. I'd wake up some nights to her drenched in sweat which in turn had me sweating from the heat radiating off of her. She used to argue with me that I was the reason she got so hot at night, but I never had a problem when I was in bed by myself.

I hated to wake her up, but I needed to make things right between us, and I needed her.

Her skin glistened from the moonlight, reflecting off of her sweaty chest. Her nightgown was pulled down, showing the top of her breasts, and it stuck to her skin.

I gently ran my hand across her forehead as I said, "Violet."

Her eyes shot open and met mine. Such a light sleeper. She didn't say a word but scooted over to allow room for me to lie next to her.

I lay next to her, our faces only inches apart as we stared at each other in silence. I knew I needed to say something, but the words I wanted to say had slipped my mind as soon as I entered her room.

"You've been avoiding me," she whispered, barely audible.

"I'm sorry. It's just that everything I've said to you lately has seemed like the wrong thing."

"I'm just scared, Calum," she said as tears began to fall from her eyes.

I leaned forward and kissed them away before grabbing her in my arms and pulling her close to my chest.

She was right, the inevitable was coming. I would have to wed someone, but I wouldn't let it happen. Not yet.

24

Chapter 24

Violet

The pastries filled the air with a fruity scent and intertwined with the faint scent of violets coming from the garden. That was the only enjoyable part of breakfast today.

I readied myself early this morning and rang for Yara well before she would have brought me breakfast. I wanted to eat with Bronwen. I shouldn't spend the limited time I had here wasting it in my room. Even if we stayed in touch after I went home, it wouldn't be the same as the days spent here with her, and in the years to come I didn't want to regret my time here.

I wasn't even sure if Bronwen sat down and ate a formal breakfast, or if she had other plans, but I had hoped, at least, that I could join her in whatever she was doing.

Instant regret.

She ate breakfast with Adar. Her brother. Her *twin*.

I still didn't understand it. Even if they weren't fae like she said, and their actual appearance was hidden—for whatever reason that could be—it didn't change their polar opposite personalities.

I didn't know why she would choose to start her day with such darkness and gloom or how she managed to stay in high spirits after spending an hour with him.

I didn't think I could.

We ate on the patio that overlooked the garden. I would've expected to be cold from the lack of sun rays and the cool breeze in the air, but it was refreshing.

"Have you had any luck finding it on the castle grounds?" Bronwen asked Adar while she plucked a grape from the assortment of fruits sitting in the middle of the table and inspected it between her fingers.

His eyes shot up and looked at me before bringing his focus to Bronwen.

"She knows about the object. We can speak freely in front of her," she said, never looking up from the grape that seemed so interesting to her. "I trust her."

Bronwen trusted me. How could she possibly trust me when I kept my relationship with Calum from her? And I was still keeping secrets from her. She didn't know how I knew about the object, yet she didn't care.

She trusted me.

"Well, good for you, sis. But I don't," Adar said as he slammed his fists on the table before he stormed off.

"I'm sorry about him." Bronwen looked at me as she reached for my hand.

"Why does he hate me? He doesn't know me." I didn't understand it. We hadn't even had a conversation and yet he had already formed his opinion on me.

"He thinks he does. But don't give him a second thought. He can go brood in his room alone. It shouldn't damper your day."

She was right. His anger seemed innate, and I just seemed to get the brunt of it.

"So are you no closer to finding the object?" I asked, trying to steer the conversation away from Adar.

She paused for a moment before simply shaking her head no.

"What will happen if you never find it?" I asked.

"He will be weak enough to kill. And I'm sure whoever is behind this will come forward to kill him themselves."

My stomach dropped at what she said.

Bronwen sat up straighter as she said, "But don't worry. If it comes to that, which it won't because we will find it, but if it does, I will bring hell to this world before I let something happen to him."

I didn't know how she could do that, but I believed her.

After we finished eating, Bronwen left to do some finishing touches on the decor for Lulenacht, which was tonight, and I decided to go to the library:

I had not yet been able to explore the massive library the way I wanted to. The last time I was in there, I only made it through a few sections before Sebastian interrupted that. I wanted to read the title of every book that filled the two-story walls and find one that I could sit for hours and read—one that I hadn't read before. Yara had only brought me books about the Night Realm and the rest of the volumes of the *Book of Healers.* I didn't ask her for anything different because I already felt guilty for having her bring them to me in the first place.

I headed straight for the right wall this time and found one in the first section that sparked my interest just by the look of it. It was an older book, based on the wear on the binding. One half of the front was covered with etches of fire and the other half, water.

A few chairs sat at one end of the library. I chose the one tucked in the corner hoping that if anyone came in, they wouldn't notice me so I could read undisturbed.

It told a story of two feuding tribes who were polar opposites. One tribe controlled fire while the other controlled water. They feuded for thousands of years causing mass destruction to the homeland they shared.

"Did you have enough alone time yesterday or are you going to kick me out of my own library?"

I had managed to get almost a quarter through the book by the time he interrupted me.

"I guess you can stay," I said before I continued reading.

Silence filled the air, and I looked up, thinking he must have left or had gone to another part of the library.

Nope. He was just standing there, looking down at me.

"What?" I meant to say that with more of a bite than I did, but instead it was more of a murmur as his dusty-blue eyes seemed to stare straight into my soul.

"How's your heart?" he asked with a smug look on his face.

I slammed my book shut. "Seriously?" There was the bite.

"Have you ever skipped a pill just to see what would happen?"

"Do you not see me trying to read a book?" I asked while I waved the book at him.

Ignoring my not-so-subtle hint to leave me alone, he said, "Have you, though?"

"Um, no. I do not wish to die."

"But you won't," he said as he shook his head.

"Yes I will! My father said—"

"What your father said is bullshit. I," he paused and let out a sigh before continuing, "I have spent countless hours contacting healers and reading bloody books trying to find proof. Proof that your heart is broken and that you need those pills."

"And?"

"And the only explanation I can come up with is if your mother was human, and I don't believe your father traveled through the Sea of Mavrola to fuck a human."

I rolled my eyes.

"One day your eyes are going to get stuck like that."

I shot him a glare.

"You should be spending any free time you have trying find the object that's draining you instead of putting your nose where it doesn't belong," I said, looking back down at my book.

"Are you worried about me, love?"

"I could ask you the same thing," I snapped back.

Something crossed his eyes, but he didn't say anything.

"Can I please get back to reading my book in peace?" I asked, breaking the silence.

"Sure," he said as he turned to the bookshelf right next to him and grabbed the first book he saw. He then took the seat directly in front of me before he opened it and started reading.

I waited for a moment, watching him to make sure he wasn't going to say anything else before I started reading again. Nothing irritated me more than being interrupted while I was deep into another world of a book. After he seemed to have read a couple of pages of his book, I slowly opened my book and began reading where I had left off.

"I never asked you how your little shopping trip went with the witches."

Before I could stop myself, I slammed my book shut and threw it at him. He caught it inches from his face, never taking his eyes off his own book.

"Was it not a good book?" he asked while bringing his eyes to meet mine with a look of concern.

When he saw the look I was giving him, the worry left his face, and he quirked a real smile.

I was reacting exactly how he wanted me to. I couldn't do that. I couldn't let him have the satisfaction. I remembered what he had asked me and decided to answer him before I let his little game aggravate me anymore.

"It was hell, which was expected. But what I didn't expect was Bronwen showing up."

"Oh, you saw Bronwen?" he asked, bringing his attention back down to the book in his hands. "Strange."

My eyes narrowed as I said, "She told me you sent her."

He stopped flipping through the book at my response but kept his focus on the book.

"You told me you'd protect me, so you sent her. Did you think they would hurt me?"

"I wouldn't put it past them," Sebastian mumbled.

"Why didn't you just kill Nathara and Lilian after you killed your father?" I asked. I didn't even know where that came from. Their deaths would have made my life a lot easier. I wouldn't be in the position I was in right now if they were dead. But would I really wish someone to be dead?

He brought his gaze to meet mine as he said, "Nathara was still in infancy. Do you really think that low of me that I would kill a faeling?"

With the look he gave me, I instantly regretted what I had asked. "No, I don't. I'm just angry at my life. Why didn't you just send them away, then? You could've sent them to Lilian's home realm."

"I'd rather have my enemies close to me. Where I know everything that goes on."

"What do you mean?" I asked.

"Nathara is the true heir. With her here, she has no connections, no one that would dare to go against me. If I sent her away, that would risk her gaining allies and she would attempt to come for me."

"Do you not suspect Nathara could be behind your weakening powers? If she wanted the throne, that would give her means to hurt you."

"Nathara and Lilian were the first I suspected, but they have done nothing but focus on this engagement since Calum's father died."

"I just don't understand. If you don't want her out of your control, why would you make a deal for her to marry Calum?"

"Because the Mountain Realm does not believe in female Sovereigns. While every other realm's line of succession goes to the firstborn regardless of gender, the Mountain Realm doesn't believe a female has any claim to the throne because they are only meant for breeding and taking care of the house. Calum's father was the only ally I had. He believed that even if I wasn't legitimate, I was the only male heir, so it was my right to the throne."

I was shocked at the last little bit of information he had given me. Sebastian knew Calum's father personally? And if that was the case, did Calum's father have a part in this engagement? I had assumed that this was all Celine's doing, but maybe I was

192

wrong.

Maybe this engagement was planned far before mine and Calum's relationship began.

Sebastian continued, "So I feel with the values of the Mountain Realm, they would never support Nathara's claim to the throne. They would just want her to submit, lie on her back, and make little Mountain Realm babies."

I grabbed the book sitting on the small table next to me and began flipping through the pages. I needed something to focus on. We sat in silence for a while. It seemed like we both weren't sure what to say after what he had just told me.

I now understood what the most powerful and feared realm wanted with a marriage alliance with our realm.

The only thing Sebastian needed was to be rid of the headache that Nathara and Lilian gave him, and the Mountain Realm was the perfect place to send them to.

Even so, it would have been simpler to kill them. Sebastian wouldn't have had to deal with unwanted guests in his home or had to plan and pay for a wedding for someone he didn't care about.

The shadow king wouldn't have given it a second thought. Nathara and Lilian would be long gone. Maybe there *was* good in him.

Or maybe he saw the Mountain Realm as more torturous to them than death. Two ladies being forced into a life of submission where they would have to be given permission from Calum before they did something as little as buy a dress.

That would make more sense. If Sebastian knew Calum's father personally and they agreed on some things, that could mean that Sebastian viewed females as objects. Objects used to satisfy male needs.

193

I got up and walked over to the wall of books to my left. I ran my hands down the binds trying to keep my focus on anything other than what I was thinking.

But I just couldn't help myself.

"Since you had a friendship with Calum's father, do you hold the same values as him?" I asked, breaking the silence.

"If you're asking if I feel that females are less than, I don't. Females are just as capable as males to rule kingdoms and to lead armies in battle. The only time a female should submit is . . ." he paused as he stood up and closed in the distance between us, "in the bedroom."

He looked down at me and watched me squirm as a grin crept across his face. He knew what he was doing. He knew what to say to make me uncomfortable.

"Why do you always do that?" I narrowed my eyes.

"Do what?" he asked innocently.

"We have a normal conversation, and you say something like that to make it inappropriate," I said, crossing my arms.

"Are you that naive, love?"

Butterflies formed in my stomach at his response. But before I could give it a second thought, I said, "I'm . . . with Calum."

"And do you think he is the one that you can truly be happy with? As his mistress, while you watch him for the rest of eternity be in love with Nathara?"

"He doesn't love her," I blurted out before I could stop myself.

"What?" He asked, taking a step back from me.

"He's faking it. Nathara and Lilian found out Calum had a lover. Calum overheard them talking about how when they figured out who it was, they would kill her. So Calum started to fake being in love with her so they would stop looking for me."

"So does he expect Nathara to immediately submit and not try to hurt you when you get back home? I know she will have to eventually, but she's headstrong and it will take some time." I stayed quiet for a moment too long. Sebastian's eyes narrowed as he said, "What else are you not telling me?"

I looked down as I felt the tears form. I didn't understand how I always got myself in positions like this with him.

"I thought we were past this," he said as he gently grabbed my chin, forcing me to look back into his eyes. I knew I couldn't lie to him.

A few tears fell from my eyes before I said, "Calum isn't planning on following through with the marriage."

"He doesn't have much of a choice in that, love." Sebastian stared at the tears on my cheeks before he raised his thumb and gently wiped them away.

"He's the reason I know about your weakening powers. He overheard someone talking about it and he is trying to find the object. He hopes that you two can form an alliance without the marriage and that would be enough to satisfy Queen Mother and his council to get his throne."

He paused for a moment before he said, "Do you honestly believe that if I can't find the object, that he will be able to?"

His question forced me to think about something that I had tried to push away for so long. Something I knew deep down, but didn't want to admit to myself.

Calum wouldn't find it.

He would marry Nathara.

25

Chapter 25

Violet

I left the library without saying another word to Sebastian. He was right: I had been living in delusion. It was only a few short months before Calum would have a wife, and I would officially be his mistress.

That was, if Nathara allowed it.

Even if she became a lady in the Mountain Realm, she would be the Sovereign's wife and as I'd seen with Celine, they had more control of the castle—and the fae within it—than the Sovereign himself.

Not to mention Celine would back her.

I may not even make it a week back home before I had a "tragic accident."

Now wasn't the time for me to dwell on this, though. It could wait until tomorrow.

I went to my room and grabbed the dress I had set aside to wear to Lulenacht before heading to Bronwen's room. When we talked about the ball, she asked that I come to her room to get ready so we could be each other's escorts. I didn't object because walking into a ball alone filled with beautiful fae ladies sounded like a nightmare. At least if I went in with Bronwen, everyone's eyes would be on her, and I could hide behind her.

Lulenacht gave me an uneasy feeling. From what Bronwen told me, it seemed like a worse version of the balls I'd never been allowed to go to back home.

At least I didn't have to worry about the ladies flirting with Calum.

Just Nathara.

Even so, I still didn't like the idea of the ball. I would have preferred to stay in my room and attempt to pretend like it wasn't happening, but the thought of not knowing what was happening or . . . or who he chose as his favorite lady of the night would kill me.

Fuck.

How did I go from Calum to him?

When I walked into Bronwen's room, I realized this wasn't going to be like the times before when we got ready in her room.

There were two chairs set up with faeries standing around.

"There you are!" Bronwen said as she stepped out of her bathroom.

"What is all this?" I asked.

"This is the biggest event we have every year in the Night Realm. Fae from every realm come here, so we have to ensure that we look better than them."

Bronwen motioned to one of the faeries, and they grabbed me and pulled me into the seat before they began working on my hair.

Another faerie began painting my face, which was something I wasn't used to as I only wore minimal makeup at home.

I had never been pampered like I was today, but I could get used to it.

Once we were ready, Bronwen and I stopped by my room so I could take my medicine. She gave me a look but didn't say anything. It didn't matter; I knew what she was thinking.

Drums echoed through the hall, growing louder as Bronwen and I got closer to the doors of the ballroom. A pit formed in my stomach at the thought of walking into whatever was behind those closed doors.

I just hoped with the dress I had chosen that I could blend in with the crowd and not look like an outsider.

But when I walked in, I realized that it didn't matter what I wore, everyone's eyes were on Sebastian, too concerned about how they presented themselves to him to notice anything else.

It was mostly ladies, who had come from every realm, with a few men scattered throughout. I had never seen a more diverse group gathered, and it was wild to think that all of this was because of him.

The most feared and powerful Sovereign brought in ladies from all over the kingdom for a chance to be with him.

He was an anomaly.

A Sovereign who had no plans to follow Queen Mother's rule of marrying from the royal lines, he was a chance for any fae to up their family's station. And he was beautiful, which helped.

Sebastian sat lazily on his throne, staring at the glass wall across the room. It seemed like his go-to move; he showed no emotion on his face. It was odd to see him like that when he showed a completely different side to me when we were alone. It seemed as if he had an internal switch that he could flip in a second to become what the kingdom thought he was.

But he had become so much more than that.

He was dressed more formally today in a solid black suit that was tailored to fit him perfectly. It would have any female stumbling when they caught sight of him.

Which it did.

Most of the ladies stood back but the few that were brave enough to approach him were given nothing more than a glance before he fixated his gaze back on the spot outside that seemed more interesting to him than the fae fawning over him.

But the part that had my eyes locked on him was something I hadn't yet seen during my stay here: his crown. The crown of the Sovereign of the Night Realm. The crown that was given to the first Sovereign of the Night Realm after his victory over the others in Queen Mother's games. A symbol that showed his station and superiority over everyone else in the room.

Even with everything I knew about him, it was easy to forget who he was in our day-to-day conversations.

But with his crown, he looked like nothing but power.

I stayed with Bronwen because even with her wanting to mingle with others, it seemed like a better choice than my other two options: sulking awkwardly in the corner or finding my father and staying with him, which would mean being near Calum and Nathara.

No, thank you.

Bronwen looped her arm in mine as we walked through the crowd. She spoke to a few ladies from other realms, but nothing seemed significant enough for me to pay attention to until she stopped behind a tall, statuesque female with long white hair that was tied back in braids. When my eyes met her gray eyes as she turned around, I knew exactly who she was.

Eira. Calum's cousin from the Ice Realm.

She was the firstborn of Celine's older brother, who was the current Sovereign of the Ice Realm, and she was next in line to the throne.

Eira had the same purpose as every other female here today, except she had the upper hand. She was strong as she can wield ice and transfer, and, possibly the worst part, she may have been the most beautiful female I had ever seen.

Eira was poised, elegant, and powerful. She would be a perfect match for Sebastian.

Even though I had no right, and frankly no reason, I didn't like her being here. I didn't want him to see her. I didn't want him to spend the night with her.

"Violet? I didn't know they would bring you here with them. That's . . . odd," she said as she cocked her head to the side. She knew of our relationship, and even though I had never experienced any ill will from her, I never forgot who her aunt was and where they both were raised. There was ice in the hearts of the females of the Ice Realm.

I had read about it before. It dated back to the first Sovereign of the Ice Realm. He was a very charismatic fae who had plenty of fun before, during, and after his victory. He charmed every female he met, except his wife.

Each of the first Sovereigns married from their respective realms to begin their bloodlines, but the Queen Mother hand-picked each of these females to ensure the purest start to the bloodlines.

His wife was nothing like the fae he had his affairs with. She had white hair, gray eyes, and porcelain skin, and the Sovereign, well he enjoyed . . . a little more color.

She watched as he showed affection towards others; he had

several mistresses. His wife grew cold, even towards her own children. They said because of that, every daughter in their bloodline had a cold and bitter heart.

It sounded like a made-up story, but I experienced it first-hand with Celine. Regardless of her opinion of me, a mother should be warm and loving to their children.

Calum never received that from her. Nothing he did was ever good enough, which meant he was always fighting for her approval. I think that was why he tried so hard to become the perfect Sovereign. He hoped to gain his mother's love.

"What's odd is that after decades of rejection, you still show up to Lulenacht in hopes of finally snagging Sebastian," Bronwen snapped at her. I guess she caught on to her condescending remark.

Eira's eyes widened. "It would do him well to understand the power he could gain by wedding a future Sovereign," Eira said as she crossed her arms.

"Sebastian isn't lacking in power. It would take more than that to catch his eye, Eira."

Bronwen looked her up and down before turning away and walking off. She pulled me along with her.

It was like she didn't see what I saw when I looked at Eira. Everything about her would catch the eye of a male.

Bronwen was everything I wanted to be. She had confidence and didn't care if she offended anyone. I guess that was a privilege of being the most-trusted council of the scariest Sovereign in Alentara.

A few hours passed while Bronwen continued to pull me around the room. She seemed to know everyone in attendance, but the few that she didn't, she made sure to introduce herself and get their entire life story.

I listened to the fae talk about themselves, but they were so boring they barely held my attention. There was something much more interesting in the room: him.

Sebastian never changed position and only shifted his eyes every so often to look at the female standing before him.

And when he gave them only a glance, it seemed to crush their spirits every time.

He caught me staring one time to which I quickly looked away. A few moments later, I glanced back to see he was still looking at me. Even though his face didn't give any sort of emotion, I could see the smile in his eyes.

I saw Calum and Nathara a few times throughout the night. Once when they were getting food and the rest of the time they were dancing. He either never saw me, or he was doing a good job at avoiding looking at me because he seemed completely focused on her.

My father was dressed for the ball, and he seemed a little less on guard than he had been. It was probably because there were several guards standing at the exits due to the volume of foreign guests. I even saw him smile once while he was talking to Adar and a few ladies that must have already been rejected by Sebastian.

It made me happy to see him like that. He hadn't been like that since Calum's father died, and he deserved happiness, even if it was only for a night.

The drums slowed their pace, and the loud conversations turned into whispers as everyone turned to Sebastian.

The night was coming to an end, and it was time for him to choose his favorite.

He stood up from his throne and walked down the steps to the middle of the floor where everyone backed away, forming a circle around him.

Bronwen grabbed my hand and pulled me with her as she pushed her way through the crowding fae so she could get a better view. We made it to the front of the circle where she looped her arm in mine and pulled my body close to hers.

"My favorite part of the night," she leaned in and whispered.

Dread formed in my stomach as I looked at the ladies and tried to figure out which one he would pick. He scanned the room, slowly looking at each lady that had pushed their way into the front of the circle. Their faces lit up before turning to utter disappointment as he moved on to the next.

I watched as Sebastian crushed the hopes and dreams of several female fae around the room, each giving me a little relief.

When his eyes met mine and a sinister grin formed on his face, I realized what he was planning to do. The look of consideration he gave the ladies was just for show.

Please, no. I shook my head and pleaded with my eyes.

But that only made his smile grow as he walked towards me. I saw looks of disgust and shock on the ladies' faces around me.

I knew exactly what they were thinking because I was thinking the same thing: how could he overlook them and choose someone like me?

My grip was tight on Bronwen's arm, but as Sebastian stopped in front of me and reached out his hand, I knew I had no other choice.

This was the last thing I expected tonight. The attention I got from him was always when we are alone, and he always managed to disappear before anyone could see.

But this . . . this was different. No hiding. No secrecy.

And he smiled when he picked me—something I didn't think he did in front of others too often.

I placed my hand in his and his cool touch sent flutters through my stomach. After following him to the center of the floor, he put his other hand on the lower part of my back and pulled me in close, never taking his eyes away from mine. I gently laid my other hand on his chest and between feeling the muscle beneath and the look in his eyes, my chest tightened.

We danced for a while, and I did everything I could to focus on the sound of the music instead of the whispers in the crowd.

His thumb started to caress my back, and his eyes shifted down before he said, "That blue . . . like the sky."

Even though I couldn't admit it, I knew he knew.

This gown was for him.

I chose it days ago. Bronwen had several sent to my room with the intention of me picking a dress. Some more elegant versions of my everyday Mountain Realm dresses, some themed around the other realms that I saw in the hidden room while dress shopping with Nathara, and some that were the perfect depiction of the realm I was currently in.

I tried my best to pick another dress, but I couldn't stop going back to this dusty-blue dress with jewels on the breast line and straps that draped down my arms.

But it wasn't for the sky. It was for the eyes that haunted my dreams every night.

I was getting too close, but I couldn't help it. Something deep inside of me was making me do it. Maybe it was in retaliation for having to watch Calum be with Nathara every day or maybe it was because I had never experienced life. Never had the chance to flirt. And now I was being tempted everywhere I turned here. Tempted by the most enchanting male I had ever laid my eyes on.

It was like he was always there, waiting for a chance to get my attention.

I could feel my cheeks redden and while I wanted to look away, I couldn't, for I knew the glares around me were far worse.

Sebastian brought his gaze back to meet mine and let out a chuckle at my silent omission. He leaned in and whispered, "You should talk to your Sovereign. He's not hiding his emotions very well."

I looked around until I laid my eyes on Calum. He was staring daggers at us. His knuckles were white from how tightly he held his hands in fists.

"Was this why you chose me? To push him? It was all a fun game because you're bored?" I asked as I shot him a look. The thought of this all truly being a rivalry between Sovereigns hurt, even though I was wrong for feeling this was in the first place.

His eyes softened when he noticed my reaction. "I chose you because I couldn't keep my eyes off of you since the moment you stepped into the room. No one here compares to you."

I scoffed. "Do you not see the ladies here? That came for you? I am nothing compared to them."

He pinched his eyebrows in confusion before shaking his head.

Slowly, a breeze picked up even though we were inside. I heard a few gasps and looked around to see everyone looking at the ground, picking up their feet as shadows slithered through the crowd.

They came together and formed a circle around us, rising high and blocking everyone's view. It was just me and Sebastian in the circle.

My eyes met his again as he said, "*This* is what I see when you walk into a room. Only you."

I had no words for what he said to me. We continued our dance while the shadows stayed around us, keeping us in our own little world. I heard the music and the voices around us, but I didn't know how long we actually danced. Far more than one song, but I couldn't tell for sure because I spent the rest of the time staring at him and trying to figure him out.

I had gone from being terrified of him, to learning to trust him, to feeling like a friendship had developed. All the while he relentlessly flirted because he knew it got under my skin.

I didn't understand why he had become fixated on me but somewhere along the way, I stopped caring because his attention made me feel alive. Wanted, even.

When he finally let up on the shadow barrier he had formed, I looked around and realized several fae had left and the ball was coming to an end.

Once Sebastian chose his favorite, there was no need for the ladies from other realms to stay. Only Night Realm fae remained, and a few from the Ocean Realm that seemed too drunk to even realize where they were.

"You may want to head to your room. I'm sure Calum plans to visit you after seeing you in that dress."

A pit in my stomach formed as Sebastian reminded me of the inevitable confrontation with Calum. He wouldn't understand. He was territorial and would not be happy about what he just saw.

Chapter 26

Sebastian

I didn't want the night to end, but Calum was currently pawning off the drunken Nathara to a few of her servants in her room, and I knew where he would be headed next.

Any other time I would have been doing everything I could to hold Violet's attention for as long as possible to prevent her from spending more time with him, but he was angry, rightfully so, and I knew she was headed for confrontation. An argument that could potentially push her further from him and closer to me, which was exactly where she needed to be.

After the ballroom doors closed behind Violet, my worst nightmare headed straight for me: Bronwen. A very pissed off Bronwen. *Fuck me.*

"A word, my lord" Bronwen said as she walked past me, heading for the garden.

I knew whatever she had to say, it was bad considering she didn't want to say it in front of the few remaining stragglers.

I nodded to the guards at the door, a silent instruction to get these unwanted guests out of my castle.

"What was that?" Bronwen said as I approached her in the garden.

"What was what?" I asked even though I had an idea what she was talking about.

"The little shadow show you put on for everyone? Did you enjoy yourself? Just using your powers since you have an endless supply? Oh, wait!" she said, slamming her hands on her thighs. "That's right. You don't!"

"I can't lose her," I mumbled. I'm not sure if it was more of a response to her or more for me, finally admitting it to myself.

"What?"

"I thought I would be okay, if she chose to be with him. If he truly made her happy and that's who she wanted, I thought I could let her go. But the more time I spend with her, the more I realize that letting her go would be the hardest thing I'd ever have to do. I won't force her, but I'm going to make it hard as hell for her to choose him."

Bronwen let out a sigh. "Well, did it work?" she asked as she crossed her arms.

"I . . . don't know."

"Sebastian, all you want to do is protect her—protect all of us. How will you do that as you continue to grow weaker?"

"It was a moment of weakness," I mumbled, turning away from her.

"You can't afford to be weak," she shot back.

She was right, and her words were like a knife to the stomach. I wasn't thinking, but I couldn't stop myself. "She's had her time with him. It's my time now."

She let out a sigh before placing a hand on my back. "You

can't take away her love for him."

"I can accept that she loves him. I know a part of her always will. He was her first love. But it's my fucking time. I've waited long enough."

27

Chapter 27

Violet

I took my time walking to my room. I studied the artwork on the walls and counted every stone I stepped on in the hallway, anything to push the argument waiting for me farther into the future.

Calum had always been jealous and territorial when it came to me, even if he had no reason. One time a servant kept his gaze on me for far too long while serving dinner, and he was sent to care for the horses. Another time, while I was watching Calum train with a few young soldiers, one of them took a break and chose to spend it sitting next to me, flirting relentlessly.

I never saw him again.

This all happened years ago, and I'd like to believe he had grown out of this immaturity, especially considering the position he was in and what I had to endure every day, but Sebastian doing that in front of others, when Calum could do nothing but watch? I knew he was pissed.

"What the fuck was that?" Calum asked as soon as I shut

the door behind me.

I didn't know how long he had been here waiting for me, but by the look in his eyes and the way his hair was disheveled, it seemed like he had been here long enough to work himself up.

"I don't know," I said as I looked to the ground. I had an idea of what it was—and why he did it—but telling Calum any of that would do no good.

"You're telling me he just randomly chose you, out of all of the ladies he could have, he chose you?"

That hurt. Even if he didn't mean it like I was inferior to every other female in the room, that was how I took it.

I constantly reminded myself how less than I was to every-one around me. I didn't need his help.

"He beds them, you know. His favorites. Are you waiting to be summoned?" he asked as he came closer to me.

"It's not like that!" I replied, fighting back the tears.

"What else could it be? I've seen the way he looks at you, Violet. You are something new for him to toy with."

I shook my head. "We have developed a friendship."

"A-a friendship?" Calum scoffed. "When are you ever around him?"

"The night at the bar, the library, the garden," I mumbled.

"He is an emotionless killer! You can't have a friendship with him!" If he hadn't placed a sound ward on my room, everyone in the castle would have heard that.

"He's not as bad as he puts on to be," I whispered, hoping it would bring his volume down.

"There is no way he just wants a friendship with you. He chose you as his favorite. Is that what friends do?"

"He did it to get a reaction out of you." I couldn't stop myself from saying it. Admitting that there may be more to

Sebastian's feelings would be far worse. Blaming it on a deep-rooted rivalry between Sovereigns seemed like the easier way out.

It was the truth, though. Even if that wasn't the entire reason Sebastian chose me, I know he enjoyed watching Calum squirm.

"What?" he asked, confused by my confession.

"He knows. About us," I said as I rubbed a piece of the fabric of my dress between my fingers.

"How?" he asked as his eyes widened.

"A paramic, disguised as you, lured me out of my room and tried to kill me. Sebastian saved me, but he saw what the paramic had shifted into, so he figured it out. He promised he wouldn't tell Nathara. I don't know if you've noticed, but he hates her and he didn't want our secret to risk the engagement. He wants nothing more than to get rid of Nathara, so our secret is of no use to him."

"So all this time that I thought you've been alone, you've been with him? Forming a 'friendship,' as you call it?" His emphasis on friendship told me nothing I had said was helping him to calm down.

"I called it a friendship because that is what it is. And I am not always with him, but why does it matter? Can I not have friends? You can spend your time with her, but I'm not allowed to have a friend because he has a penis?"

"I don't trust him," he replied.

"You don't have to trust him. You have to trust me." I placed my hand on his arm.

He clenched his jaw and had a wild look in his eyes, animal-istic almost. "And if he tells you to lie down and spread your legs?"

212

"Are you serious? Do you think I would just submit and do whatever he says?" I asked.

"That's what you were taught to do," he said as he narrowed his eyes.

I slapped him in an instant. I couldn't believe what he just said to me.

"How dare you," I said.

He didn't falter from my slap and deepened his gaze into mine.

"Do not be alone with him again."

"Get out," I said between my gritted teeth. I was so angry and hurt but I didn't want to break down in front of him. I wasn't backing down.

Not this time.

"As your Sovereign, I command you."

"What is wrong with you?" I said, taking a step back from him.

"I mean it, Violet."

"Get out!" I screamed as I shoved him in the chest.

Tears began flowing from my eyes as he transferred out of my room. I ripped my dress off and threw it on the floor before heading straight for the bed, burying myself within the blankets.

My Sovereign. Not my Calum. That was who just spoke to me.

I could feel his eyes boring holes into me the entire time I sat at the dinner table, but I couldn't look at him. Not until he apologized for the things he had said to me last night.

I did nothing wrong.

But I also couldn't look at Sebastian. Looking at him would add more fuel to Calum's fire, and I just wanted it to be over with.

He was angry. I knew deep down he didn't mean it, but he had never been good at expressing his emotions and the only way he seemed to settle things was always by enforcing his authority. He would apologize eventually. He just needed some time to cool off. We were in uncharted territory with all of this. There had never been others inserting themselves in our relationship, and we had never had the challenges we faced now.

I sat, staring at my hands in my lap while the servants came around and replaced our empty dinner plates with small plates with pieces of cake on them.

Out of the corner of my eye, I saw a small trail of shadows slithering towards me. Small enough that they would go unnoticed to anyone around me.

He was trying to get my attention, begging me to look at him.

But I couldn't.

I didn't want our friendship to end, but I also never wanted to see the side of Calum that I saw last night again.

Calum had to apologize and admit what he said was wrong. If he did, I wouldn't see Sebastian again. Even though a little piece of my heart broke at the thought of it.

Later, I stood at my bedside table and twiddled with the small pill between my fingers—it was a constant reminder of how weak I was.

I heard a knock at my door, startling me into dropping the pill on the floor. I wasn't used to someone knocking this late at night, only transferring unannounced. I quickly found the pill on the floor, swallowed it, and took a sip of water from the glass that sat next to the pill bottle before going to my door.

I ran through the possibilities of who it could be in my mind. Bronwen? Yara ? My father?

What I didn't expect was to open my door and see Nathara standing there.

"Oh, um, can I help you?" I asked as I kept my grip on the door handle.

"We have some things to discuss. Can I come in?" she asked with a solemn look on her face.

I couldn't speak. I couldn't figure out why she would possibly need to talk to me. But I couldn't do anything but nod and allow her entry.

I closed the door behind her and turned to see her walking around my room, inspecting every inch of it. Even picking up my bottle of pills and looking at it, confused.

"What do we need to discuss?" I asked, even though the pit in my stomach told me I didn't want to know.

"Oh, I'm just waiting for someone to arrive before we discuss some things," she said as she placed my bottle of pills down and brought her attention to me.

Before I could even fathom saying anything, Calum was standing between us.

"And here he is."

Calum quickly turned around to see Nathara, realizing we weren't alone. He glanced back at me, his eyes wide at the realization that we were fucked.

"What are you doing here?" Calum asked.

"I should ask you the same thing," Nathara replied as she crossed her arms.

Calum and I stood in silence as we both knew there was no way out of this.

"I know about you two," she said as she shot a look of disgust between the two of us.

"What about us?" Calum asked.

"You two have been together for years."

My eyes widened, but I kept silent. I had no way out of this, and I knew in the end it would be me who took the blame and punishment.

"Nathara—" Calum said, walking towards her.

She took a step away from him, causing him to come to a halt. "Don't try to talk your way out of this. Are you in love with her?"

"Of course I'm not in love with her. She is nothing but a fuck."

That hurt. I knew it wasn't true, and he was trying to get me out of this situation. But it still hurt.

Calum grabbed her hands in his as he said, "I'm in love with you. I am going to spend my life with you. Violet means nothing to me. She never has."

"Prove it," she said as she stared back at him.

He paused for a moment. "How?"

A wicked grin came across her face. "Make love to me."

His eyes shifted towards me, and I saw a glimmer of remorse before they shifted back to her. He had no choice. The one thing he promised he wouldn't do. The one thing that would shatter my heart into a million pieces.

"Fine. Let's go," he said, wrapping his arm around her.

"No—I want to do it here," she said as she pushed his arm off of her. "You may not care about her, but I can tell by the way she looks at you that she cares about you. So I want her to watch."

I shook my head, trying my hardest to hold back the tears. I knew there was a possibility that this would happen one day, especially knowing now that his chances out of this marriage grew slimmer by the day.

But this—having to watch—this was something I was not sure I could ever recover from.

"There's no need for that. I think she understands," Calum said as he looked at me again.

"I could have her killed for treason. So it's this or death."

I looked at Calum, hoping he could save me from this, but he was at a loss for words. There was no way out. He looked back at Nathara and began unbuttoning his shirt.

My eyes filled with tears. I squeezed them shut and tried to picture something—anything else.

"No, keep your eyes open," Nathara said. I opened my eyes to see her smiling at me. "I don't want you to miss this."

I stood there, staring them down and watching them take each other's clothes off. Every chance Calum got, he would look at me and mouth, "I'm sorry."

They were completely naked now and all that sadness I felt was turning into rage. I wanted to rip her head off of her body.

Nathara grabbed his face and started kissing him before pulling him onto the bed with her.

All of a sudden, my eyesight started to darken, but I knew my eyes were open. I never closed them. My hearing, too, began to go away. *What was happening?* I couldn't see or hear anything that was going on. Just before I truly panicked, I heard *him*.

Stay calm and don't move, love. You're still looking at that disgusting atrocity, but you're not going to see it.

Sebastian. He was in my ear talking to me. He was protecting me. Like he always had.

I hesitated for a moment because my father had always told me to keep my mind guarded, especially around someone who had power like Sebastian, but I let my walls down to let him in so I could communicate back to him.

Why are you doing this? I said back to him in my mind.

You don't deserve this. And I could only see two ways out of it: This or I come in there and kill them both. But if I saw them naked, I would have to take away my own eyesight.

I smiled at what he said before I quickly stopped, remembering what was happening in front of me, even if I couldn't see it. I began to breathe heavier, thinking about the point they were currently at.

What felt like a finger caressed the small of my back. I had forgotten that in letting Sebastian in, he could hear every thought I had.

I had to take my mind elsewhere if I was to make it through this.

What were you doing before this act of chivalry intervened? I asked Sebastian.

Well, I'm currently swimming.

You like to swim? I asked. I'm not sure why, but the thought of the big bad shadow king swimming seemed funny to me.

Yes. Every night. It calms me, he said, still rubbing my back with his shadows.

I haven't seen any body of water around the castle, I said.

I'm outside the walls. My secret place.

That sounds nice.

I thought about it. A place away from everything and everyone. Away from what was going on right now in front of me.

You'd like it. It's a place to be alone with your thoughts.

I wish I was there right now, I said back, begging for this to be over.

218

28

Chapter 28

Violet

When my eyesight came back, Calum and Nathara were lying in my bed under a blanket, both panting.

Calum's eyes were filled with sorrow as he stared at me.

"Do you get it now, Violet?" Nathara asked as she sat up. "You are nothing."

I glanced between the two of them and nodded, feeling numb.

"Never forget what you saw. Next time, as his wife, I won't be so kind with you," she said.

I couldn't look at Calum again before I turned around left. I know we weren't home, and he had no authority here, but how could he allow that to happen?

I had to get far away from there and find some way to take my mind off of what just happened. The reality of it hurt too much.

I slammed shut the door to my room and leaned against it with my back. I didn't even want to go back into my room after they left. What had become my safe haven had now been destroyed.

Holding my eyes shut, I tried to picture the swimming hole Sebastian was telling me about moments before. Far away from the nightmare I was living.

"Let's go."

My eyes shot open to see Sebastian standing in front of me. I knew he could transfer, but he was just at his spot, swimming, and now he was standing in front of me, completely dressed and completely dry.

"Go where?" I asked, standing up straight. I really didn't care. He could take me to a fiery pit right now, and I would willingly go because anywhere sounded better than where I was right now.

He grinned as he looped his arm around my waist.

The next moment we were standing in front of a body of water the size of a small pond, but nothing like anything I'd seen in the Mountain Realm. It was the brightest blue and looked like it glowed.

"Your wish is my command," Sebastian said as he winked at me.

"Your . . . your secret spot."

"*Our* secret spot now," he said as he grinned before pulling his white shirt over his head.

I watched as he walked towards the water, his muscles in his back flexing with every step he took.

Before I realized what he was doing, he pulled his pants down and stepped out of them. I quickly glanced away when I caught a glimpse of his bare butt.

Of course, he swims naked.

"Sorry, love. I didn't have time to grab you a swimsuit."

My cheeks reddened, and I realized that I hadn't put my walls back up after letting him in. I closed my eyes and quickly put them back up. I looked back at him to see he was wading in the water.

Any other time I would have objected and started walking back to the castle, even though I had no idea where we were or how far away we were, but I needed a distraction.

"Turn around," I said.

"Even if I turn around, I can still see you through my shadows, you know," he said, winking at me.

"Well tell your shadows to turn around too!" I demanded as I crossed my arms and glared at him.

He let out a laugh before he turned to face the other direction.

I let my dress fall to the ground, pulled off my undergarments and quickly got in before he had the chance to turn around.

"What is this?" I asked as he turned to face me.

"It's a starlight lagoon. There are a few in the Night Realm, and they used to serve a purpose more than they do now. Centuries ago, when darkness covered the realm, faeries would bottle up the water and use it to see. Now that there is light in the sky, they don't serve a purpose, so they usually go untouched. Except for the occasional swim, of course."

I looked at the sky to see it covered in stars. I had gotten used to it since my time here, but it was odd to think about considering the Night Realm was known for total blackness. No sun, no moon, no stars. At least, that's what I had read in my books, but I was sure most of the books in our library were out of date when it came to information about other realms.

I looked down from the sky to see Sebastian's eyes locked on me. Those blue eyes.

I was swimming in the most vibrant blue I had ever seen, what most would call the most beautiful blue, but nothing compared to his eyes.

The light from the water reflected on his eyes and made me feel like he was staring straight into my soul.

We swam in a circle just staring at each other, never faltering in our gaze.

I wasn't sure who would break the silence first until he asked me something I never thought he would say. "Why haven't you asked me to end the engagement?"

"What?" I asked. I wasn't sure why he would bring up something that would remind me of the torture I just went through, or why he would have even thought about something like that in the first place.

"You know I have the ability to end this and send you and Calum home and yet you haven't asked me to," he explained.

I had thought about it quite often actually. That there was a chance that Sebastian would end the engagement for me because for some reason he had a sweet spot for me. But every time I thought about asking, I couldn't do it. Because if he did end it, I would lose my freedom and the moments like this that I had with him. And I wasn't ready to let go of that just yet.

"I didn't think you would do that for me," I lied.

"If you can tell me that you know without a doubt that you want to spend eternity with him, and you believe no one could ever make you happier than him, then just say it and I'll end the engagement. But if there is even an ounce of doubt in you or a small part that feels anything *for me*, then I will fight until the last second to make you see what I see and feel what I feel."

His response had left me speechless. All of this time I had downplayed the looks, his actions, and his endless flirting as nothing more than a fascination. That I was something new for him to toy with to let the time pass by, but his confession turned that into so much more. He had feelings for me, and I, well, I was falling for him. Even if I had denied myself that confession for so long.

"Sebastian," I said, even though I feared the next words to come out of my mouth.

"Say it," he said with such hunger in his eyes as he swam closer to me. Like he knew what I was thinking but needed me to admit it to him. To make it real.

"I—" I tried to say something. Anything. But I couldn't.

He leaned in so there was little room between our lips.

"Tell me to stop. Tell me this isn't what you want. And I'll stop."

I should've said stop, I should've gotten out the pool and run back to the castle, wherever it was, and finally put an end to this game we had been playing.

But I didn't want to.

He took my silence and my glance down to his lips as an invitation. He kissed me softly before pulling away to gauge my reaction, but before he could say anything, I grabbed him and our lips came crashing together.

The touch of his lips left me aching for more, and I didn't want to waste a second of missing his touch. One small kiss had set my body on fire.

He reached down and grabbed my legs to wrap them around his waist. The cool touch of his body on mine reminded me that we were both naked with nothing between our bodies. I pushed my hands into his hair as he kept one hand on my thigh and brought up the other to hold the back of my neck.

There was so much passion in his kiss, like he had been

wanting to do this for so long. It escalated quicker than I could wrap my head around it.

His hand on my thigh started inching farther up, and I began to ache between my legs. I brought one hand down onto his chest, feeling the tight muscles underneath. My body was begging my mind to let go.

To give in to him.

I knew if we went any further that there would be no stopping. No turning back.

I didn't want to stop. I wanted it all.

But I *had* to stop.

"Stop," I whispered.

"What?" he said as he pulled his lips from mine and locked eyes with me.

"I-I can't do this to Calum," I said as I unwrapped my legs and swam away to get some distance between us.

His eyes darkened at the sound of his name. "You're still worried about Calum? After all he's done to you? After you had to be in the room while he fucked his fiancée?"

"He did that to protect me," I mumbled.

"Oh, so that's what he's doing at his very moment? Round two to protect you?"

I scrunched my eyebrows at what he had said. How could he say something so cruel to me? Was it true?

It couldn't be.

Calum wouldn't do that to me.

He had such hunger in his eyes for me that it seemed like my rejection made him want to say anything to hurt me.

Like I had just hurt him.

"Fuck you, Sebastian," I said as I pushed past him and made my way to the shore to find my clothes.

I felt the tears well in my eyes as I got out of the water and walked to where I had dropped my dress.

"Wait, I'm sorry," Sebastian said from the water. "I didn't me—"

The next moment he was in between me and my clothes. He had transferred and managed to get completely dressed and dry in the time it took me to get out of the water.

"Do you know there is a glamour on your back?"

His question and look of concern on his face, such a change from the look he was giving me moments ago, had caught me off guard so much that I had forgotten how mad I should've been at him.

"What are you talking about?" I asked.

He spun me around and placed his cool hand on my back. I turned my head as far as I could to see his shadows covering my back. A faint pulling sensation brought tingles to my back. They were removing the spell that I had no idea someone had put there.

The shadows retreated back into Sebastian's hand just as he said, "What the fuck."

"What? What's wrong?"

I turned back around to see his dusty-blue eyes were completely black, and the sky was darker than it was moments ago. The starlight was gone.

"There . . . there are scars all over your back," he said as he seemed to stare through me.

"Scars? How are there scars on my back?" I asked.

"Did Calum do this to you?" Shadows began radiating from Sebastian.

"No! Of course not!"

"Then who did this to you?" he asked as the shadows

225

continued to spread farther from him.

"I . . ." I realized then that I had no idea when it even happened. "I don't remember."

"If you don't tell me who did this, I will kill everyone in the fucking Mountain Realm so I will know they are dead," he yelled, anger seething in his words, and I knew he wasn't bluffing.

"I don't know who did this. I don't even remember it happening."

Sebastian grabbed my head with both of his hands and said, "Drop your walls."

I let him in without a second thought and waited as he searched my mind for the thing I couldn't remember.

"There's a spell in your mind. It's altering your memories."

"Well, get rid of it!" I said.

"It's going to hurt."

"I don't care. I have to know what happened." I wrapped my arms around my body, realizing that I was still naked. I felt so vulnerable in this moment.

Sebastian was still in my mind, and he heard what I was thinking. He placed his hand on my shoulder and suddenly my dress was back on, and I was completely dry.

He closed his eyes and took several deep breaths. When he opened his eyes, they were back to blue, not the usual dusty blue, but a dark blue and the stars were back in the sky. He knew I was scared, and he was trying to keep his composure.

He placed his hands back on my head and looked into my eyes. "I'm sorry, love."

"Wh—" I heard the loudest shrill inside my mind and a sharp stabbing pain radiated through my head. It was like he was standing in my mind and with a dagger was tearing through the spell that was blocking the memory of what happened to me.

I screamed out in pain as the stabbing continued, but the pain of that was nothing compared to the pain of the truth.

I remembered what really happened.

Removing the spell took me back to the weeks after Calum left the Mountain Realm.

29

Chapter 29

Violet

Three weeks. It had been three weeks without Calum. Three weeks without leaving my room. I'd cried all I could cry. I'd solved every damn riddle book the servants have brought me. I'd reread all of my favorite books from the library. I'd counted every star I could see out of my window.

Three weeks down. Only twenty-three weeks to go.

But I could not stand it any longer.

I had to go outside. I loved being outside. I used to lie in the grass for hours reading about new things while Calum attended meetings with his Advisors or traveled around the Mountain Realm making appearances, kissing faelings—or whatever he did.

Would Celine really hurt me? For all she knew, her son was in the Night Realm, falling in love with the one she picked.

That hurt to even think about.

But there was no way she's thinking about me. I could just sneak outside and go past the horse stables. She would never go over there. It's "beneath" her.

I was going to do it. If I stayed in my room any longer, I would go insane.

I held my breath as I unlocked the door and slowly pulled it open. What was I doing? Celine would never be down here.

Again, it was beneath her. Literally.

As soon as my foot hit the floor in the hall, a ripple broke out like I had just stepped on water, and I fell straight through.

After falling for what felt like one hundred feet, I hit the cold, hard ground. It felt like concrete, but I couldn't tell because it was pitch black wherever I was.

"Help—" I started to scream out, but then I remembered what my father said.

"Do not leave your room."

He was right. Celine was after me. He must have had a witch protect my room, put a spell on it that wouldn't let danger in. But as soon as I stepped out of the room, I left the protection and fell right into Celine's trap.

I slowly stood up and reached my hands out to feel around.

I walked a few feet and felt a wall. I started to inch my way around to see if there was a door anywhere.

Corner. Corner. Corner. Corner. Four corners. Four concrete walls. No door.

What was Celine going to do? Leave me in here to starve to death? A slow painful death?

No, my medicine. Father always said that missing one pill would kill me.

Well, it was just after midday when I stupidly decided to leave my room, so in about eight hours I'd miss taking my pill and I'd be dead.

Death by my heart stopping sounds better than death by starvation.

229

All of a sudden, a bright light turned on. I shielded my eyes while they adjusted to it.

I was right. I was in a concrete box with no way out.

Like I'd always said, I really wished I could transfer.

As if it couldn't get any worse, Celine walked through the wall and stood in front of me.

"You've made me wait three weeks for this. I was starting to get impatient, my dear Violet."

"What are you doing? When Calum fin—"

"Oh, I'm not worried about Calum. I have no doubt he will fall in love with his fiancée and realize all that he wasted on you. I'd been planning this since that dinner he said 'he was in love with you.' You are finally going to be punished for the crime of treason."

"Treason? What are you talking about?"

"Calum was always going to marry the daughter of a Sovereign. You throwing yourself at Calum, causing him to lose sight of his duty as Sovereign is treason."

Celine raised a hand to motion someone to come forward from the wall she walked through.

Just then a fae with a horned mask walked through the wall and stood next to Celine.

The mask was so frightening that I shifted my eyes down.

I really wish I hadn't.

Because what was in his hand was so much worse than the mask. It was a whip covered in spikes.

"Fifty-two years," Celine began to speak, causing me to look at her again, "you've been living in our castle corrupting my son for fifty-two years. So, I can't think of a better punishment than one whip for every year."

I felt like I was going to throw up. This had to be a nightmare. I was going to wake up any second, back in Calum's arms and realize this wasn't real.

"Take off her clothes."

The masked fae walked over to me and ripped off my dress. When he got close to me, I realized he wasn't wearing a mask. It was his face.

I was so shocked that I couldn't move. Only fae look like humans. Our servants are other types of faeries and creatures. Some made of stone, some covered in fur, and some that could hide in a flower garden and you would never know they were there.

But this . . . thing was different. He had the face of a wild beast with black horns, but the body of a human. I'd lived in the Mountain Realm for as long as I could remember and I'd never seen anything like this creature before.

I was so taken aback by this creature that I didn't even realize I was completely naked until Celine spoke again. "Turn around and put your hands on the wall."

I had wrapped my arms around my body. I'd never felt so vulnerable and scared in my life.

Calum was the only one who had ever seen me naked before. But here I was, living in a nightmare.

"Now!" *Celine screamed.*

I knew there was nothing I could do. Even if I could fight, which I couldn't because my father had never taught me anything in fear that my heart couldn't take it, there was no way out.

A witch had allowed Celine and this creature to walk through a concrete wall. I was trapped.

I turned around and did as she said. Maybe if I was obedient, this would be over quickly and she would let me go.

Crack! I let out a scream as the whip hit my back. I felt a warm liquid inch down my back.

"Oh! You were right. The spikes ripped right through her skin.

That's so much better than a basic whip," Celine said to the thing that hit me.

"Again!"

Crack! I screamed again. This time it hit a different part of my back, but it had the same effect. I could feel the blood running down my back.

"Again. Again. Again. Again." Celine said it every time. She was enjoying it too much.

I could feel myself getting light headed but I fought through it. I just kept telling myself that it would be over soon and when Calum was back, he would punish her.

"Again!" Crack!

My knees buckled at that last hit. I wrapped my arms around my legs and pulled them close to hide my face. I couldn't look at her.

Celine let out a laugh before I heard her walk away. I looked up and saw that I was alone in the concrete box again. I couldn't stop the tears from coming. That was the most painful thing I'd ever felt.

The light turned off, and I was alone in the darkness.

I curled up into a ball and sobbed. My back burned. It was already starting to heal but with a faerie's ability to heal faster comes the pain from your body working in overdrive.

I wanted to scream for Calum, for my father, for anyone that could get me out of here, but it was no use.

I was alone.

When Celine and the creature walked through the wall and left me alone, I knew that she wasn't planning on letting me go.

She wasn't worried about Calum finding out because he would never find out.

She got her revenge and now she was leaving me here to die. At *least it wouldn't be long.*

It couldn't have been more than a few hours when the lights turned back on. I lay there unable to move or look around. I was too scared to see who—or what—it was.

"Vi-violet?" A familiar voice. A voice I hadn't heard in almost two decades.

"Astrid?" I sat up to see my nursemaid. The closest thing I'd ever had to a mother. We kept in touch through letters, but this was the first time I'd laid my eyes on her since the day she left almost a decade ago.

Astrid was fae, but of the lower class which was why she became a nursemaid. She was very short and stocky with light brown hair that she always kept tied in a braid.

"Are you really here?" I asked.

"Yes. I got a letter from Calum saying you were sick, that your heart condition had gotten worse and wanted to say your goodbyes. It wasn't until I arrived here that I realized that was a lie." She wrapped a blanket around me and held me in her arms.

"You . . . you shouldn't be here."

"No, but you shouldn't be here either." Astrid waved her arm around before sitting me up to look me in my eyes.

"Where is Calum? He promised me he would protect you." I could see the anger in her eyes. She was the most loving woman I'd ever known, but she was sassy and opinionated. Even though she was from the Mountain Realm, she didn't have a problem telling Calum and my father how she felt. Especially when it came to me.

"He's in the Night Realm getting to know his fiancée."

"And your father?" She asked

"Protecting Calum."

Astrid scoffed. "And not protecting his daughter. I will have a long talk with him when he gets back."

"Celine sent that letter. But why would she bring you here?" I asked.

"She told me that you were in trouble and being punished for your crimes. She needed to make sure that you took your medicine because she feared that you would end your life."

"Why would she care? If I died, it would make her keeping control of Calum and the realm so much easier."

"She knows he would never forgive her if something happened to you."

"He will never forgive her for this," I said as I felt the anger build inside of me. He would punish her.

She moved my hair out of my face. "Maybe, but we have to get you through this first."

"Through this? I–I'm not done?"

Astrid looked at me with such sadness in her eyes. "I fear this is just the beginning."

I couldn't breathe. It had only been three weeks since Calum left. Was Celine going to keep me here, torturing me, until he returned?

She pulled an apple, a waterskin, and my medication out of her satchel. "You have to stay strong, Violet."

She sat the apple and water on the ground, then she took a pill from the bottle and placed it in my hand.

"I'm not strong. I'm weak."

"You are stronger than you think. You will get through this, and one day you will get your revenge on Celine."

Astrid sat with me while I ate the apple and forced me to drink every bit of water. She then looked at the wounds on my back and told me that they were almost gone.

Even though fae were immortal in the sense that we couldn't die from old age, we could still be injured or killed if someone wanted us dead. Our wounds healed faster than they would on a human and it took a lot more to kill us.

Well, except for me and my heart. All you would have to do is throw away my pills.

Eventually the lights flickered, and Astrid told me that she had to go. I didn't want to be alone, but I was more afraid of what would happen if I wasn't obedient in this sick game Celine was playing with me.

As soon as Astrid left, the lights shut off again. I lay on the cold hard ground on my stomach because my back was still in so much pain and covered myself with the blanket Astrid left me.

I must've fallen asleep from the pure exhaustion, and I had no idea how long it had been but I was awoken by the lights turning back on.

After my eyes adjusted, I saw Celine and the creature standing over me. Before I had time to react, he bent down and snatched the blanket from me, leaving me lying on the floor completely naked and exposed again.

"Well, it looks like you're already healed from yesterday. Not even a mark left on you." Celine seemed disappointed.

When she said that I realized my back wasn't even sore anymore. I reached back to find it as smooth as it always was.

"Stand up, Violet. It's day two of fifty-two."

"Fi . . . Fifty-two days?" I slowly stood up, still trying to cover my body with my arms.

"Oh, did I not mention that yesterday? Fifty-two whips for fifty-two days for the fifty-two years of treason that you committed."

"You left out the fifty-two days part yesterday."

Celine smiled as she said, "Well, my mistake."

She purposely didn't mention it yesterday. She enjoyed adding to the evil.

235

"Turn around."

Fifty-two days. I was whipped over and over again for fifty-two days. With every day, my healing process slowed. About halfway through, it had slowed so much that my wounds were still open when it was time to be whipped again. That just made Celine happier.

The pain was so excruciating that it got to the point that I was unable to stand up on my own. That didn't stop them. They put hooks in the ceiling and tied me up so I couldn't fall while the creature whipped me.

The only thing that kept me going was the visit from Astrid every day and thinking about being with Calum when this was over. Astrid was only there long enough to make sure I took my medicine and to practically force-feed me food and water, but that little bit of familiarity gave me enough comfort to keep pushing through.

The rest of my days and nights were spent in silence and darkness. I would just picture being reunited with Calum. He would find his way out of this marriage and come back to me. I would tell him what his mother put me through, and he would punish her.

As good as he was, there was no way he would be okay with what she had done to me.

I didn't know why Celine had Astrid there. She said it was to ensure I took my medicine, so I didn't die, but I felt like Celine could've found a way to force the medicine in me.

I didn't want to question it though because I knew I would've lost my sanity during this time if it wasn't for Astrid. She gave me something I needed so badly—hope.

It was day fifty-two. At this point, they didn't even try to let me stand on my own. They tied me up as soon as they came in. With every whip, I could feel the end of this hell getting closer and closer. All I could do was picture Calum. I had found a way to dissociate ten or so days ago. Every time, I pictured myself with Calum, lying in the grass under our tree.

I had such a small piece of myself still holding on through all of this.

After the fifty-second whip, the creature untied me, and I fell to the ground. I looked at the ground waiting for them to leave and for the lights to shut off, but they didn't. They usually immediately left. Maybe it was because this was the last day. Maybe they were waiting for me to stand so I could leave this place with them.

"Violet."

My eyes shot up when I heard my name. It was Astrid. What was she doing in here? She'd never been in here with them.

"Since it's the last day of your punishment I have one more, well, I guess you could say surprise, left."

The creature was holding Astrid by the back of her neck. No. They couldn't do anything to her.

"Please let her go. She hasn't done anything wrong," I begged as I stood up.

"You're right. She hasn't done anything wrong, but she means something to you."

"Please . . . just kill me and let her go."

"Violet, you know I can't do that. While I'm sure Calum has long forgotten about you, he might be a little upset with me if he came home and you were dead."

"You don't think he will be upset with the hell you've put me through already?"

"Oh, I'm not worried about that."

"Please, let Astrid go."

Celine nodded at the creature, and he released Astrid from his grip.

Astrid and I both let out a sigh of relief but as she took a step towards me, the creature lurched forward and slit Astrid's throat. I screamed as her lifeless body fell to the ground. I crawled over to her and wrapped my arms around her just as she had done for me for the past fifty-two days.

I sobbed. I would've taken a lifetime of whips if it meant I could bring her back. She didn't deserve any of this. Her love for me cost her life.

Celine knelt down next to us, holding her dress up to make sure none of Astrid's blood got on it, and grabbed me by the chin so I had to look her in the eyes. "I will make the rest of eternity hell for you."

She stood up, adjusted her dress, and walked through the wall, leaving me alone with Astrid.

Celine left me in my cell overnight. Unlike any other time when she would have turned the light off, leaving me in total darkness, she left the light on. I sat up all night, staring at Astrid's lifeless body and thinking of every possible way I could hurt Celine.

This torture wouldn't be enough punishment for her. I wanted Calum to rip her limb from limb.

She broke me. The last fifty-two days were horrible, but they were nothing compared to having to watch Astrid die. She was the closest thing I had to a mother.

Now I understood everything Celine did was a part of a bigger plan. The fifty-two days of whippings was just fun for her. The real punishment was bringing Astrid back into my life just to take her away for good.

The next morning, Celine came through the wall with a couple of servants. As the servants took Astrid's body from my concrete prison, Celine said, "Your punishment is over. You are released from your cell."

The concrete walls began to fade in front of my eyes and what was left was all too familiar.

We were in my room.

Did we transfer from the cell to my room? I looked down to see a blood-stained wood right where Astrid's body used to be. I quickly realized that I was never trapped in a concrete room, someone got into my mind and made me believe that I fell through the floor into a cell. I'd been in my room this whole time, but someone made me believe that I was in my own hell.

Some faeries and other creatures have mind reading and manipulating gifts, but I'd never encountered one.

They may have faked the concrete room, but the blood-soaked floor and the pain radiating from my back told me everything else was real.

"Okay, Violet, we've had enough fun, but unfortunately all good things must come to an end. I need you to forget everything that has happened. I don't want Calum finding out about this."

"Forget?" I stood up from the floor, still completely naked. "You expect me to forget everything that you've done to me?"

As I began to walk toward Celine, I stopped when I saw an unfamiliar female walk into my room. I couldn't move. It felt like someone had locked every joint in my body. I realized then what this female was.

The witch walked up to me, raised her hand, and said a few words.

And just like that, I had forgotten those fifty-two days, and the memories were replaced with a narrative that Celine chose.

30

Chapter 30

Violet

After reliving everything that happened, I was back to reality, standing in front of Sebastian.

I fell to the ground and sobbed. Celine did all of that to me and then just *took* those memories from me to ensure that Calum never found out.

I had been living the last few months as the same, timid, obedient Violet that I'd always been.

But I wasn't that Violet anymore. Celine broke me, and I'd never be the same.

I looked up at Sebastian who was still standing in front of me. His hands were balled up into fists and his shadows were circling around us. The wind started to pick up as if he was causing the weather to change.

The wind and shadows started to circle faster and faster around us as Sebastian looked ahead deep in thought, in anger. I noticed then that his eyes were completely black again and as I looked up higher, so was the sky. The once starry night was gone and replaced with total darkness. The only reason I could see was because of the glow of the pool.

He was in my head. He just lived through what happened to me. Felt every whip I endured and the pain I felt when Astrid died.

I started to hear several different screams and howls from the woods surrounding us. I heard a woman's voice starting to whisper something in a language I had never heard before. But no one was there. This. This was the Night Realm I had read about.

"Sebastian." I was scared. The Sebastian I had gotten to know the last few weeks was gone and replaced with someone completely different. The shadow king. The one that cornered me in the hall, threatening me on my third day here.

And then I remembered him telling me that he could control the Night Realm without lifting a finger. Because his *emotions* controlled the realm. And right now, I was about to see every one of my nightmares come to life.

"I am going to kill that bitch. No—death would be too merciful. I am going to torture her worse than anything she could imagine and let her biggest fears consume her. *She* will be living in hell for eternity."

The screams and howls seemed to be getting closer. I was terrified to see what creatures were making those dreadful noises.

"Sebastian, stop, please." I reached up and grabbed his hand, and he immediately started to relax. The wind slowed but the shadows were still floating around us. The creatures seemed to disappear immediately, but the sky was still black. He knelt down and cupped my cheek with his hand. Just like the sky, his eyes were still black. He wiped my tears and started taking deep breaths trying to calm himself because he could see the fear in my eyes.

"I'm sorry you had to see that," he said. His eyes started to lighten, and the blue slowly started to show again. So did the stars in the sky.

"I-I don't want you to be afraid of me. I would never hurt you." He looked so worried.

"I was afraid, but I'm not afraid of you hurting me. I know you won't hurt me. I'm afraid of whatever creatures I just heard, and I'm afraid of what you might do to Celine. I don't want you starting a war between the realms."

He looked at me confused as he said, "But she deserves to be punished."

"Yes. But Calum needs to handle this. It needs to be kept within the Mountain Realm." As soon as I said Calum's name, Sebastian's demeanor changed. I hurt him. We had gotten so close and just went through so much together and no matter how right I was about handling this within the Mountain Realm, all he heard was me choosing Calum, again.

Sebastian looked away from me before standing up. "You need to get back to your room and get some sleep."

"Sebastian."

"What? Do you want me to summon Calum for you?" He looked angry again.

"No, I don't want to see Calum," I said as I stood up.

"Then what do you want, Violet?" He used my name. I couldn't remember the last time he called me anything besides love. He looked into my eyes, waiting for my answer. I knew my answer was important to him, but I didn't know what the right answer for me was. I only knew one thing in that moment.

"I-I don't want you to leave me," I whispered.

All of those memories hitting me at once was a lot to handle. I could feel the tears building back up. I was alone in a dark cell for fifty-two days other than the short visits with Astrid. I was afraid to be alone again, and I didn't want Sebastian to leave me.

All of the anger left his face, and he wrapped his arms around me and transferred us to my room.

I stood there and looked around my room. I was so flustered by everything that happened that I wasn't sure what to do.

"Do you need to take your medicine?" he said as he pointed to my nightstand.

"I take that at nine. Did you forget?"

I could tell by the look on Sebastian's face that he had another smart comment to say about my heart condition, but he knew it wasn't the time.

But I also knew he hadn't forgotten. He only said that to get my mind off of what just happened.

And it worked for a moment.

"Sebastian," I said.

"Yes, love?"

I paused, contemplating my next words. How do you ask someone that you just did unspeakable things with less than an hour ago to sleep in the bed with you because you're scared to be alone?

"Fine, I guess I'll sleep in the bed with you."

I looked at him with an annoyed look.

Get out of my head, I thought, knowing he would hear it.

"You let your walls down to let me in, and you haven't put them back up. And when you say my name like that," he paused, "and look at me like that, I can't help but look to see what you're thinking."

I rolled my eyes at him.

"You look exhausted."

I didn't argue with him about that. After everything that happened tonight and the pain I endured for Sebastian to remove the spell, I could barely hold my eyes open.

As I took a step towards the bed, Sebastian said, "Wait." He waved his hand towards the bed, and the sheets—the disgusting sheets where Calum and Nathara once were—disappeared and were replaced with clean ones. I had almost forgotten what had happened only hours ago in my room.

I crawled into bed and Sebastian followed me. He lay on one side of the bed with his arms glued to his sides.

He looked as if he was afraid to do something wrong, worried I would push him away again like I did earlier. Like I'd done every time he'd gotten close. But he was the only one who knew what I went through, and I knew that if I was with him, I was safe—something I hadn't felt in a long time.

I pulled his arm away from his side so I could lay next to him and lay my head on his chest. The coolness of his body was such a comfort to me. Being able to sleep tonight without waking up in the middle of the night covered in sweat was welcome.

Once I allowed my body to relax, my mind went back to Astrid, and I couldn't stop myself from sobbing.

"I'm so sorry that happened to you," he whispered as he ran his fingers through my hair.

"I don't care about what happened to me," I said between the sobs. "Astrid was the closest thing I ever had to a mother, and she's gone. I would rather endure a lifetime of torture if that meant she would still be alive."

244

I felt Sebastian tense underneath me. If anyone was to understand how I felt, it was him.

I kept reliving the moment of her death over and over again. No matter how hard I tried, I couldn't get the image of that creature slicing open her neck out of my mind.

That creature.

I sat up to look at Sebastian.

"That creature," I said as I tried to wipe the tears from my face. "What was that?"

"It looked like a dovamin, but it could have been anyone with a glamour. And the witch, well she could've done anything. Whatever she did to make you believe you were in a cell, she could've also made you believe the dovamin was there."

"Does that mean they could've faked Astrid being there. And maybe she's still alive?" I asked.

He paused as he searched over my face, seeing the hope form. "I will find out tomorrow. But please try to get some rest now."

He pulled me back into him and began rubbing his hand up and down my back.

The small sliver of hope that Astrid was safe somewhere with her new faeling gave me enough peace to fall asleep.

I don't think I moved a muscle during the time I slept that night. With Sebastian's coolness and overall comfort of knowing he was with me, it may have been the best sleep I'd had in a long time.

When I woke up, Sebastian was in the same spot with his arm wrapped around me. I looked up to see he was staring off, deep in thought. His eyes weren't the usual dusty-blue, but they also weren't the black I saw the night before. They were a deep blue and his eyebrows were scrunched so I knew whatever he was thinking about wasn't good.

I reached my hand up and placed it on his cheek. He immediately relaxed and smiled as he looked down at me.

We had become so close over the last few weeks. I knew it was wrong. I loved Calum. But no matter how hard I tried, I couldn't stay away from Sebastian. He consumed every thought I had, and now, he was starting to consume my time physically, too.

"How are you feeling this morning?" he asked.

"I don't know how to feel . . . not until you find out about Astrid," I said.

"I've already talked to Adar, and he is sending a few spies to look for her."

I nodded. Now it was just a waiting game. A time of limbo until I knew how deep my wounds really were.

"So before you became Sovereign, it was always dark out-side?" I asked as an attempt to change the subject. I wanted to see those dusty-blue eyes again.

Sebastian raised an eyebrow. "Yes."

"And now your emotions control the Night Realm so when you're angry or upset, the darkness comes out?"

He left out a small laugh. "It didn't take long for you to figure that out."

I rolled my eyes. "I like to consider myself smart."

"You are very smart," he said as he looked down at me and smiled.

"How did that happen, though? I don't understand how that gift developed."

He shrugged his shoulders. "I don't understand it either."

"The things I heard last night, the ones that live in the darkness, what do they do the rest of the time? Like when you're not angry?"

"They go into a slumber and when they are awoken, they don't realize they have lost time."

"But the paramic?" I asked, "Were you upset about something that night?"

"A paramic is not one of the creatures I'm talking about. The creatures in the darkness you heard last night make a paramic look like an angel."

Chills went down my spine. "So when you're angry, all hell breaks loose, and no one is safe?"

"Yes, but what you saw last night . . . I haven't allowed myself to bring forth that darkness for over a century."

"Then why did you do it last night?"

He paused for a moment, clenching his jaw. "Because someone hurt you."

I stared at him for a moment, my head still resting on his chest. Too close, I was getting too close again.

I got up and went to the bathroom to freshen up, but I had another pressing matter that I needed to ask him about.

"Sebastian?" I asked from the bathroom.

"Yes, love?"

"Last night, when you insinuated that Calum was . . . with Nathara. Was that true?"

He didn't say anything, which told me everything I needed to know.

"I'm sorry. I shouldn't have told you like that."

"No, I needed to know," I said as I ran my fingers through my hair, trying to work the tangles out.

"Violet?" Calum called.

When I heard his voice, I ran out of the bathroom. I looked down to see Sebastian was nowhere to be found. I guess his shadows told him Calum was coming so he left before he got there.

"What are you doing here?" I asked.

"We need to talk about what happened. I haven't had a chance to get away from her since . . ." he paused, glancing at my bed, "you know."

"Since you fucked Nathara last night? Just say it. You fucked Nathara. In front of me."

"I wasn't given a choice, Violet. If I had told her no, she would've had you killed."

No. He wasn't going to convince me to just get over it.

"That doesn't make it hurt any less. I've had to watch you make over her for weeks, and I found a way to get over it. But this is different. I can't even look at you the same."

"I did that to protect you." He took a step towards me, but I took a step back, keeping the distance between us.

"Had you been with her before?" I asked.

"What?" His eyes widened.

"I haven't put out for you lately, so did you go to her instead?"

"No, I haven't. That was a one time thing."

I didn't know who to believe. Calum had never lied to me or given me a reason not to trust him, but Sebastian had protected me every chance he'd gotten, and I'd learned to trust him too.

I should tell him what his mother did, but how could I tell him I just remembered it? I couldn't tell him about Sebastian. That would only make it worse.

We still hadn't talked since he commanded me to stay away from him, and if I brought him up now, I didn't know what Calum would do.

"I don't want to see you right now. I can't keep doing this back and forth while we are here. And now that she knows, she will be watching closer." I needed him out of my room.

"So what? You're done with me now? Everything I've done has been to protect you."

"No. Get out of the marriage and then we can work on this. But until we are back in the Mountain Realm, I don't want to see you." I was grasping at straws with that. I knew it would take a miracle for him to find his way out of this marriage, but I couldn't continue this conversation with him now.

The longer he was around me, the more opportunity he would have to notice something else was wrong. He had always been able to read me based on my facial expressions. My mind was so clouded, and I needed space from him.

"Violet," he said, pleading with his eyes.

"Leave, Calum."

He knew I was serious, and he knew I was right. Nathara would be watching his every move now, and if she found out he was still coming to my room, there would be no protecting me. I watched as Calum transferred out the room.

"Why didn't you tell him what his mother did to you?"

Sebastian had transferred unannounced enough times now that I'm not even startled when I heard his voice.

"How did you hear that?" I knew the ward on my room worked because he didn't find out about mine and Calum's relationship until I followed the paramic to the woods.

"I broke through the ward in your mind. Do you really think a simple sound ward could keep me out?"

"When did you break the sound ward?" I asked without turning to face him. Did he do it as soon as he found out about me and Calum? Had he heard me and Calum being intimate?

"I asked first. Why didn't you tell Calum?"

"I will tell him when we are back home. He has enough to

deal with right now."

"So you're still going back to the Mountain Realm?" he asked as he transferred to where he was standing in front of me. "After he's been fucking Nathara and everything his mother did to you? And you know he isn't getting out of the marriage."

"What other choice do I have, Sebastian?" I asked, throwing my hands in the air. I had nothing to my name and nowhere to go.

"Stay here," he said, grabbing the side of my face and bringing it closer to his.

"What?"

"Stay in the Night Realm."

31

Chapter 31

Violet

Stay in the Night Realm. Those words were the only thing I could focus on for the rest of the day and then they kept me up all night.

Sebastian said I could stay here, be able to do whatever I want and live however I want free of the strict rules of the Mountain Realm.

I knew I needed to tell Calum what his mother did. I wanted to know how he would handle it. I'd been so lost with our relationship and now I didn't even feel like the same Violet. There was so much darkness in my heart.

Darkness his mother created.

I wasn't going to tell him until we returned home, but Sebastian's offer changed everything.

How Calum chose to punish his mother was going to give me my answer as to whether I stayed in the Night Realm.

But I wasn't ready to tell him yet. Not until I knew for sure about Astrid.

I asked Sebastian to give me some space unless he got word about Astrid. I needed time alone to process everything.

In the matter of a day, Calum and Nathara had sex in front of me, Sebastian and I kissed, and I found out I had endured weeks of torture after which a witch tampered with my mind to cover it up. A week ago, just one of those things, let alone all three, would've had me hiding out in my room.

I had already pushed Calum away and if I continued to spend more time with Sebastian, the tension between us might become more than I could bear. I couldn't risk complicating things more than they already were.

Sebastian seemed like he understood so I didn't worry about him showing up wherever I went, like he previously seemed to enjoy doing, so I decided to go to the library and find a few books to take to my room.

As I was walking down the hall, I heard Bronwen yelling at someone from a room I hadn't been in before. "What is this? I said silver finishes not bronze! Where do you think we are? The Forest Realm? Please! We have more class than that!"

I pushed the door open a few inches to see what she was doing and there were several fae running around at her instruction. Some were taking off drawer knobs on the giant dark oak desk that sat in the middle of the room while others were packing up trinkets from the shelves that covered the walls.

"Violet, come here, I need your opinion," Bronwen said as she faced the other way.

"I'm sorry, I shouldn't have been spying but fae in the Forest Realm could probably hear your yelling," I said as I walked in.

"I wouldn't have to yell if anyone here had a brain," she said while pointing at a bronze knob the fae removing them must have missed.

I couldn't help but let out a small laugh when a fae walking past me gave Bronwen the dirtiest look.

"Anyways," she began as she walked over to the chair sitting in the corner of the room. She leaned over and picked up two small pieces of fabric. "Which one for the window drapes?"

I squinted my eyes and looked between the two. "They aren't the same?" I asked. They were both black and there was nothing to set the two apart from each other.

Bronwen let out a loud huff and threw the two fabric samples in the air.

One of the fae servants in the room let out a quiet laugh, and Bronwen shot them a glare.

"Well, you're no help either," she said.

"What are you doing anyway?" I asked while I turned around to take in the servants busy at work replacing some things and removing others all together.

We were clearly in an office of sorts, but I wasn't sure who was using it.

"I am . . . cleaning out the old and bringing in the new," she said. I knew by her pause that she was carefully choosing her words so as not to give too much away.

But I knew exactly what she meant. She was replacing the items that could be the object filled with black opal that was absorbing Sebastian's powers.

"How many rooms are left?" I asked.

"Four."

My heart sank. Four rooms left. What would be the odds that out of the entire castle the object was somewhere in one of the very last rooms they went through?

Maybe they had it wrong. They could be looking for something that wasn't here, and it could be something else tearing Sebastian apart. They had been blindly following the words of a healer, and they could have wasted their time.

"That is one good thing to come out of this predicament. I'm able to redecorate," Bronwen said, trying to muster up a smile.

She was always trying to lighten the situation, even if deep down I knew she was worried.

I left pretty quickly to continue my walk to the library.

As I stood there, trying to narrow down the selection of books I had pulled, I felt the presence of someone behind me.

I turned around quickly to see it was Sebastian. I stared at him, afraid to say anything as I waited for what he had to say because I knew he had the answer I desperately needed.

His face was solemn as he opened his mouth to speak before quickly shutting it again. He looked down at the ground for a moment, and my heart raced, waiting for an answer.

He looked back at me and slowly shook his head.

This confirmation was all it took to have me falling to the ground. The little bit of hope that I was desperately holding onto was gone.

Astrid was gone.

Before my knees hit the ground, Sebastian had me in his arms and fell to the ground with me. He held me tightly while he ran his fingers through my hair.

I held on to him as I sobbed into his chest.

I was broken, truly broken.

32

Chapter 32

Calum

Days had passed since Violet told me she wanted no contact with me.

She'd skipped dinners.

She was slowly pushing me further and further away.

It was eating me alive, but I knew it was for the best. Nathara was watching, and I couldn't risk her thinking I was still with Violet.

I knew now more than ever that I had to find my way out of this. Time was running out, but I couldn't bring Nathara back to the Mountain Realm. Even though I'd gain full control and authority of her and her mother, they were sneaky.

They would find a way to hurt Violet and not leave a trace of proof that it was them. I had lost hope that I would find the object draining Sebastian. Alastor and I had listened to every little conversation between staff and servants, I'd contacted some allies in other realms trying to see if anyone knew who was behind it, but there was nothing.

And frankly, I didn't want to save the bastard now. The way he looked at what was mine, I'd rather see his demise.

I had barely slept these last few nights as I'd tried to lock in plan B. I'd been to the other realms, had secret meetings, trying to find another engagement. One to create an alliance that would satisfy my council that would include a more even-tempered lady. One that wouldn't dare to come between mine and Violet's relationship.

But with every meeting, I'd come up short. Everyone feared Sebastian's retaliation for going behind his back. Even with the knowledge that he was growing weaker by the day, they said they wouldn't do anything until he was dead.

I allowed my breakfast to grow cold as I was overcome with exhaustion. All I wanted to do was sleep for the entire day after spending the entire night trying to convince the Flower Realm of a betrothal, but Nathara was at my door first thing this morning with a full schedule for today.

Breakfast with her mother, always.

Dance lessons.

Band selection.

And because the castle grounds weren't big enough, a trip to a nearby village for a "stroll."

The terrace must be Nathara's favorite spot because we seemed to do everything out here, overlooking the maze of hedges with the weirdest little flowers.

I knew I needed to sleep when I started hallucinating Violet.

No, wait. I wasn't hallucinating.

The first time I'd set my eyes on her in days, and she'd never looked so bad.

She was headed straight for me and Nathara. I felt Nathara's grip tighten once she noticed Violet.

"Oh, this will be fun," she whispered in my ear.

I gritted my teeth. It took every ounce of restraint I had not to snatch my arm out of her grip. Every time Nathara did something like this, I had to think of my realm, of the purpose I had and why I was here. I was Sovereign, and the needs of my realm came before my own, no matter how hard it was to do this to Violet.

Violet stopped a few feet in front of us but kept her puffy eyes with dark circles underneath looking ahead, refusing to look at either of us.

"Can I spend some time alone with my father?" she asked.

"Yes," I said before looking at my Commander. "Go ahead, Alastor."

That was odd. They barely spoke unless it was a matter of importance or anything to do with Violet's well-being.

Her hair was slightly disheveled, and she had an overall look of defeat on her face. I couldn't blame her after she had to watch me be intimate with Nathara, though.

That still didn't explain her wanting to speak to her father. She wouldn't tell him what happened.

They walked through the garden and continued into the woods until they were out of my sight.

What I would give to hear that conversation.

They were gone for a while, though I was glad my Commander didn't watch me trip over my feet trying to learn the intricate dance Nathara wanted us to do at the party after the ceremony.

I was trained to fight, not dance.

When Alastor finally made it out of the woods, he was alone.

Violet needs to talk to you, Alastor said down the tether that held us together as he walked up the steps to the terrace. I scrunched my eyebrows as I glanced at him before quickly removing the look from my face.

I didn't want to raise any suspicion to anyone watching that we were talking.

She said she didn't want to speak to me until we were back home, I said back.

She changed her mind. You need to go to her as soon as you can tonight. It's important.

I gave him a slight nod, barely noticeable to anyone around before standing up to follow Nathara to the next part of the scheduled day.

I had become a fucking lap dog.

33

Chapter 33

Violet

I sat up, waiting for Calum to come. I didn't know how long it would take before he would have the chance, but I didn't care. I needed to talk to him. I needed to know how he'd react.

And what he would do.

It was well into the night before he made it to my room.

"We need to talk about something that happened before I came to the Night Realm," I said, taking a step back from him as he approached me.

No matter how much I may have wanted him to hold me, to comfort me, I hadn't forgotten what he did with Nathara.

He looked at me, confused, and I started from the beginning, making sure I included every detail as it was still so fresh in my mind.

The torture, the visits with Astrid, the things his mother said to me, Astrid's death, all the way down to the witch wiping my memories.

He stood there for a moment, stunned by everything I had

said.

"If your memories were taken away, how did you learn of this?" he asked. Everything I had told him, and this was his response.

"Sebastian. He saw the glamour on my back that was hiding the scars. So he went into my mind and removed the spell that was hiding the memories."

"You . . . you let him into your mind?" he asked with a look of astonishment on his face.

"I had to know what happened," I said. I knew he thought I shouldn't have let my guard down, but nothing mattered in that moment except discovering the truth.

"Do you not realize how stupid that is? He could be lying! He could've placed false memories in there!"

I undid the button at the top of my dress and let it fall to the ground before turning around to show him my back.

"Is this real enough for you? Those are scars. Scars from something that happened months ago. Do you not understand how bad it was for me to not heal properly?"

Calum gently laid his hand on my back, causing me to jump. Even if they were months old, they were so fresh to me. I knelt down and grabbed my dress, pulling it on my shoulders.

"Your mother did this, Calum. Letting Sebastian in to show me the truth? It doesn't matter. You should be thanking the gods that he can see glamours and he told me. The only thing that matters is that you finally realize how cruel your mother is and what you plan to do with her now that you know this.

"So tell me Calum, what are you going to do about what happened to me?"

He looked at me as he ran his fingers through his hair, contemplating his next words. Considering his options.

But there was only one option that I would be okay with: pain.

"I am going to send her away," he said.

I raised my eyebrow in confusion. "Away to where?" I asked.

"To Sartova."

My eyes widened at his response. "To her *vacation home?*" *Was he fucking kidding me right now?*

"Yes. She will not be allowed back at the castle. You'll never have to see her again."

"So her punishment is to live eternity in her favorite place with an entire staff of servants?" I couldn't believe what I was hearing.

"What do you expect me to do, Violet? She's my mother."

"And what am I? Your whore?" I wanted her punished. Not sent away.

"Violet." And in his response—in his choice of "punishment" for his mother—I had my answer.

"I'm done," I said the words before I could stop myself, but I meant them.

"What?" He looked at me confused.

"I can't do this anymore. *Us* anymore." I motioned between the two of us.

"So that's it? All this time and it's just over?"

"All of this time, and you still can't choose me over her. You can't put me first. You'll never be able to put me first," I paused. "I deserve better. Better than the life I'm destined to live by being with you."

"Dammit, Violet!" Calum yelled. "It was going to be me and you forever. Remember? What happened to me being the love of your life?"

"You were the love of my life, Calum, but the Violet you loved died when she watched the life leave Astrid. Your mother killed her. She killed the closest thing I ever had to a mother. I will never be the same."

"So what are you going to do? You have nowhere to go. Your home is with me. Your father is bound to me. You have no family besides him. You have nothing to your name."

Nothing. That's truly what I was to him.

Nothing but convenience. A convenience locked away in his castle for him and him only. Nothing but an object. An object to screw whenever he pleased. Nothing but a female.

"I am going to stay in the Night Realm," I said as I fought back the tears.

His eyes widened. "So this is about Sebastian?"

I shook my head. "This has nothing to do with Sebastian."

"Oh, really?" he said as he stalked towards me. I didn't realize I was backing away until I hit the wall. He leaned in so we were only inches apart and said, "Violet, look me in my eyes and tell me Sebastian has nothing to do with your decision."

I stared back at him, unsure what to say because I didn't know the answer. If it wasn't for Sebastian, I wouldn't have been put in a position where I was questioning Calum and our relationship. I wouldn't have known what Celine did to me.

But that's not what he meant.

I glanced down, and I felt Calum's fist hit the wall inches from my head, breaking the stone wall. He had never acted like that towards me.

Before I could process what he just did, Sebastian was in my room; he grabbed Calum by the neck and slammed him into the wall opposite where I was standing.

"Are you looking to die, Mountain boy?" Sebastian said as he walked over to him.

"Sebastian!" I screamed, but he ignored me as he grabbed Calum by the throat and pushed him up against the wall.

I knew what was coming. When Sebastian sensed danger, nothing could stop him. He embodied the shadow king, and it was like he became a different being. But he couldn't hurt Calum. I could never forgive him for that.

"Sebastian, please!" I whispered, barely audible as the tears fell down my face.

In an instant, he let him go but before Calum could react, Sebastian's shadows wrapped around him. He stood there for a moment, staring at Calum as he clenched his fists.

I feared what I was about to see, but before I could say anything else, Sebastian walked over to me and placed his hand on my face, wiping my tears away.

"Are you okay?" he asked with a strained look on his face. It was as if he was fighting to push down every natural instinct he had in order to not scare me.

I nodded and said, "Don't hurt him, please."

He studied my face for a second before he walked back to Calum and said, "Leave her room and don't come near her again. Got it?"

Calum glared at him as Sebastian's shadows released him.

"And there's my answer," Calum said as he stared back at Sebastian. I knew in that moment that his anger, and punching the wall, something I'd never experienced from him, was all a test to see if Sebastian would come.

And he did.

Calum glanced back at me with nothing but hurt in his eyes before he said, "I'm not giving up on us that easily." He transferred out.

Sebastian walked back to me and said something, but I didn't hear him.

I couldn't look at Sebastian. I kept my gaze on the hole in the wall where Calum once was.

"I just want to be alone."

34

Chapter 34

Violet

I wasn't sure how many days had passed as I stayed locked in my room, allowing myself to sink into a deep depression. I had just finally forced myself out of my room and yet here I was back in it.

Yara brought me food, which I barely ate, and Bronwen tried to come in every day, but I refused to even open the door for her. I knew she would push for me to come out, push for me to go to Sebastian as I had no doubt in my mind that she already knew everything that had happened. I also knew myself well enough to know that if I let her in, I would eventually give in to her persuasion.

But I couldn't. I didn't deserve to see him. I didn't deserve to be happy.

My father came by once, but only stayed long enough to make sure I was still taking my pills like I was supposed to.

I sat in my room, staring at my clock with a pill in my hand, waiting for nine o'clock. The time had come but I couldn't move. I couldn't find a reason to take my medicine.

I had nothing to lose anymore. My entire world had crumbled and all I had left was Sebastian and the trust I had in him.

He was so adamant that I didn't have a heart condition. He had spent so much time researching and trying to prove to me that my pills were for something else. He spent the time that he should have used trying to figure out what was draining his powers.

I placed the pill back in the bottle on my nightstand and sat up against my headboard.

I stared at the clock as I watched the minutes go by.

9:01, 9:02, 9:03.

The longest I'd pushed past 9 without taking a pill was 9:15—the night I met Sebastian. That night, the only thing that happened was I got hot and sweaty, so I knew I had to wait a while if I was going to see this through.

When I was a faeling, my father would handle my medicine. I refused to swallow pills so he would crush it up and mix it into something sweet that he knew I couldn't resist.

Even well after I was old enough to be responsible for taking my medicine, he would be with me every night at nine o'clock sharp. I didn't mind it, though. I cherished those few minutes that I got to spend with him every night. It was the only time he wasn't working, and his focus was completely on me.

It wasn't until after he learned of my relationship with Calum that he stopped overseeing me taking the pill every night. I guess he passed that responsibility on to Calum even though I was perfectly capable of reminding myself.

Well, it wasn't something I ever needed reminding to do. It had always been a part of my routine, and I did it without even thinking about it.

But now . . . now, *fuck it.*

I lay on my bed, covered in sweat. My heart was racing. The last time I looked at the clock it said 9:47, but I couldn't move to check again.

Every bone in my body felt like it was on fire and every time I tried to move, it felt like I was being stabbed over and over again. I pushed through it and reached as far as I could on my nightstand to try to get the bottle in my hand. I needed to take a pill. This little experiment was going to kill me.

My fingertips touched the bottle but as I tried to grab it, it fell to the floor. I needed help. I needed *him.*

"S-s . . ." I tried so hard to say his name, but I couldn't catch my breath.

He was my only hope. The only one that could possibly hear my cry for help. That was, if I could even get a word out.

My vision started to blur, and I knew it wouldn't be long before my body gave in to the pain.

"S-Bash," was all I could say before the world went black.

35

Chapter 35

Sebastian

I heard her. Barely, but I heard her call out for me. I transferred to her room to see her covered in sweat, passed out, and her pills covering the floor next to her bed.

She did it. I couldn't believe she did it. She listened to me, but something wasn't right.

I went to her side and placed my hand on her head. She was burning up. I could hear her heart beating, but it was in overdrive. I picked her up and transferred back to my room. The last thing I needed was for someone to show up to her room during whatever this was. I had to take her somewhere no one would come to.

I lay her gently on my bed and used my shadows to push the balcony doors open. The wind rushed in, and I hoped it would bring her temperature down.

I placed my hand on her head again only to feel that she was even hotter than she was moments ago.

"Violet. Violet, wake up," I said as I shook her. A pit formed in my stomach as I thought about the possibility that I could've been wrong. That she really needed those pills.

Her eyes fluttered but she couldn't respond.

I had to shake off that thought because that couldn't be right. I just found her.

I couldn't lose her.

Even with the fear that was growing inside of me, I knew it wasn't a heart condition. A heart condition wouldn't cause her body to continue to elevate in temperature. No, whatever this was . . . it was magic.

She lay limp across my bed. I placed my hand on her head again only to immediately pull it off because she was so hot.

"I know you can hear me. I can feel some kind of energy that you're holding in. You need to let it go," I said.

Whatever was happening, or whatever those bloody pills were keeping contained, was radiating off of her. Her body may have given up, but her mind was fighting. She was fighting to keep control of whatever was eating her from the inside out.

"Violet. Let it go."

Her head jerked to the side as she fought an internal battle. Her body tensed and she seemed to be squeezing her eyes shut.

"Violet!" I yelled. "Let it go!"

Her eyes shot open, but instead of the brown eyes I had grown so fond of, they were golden and glowing. Eyes I had only heard stories about.

"Oh fu—"

Violet's body became engulfed in golden flames that shot out and consumed my room. I surrounded us with a force field to try to keep the fire in my room. No one could know what was happening. I knew at that moment why Violet's father came up with the heart condition story and made Violet take those pills. He was protecting her from the world. Keeping the world from finding out that she was something the realms thought they had gotten rid of almost a century ago.

She was a phoenix. The *last* phoenix.

Violet had eighty years of fire that was bottled up inside of her all coming out at once. If I didn't keep it contained, it would burn my realm, and everyone in it.

Nothing mattered to me as much as she did, but I knew if word got out about what she was, a war would come that I wasn't prepared for. Not when I was fighting a war within my own realm right now.

I kept the force field up and watched as the fire hit the dome around us and came back towards us. The energy pushing out the flames had created a cyclone of fire that tore through every object and piece of furniture in my room.

If it wasn't for the shield of protection that I kept on myself, I would be a pile of ashes like everything else in my room.

I could feel my power draining exponentially fast as I fought to keep the force field. Her fire was so strong that it was taking everything I had to keep the flames from breaking through.

I had been so careful about using my power since I started losing it, but I didn't care now. All that mattered was protecting her. And protecting her secret.

I knew that if she didn't stop soon, she would break through the force field. She was strong, and I was growing weaker by the second.

"Violet," I said as I panted to catch my breath.

I had to get through to her.

"Violet, I need you to stop."

My shield was starting to wear away, and I felt the burn on my cheek as her flames tore though.

I was losing it.

"Please, love."

36

Chapter 36

Violet

I woke up on the floor in a room I'd never seen before. Well, a shell of a room. Everything was charred, in a pile of ashes, or covered in black soot.

The last thing I remembered was not taking my medicine. I sat up and realized that I didn't have any clothes on, but even with the soot surrounding me, I didn't have a speck of dirt on me.

What happened here? To me?

"Good morning, love."

That voice. A voice I had grown so fond of hearing, but I had never heard it like this before.

That voice set every nerve in my body on fire, and I felt something inside of me pulling. Like it was tugging me towards that voice. Begging me to turn around.

I slowly turned to see him sitting against a wall, resting his arms on his knees.

Everything in the world faded away when my eyes met his.

Since the time I first saw him, I felt something deep down, but it was like there had been a cloak covering that feeling, and I would only get a glimpse of it every now and then.

But the cloak was gone now.

The feelings I felt were so clear.

My mate. Sebastian was my mate.

He must have noticed the look on my face because his eyes softened as he said, "It's about time."

I started to crawl towards him, not taking my eyes away from his. He seemed to look a little afraid of what I'd do next. Which made sense considering how I had tried to push him away all this time.

I stopped when I was only inches away from him and reached my hand out to place it on his face. He leaned into my hand and looked relieved by my touch.

His skin. I had never felt something so soft. Even with the coolness of it, it warmed me deep inside. I wanted to say something, but I couldn't think of anything to explain what I was feeling. All I wanted was to feel him.

Every part of him.

I placed my other hand on the other side of his face, pulled him into me and our lips came crashing together. Even though we had kissed before, it felt nothing like this.

Those fucking pills.

I'm sure they did more than take away my pull to him, probably something that had to do with this room, but I didn't care about any of that right now.

All that mattered was Sebastian and this moment I had with him.

He pulled away to say, "I have been waiting for this. For you. For so long."

I looked at him confused. Had he known this entire time?

"Since I arrived here?" I asked.

"You've haunted me for eighty fucking years, Violet."

I pulled his face back to mine, forcing our lips together as I climbed on his lap. I opened my mouth, and his tongue slid in.

I felt him harden beneath me, and I let out a moan.

I needed him. So badly.

I had denied the feelings and denied myself him for so long. But not anymore.

I wasn't in the wrong for how I felt. I shouldn't feel guilty thinking of him.

He was my mate. The one natural thing in this world of magic and power and everyone fighting for control one way or another.

I was made for him.

With my moan, he deepened the kiss, and my hands slid down, tugging at his shirt.

He pulled his shirt off over his head and wrapped his arm around my waist before picking me up and laying me on the floor. He climbed on top of me, trailing kisses down my neck before coming back to my mouth, devouring it like he had been starved.

"I want you," I said through the kisses.

He pulled away, causing me to whimper, and gave me an uneasy look.

"Are you sure?" he asked.

"I've never been more sure of anything in my life."

He stood up, staring down at my naked body as he unbuttoned his pants. He pushed them down to show his large length. My insides tightened at the thought of what was to come.

I needed him. Every part of him. Every inch of him.

He knelt down, hovering his body over mine, before slowly moving closer and closer to me, never taking his eyes off of mine. He stopped at my entrance, allowing me to only feel the tip, which only made my need grow stronger. I lifted my hips to him and begged him with my eyes. He chuckled before he obliged and thrust deep inside of me.

I let out a moan and wrapped my arms around him, clawing at his back. He pulled out slightly before he thrust back in again. Another moan escaped my lips as I tilted my head back, engulfed in pleasure.

Sebastian grabbed the back of my head, bringing me to look at him again as he stilled inside of me. "You're mine, Violet," he murmured.

"I'm yours," I whispered, "all yours."

With those words, the words he had so desperately wanted to hear from me, I felt something deep inside of me forming, connecting me to him. Our unbreakable bond.

He pulled out, then began pumping faster and deeper inside of me.

He grabbed my breast with one hand as he bent down to kiss me again. Our bodies moved in synchrony as we both came close to release.

Nothing had ever felt as good as the moment when we met our releases together.

I love you, I thought as I looked at the most beautiful male I had ever seen lying next to me.

He turned to look at me, his eyes wide as if I had said that thought out loud.

I love you, Violet, he said to me, without ever opening his mouth. He had said it through the tether that connected us—

our bond.

I smiled at him, and even though all I wanted to do was feel him again and again, I glanced around the room, reminding myself that something had happened.

"What happened?" I asked.

"You burnt down my room," he mumbled.

I sat up and looked at him worriedly as I said, "Just in here?" I imagined what the rest of the castle looked like if I somehow managed to do this in here.

"I held it in; it took a lot, but no one besides us knows what happened."

I thought about what he said about conserving his power. How whatever he used didn't get replenished as long as that object loomed in the castle.

"How much power did you use?"

"I'm fine," he said, evading the questions.

"How much?"

He paused for a moment before he said, "Most of what was remaining."

"Why would you do that?"

"You know how you're feeling right now? The need to protect me and the worry about something happening to me?"

I nodded.

"I have been feeling that since the moment I laid my eyes on you. If the roles were reversed, you would do everything you could to protect me. No matter the costs. My powers mean nothing to me without you. And allowing this," he said as he waved his hands around the room, "to get out would put you at risk, and I would die before I let that happen."

"Seb—"

"I am fine. Better than fine, actually. I finally have you."

I knew there was no point in fussing at him. It was done and we couldn't change that. I just had to trust that he really was fine.

"How did I burn down the room?" I asked.

"You burst into flames."

"So . . . no heart condition, I take it."

He let out a loud laugh. "No, love. No heart condition. You can admit you were wrong now."

I rolled my eyes. He may have been right, but I would never admit that I was wrong.

He smirked as he reached up, ran his fingers through my hair, and lifted a piece for me to see. It was no longer the dirty blonde hair that I've always had. It was a very light blonde with golden undertones.

"What the fuck," I said as I grabbed the strand of hair from him, bringing it closer to my eyes as if I was seeing it wrong.

He chuckled as he said, "You should see your eyes."

I looked around the room for a mirror but anything that was once on the walls was burnt and scattered across the floor. I saw a faint glimmer and ran over to find a broken mirror.

I wiped off the soot and what I saw in the mirror, I didn't recognize.

The piece of hair that Sebastian had shown me was only part of the flowing waves that I now had. My hair was not only lighter, but it was fuller. But the part that left me speechless was my eyes.

Golden eyes that seemed to be glowing were looking back at me.

I dropped the mirror and looked back at him to see the pure awe on his face.

Awe of me.

277

I faltered for a moment because when I looked at him, nothing else seemed to matter.

"What am I?" I finally asked.

He scrunched his eyebrows. I'm not sure whether he wasn't sure himself or he just didn't want to say, but he said, "You need to talk to your father."

37

Chapter 37

Violet

We stayed in Sebastian's ruined room until midday the next day. We couldn't keep our hands off of each other long enough to look at a clock and the only reason we found out the time was because Adar talked to him through their bond.

Sebastian didn't tell me what he said, but it was enough for him to take me to my room where he left me to meet Adar.

Before he left, he placed a glamour on me so no one would notice anything different. My eyes were brown and my hair dirty blonde again. Only someone with the ability to see glamours would notice, and Sebastian assured me that he was the only one in his castle with that ability. He didn't want anyone to find out about my powers until we talked to my father.

He seemed uneasy about the entire situation, like he knew more than he was telling me, or suspected something at least, but he wanted to hear what my father had to say first.

This may have been something I should have talked about

with my father myself, but I didn't want to be away from Sebastian more than I had to be.

Along with hiding my powers, he thought it would be best to hide what our relationship had become. Being his mate put a target on my back that he wasn't prepared to face yet.

So I could only see him in secret, at least until he was back to full power. I guess all the years of practice with Calum had turned out to be useful.

I didn't want to do it because it seemed like I was being put in the same position I had always been in, but I knew he was right.

At least until he was back to full power.

I was not sure of the last time I had attended dinner. Days? Weeks? But this may have been the first time I actually wanted to go.

It had only been a few hours since I saw Sebastian, but I needed to see him. It would take every bit of self-control I possessed not to jump into his arms when I saw him, though. I also wanted to see Bronwen. I had pushed her away recently, but now that everything seemed so much clearer in my mind, I realized how much I missed my friend.

I wanted to tell her everything that happened. Everything about me and Sebastian. But that would have to wait until we had a moment alone.

I walked through the doors of the dining room feeling more confident than I ever had. Even if no one knew, I was mated to the Sovereign of the Night Realm. I was no longer less than everyone else in the room.

Sebastian, Bronwen, and Adar were the only ones sitting around the table when I came in, and while my eyes went straight to Sebastian, my look was cut short when Bronwen jumped up and screamed when she saw me.

I looked at her with a mix of shock and confusion on my face. Her eyes were wide, and she was grinning from ear to ear. I glanced at Adar to see he was rubbing his head.

"You told them?" I asked, shooting daggers at Sebastian.

"Ye—"

"Yes, he did!" Bronwen said as she clapped her hands. "Finally!"

"Did everyone here know except for me?" I asked, throwing up my arms.

"Yep," Adar mumbled, not bringing his eyes up to look at me.

I looked at Sebastian, ready to tell him exactly what I thought about their little secret-sharing club that I wasn't invited to, but before I could say anything, he motioned to the door and said, "A conversation for another time."

Damn right.

I quickly found my seat as Nathara, Calum, and my father came in. Bronwen squeezed my hand under the table and even though I rolled my eyes, I couldn't help but smile.

At least she wasn't upset with me for avoiding her lately.

Throughout dinner, I did everything possible to keep from looking at Sebastian. I talked to Bronwen about her plans for tomorrow, I listened in on Adar and my father's conversation about their favorite forms of combat, and I even ate the nastiest looking peas I had ever seen.

I looked up to see Calum staring at me, and I felt . . . nothing. Not love, not anger, not sadness for everything our relationship had put me through, and not even the slightest bit of guilt for the things I had done in the last twenty-four hours. I was . . . indifferent.

Bonding to Sebastian showed me how minuscule everything was compared to the feelings I had for him. I knew I loved Calum, at least I loved him in the definition of what I thought love was then, but now I knew that I hadn't experienced true love for someone until now.

I just wished I had realized it sooner.

Stop looking at me, I said down the bond to Sebastian as I took another bite of roast. I didn't look at him, but I could feel his eyes on me. He shouldn't have been drawing any attention to us, and yet he hadn't taken his eyes off of me this entire meal.

How can I not when you wear something like that? You're teasing me, love.

I didn't have to think about it when I got dressed today. No one could have forced me to but on a Mountain Realm dress. Not when I finally felt like I belonged somewhere, in the Night Realm, in a Night Realm dress, with my mate.

I smiled before bringing my attention to the conversation—well, argument—between Nathara and Bronwen. I wasn't exactly sure what they were discussing, but it had something to do with the party after the upcoming wedding.

It was funny watching Nathara squirm in her seat as she had no backup today. I didn't know where Celine and Lilian were, but their absence was a good thing.

Any part of me that was upset by what Celine had done turned into pure rage since I stopped taking my pills. Any time I even thought about her, I could feel my temperature elevate and my heart rate increase. And since I still hadn't talked to my father about whatever I was, I had no idea how to control it. If Celine walked through the doors right now, I think she would be a pile of ashes before anyone could stop me.

While I wouldn't feel remorse for Celine's death, it's not what I wanted. I wanted her to live. Live in misery and suffer for the rest of eternity.

Easy, love. I knew Sebastian could feel something brewing in me, and he knew it wasn't good. Along with the glamour, he placed a shield of protection on me. It was like my own personal force field that kept me protected from any harm, but it also kept whatever was in me contained.

So if I wanted to release this fire, I would have to fight Sebastian's powers first.

I wanted revenge on Celine, but it would come. In due time.

Sebastian had a note delivered to my father telling him to come to my room after everyone was asleep. That was the only time he wouldn't be with Calum.

I feared hearing the truth. I knew that the recent events already changed everything, but I knew once I talked to my father, it would become more real.

38

Chapter 38

Violet

His eyes widened at the sight of Sebastian opening the door to my room.

My father quickly pushed past him to get his eyes on me. Relief washed over his face when he saw me standing there unharmed and in one piece. I knew that relief wouldn't stay for long.

"What's going on?" he asked while Sebastian walked over to stand beside me.

I looked up to Sebastian and nodded, a silent instruction to drop the glamour.

"Violet," my father said as he took a step back when he saw my glowing eyes and light blonde hair. "What did you do?"

"No. What did *you* do, Father?"

He opened his mouth to say something before quickly shutting it and glancing at Bash. "What is he doing here?"

"He's my mate."

He looked between the two of us in shock.

"Those pills that hid all of this," I said, motioning to myself, "also hid our bond from me."

My father began pacing the room before sitting on the edge of the bed and burying his face in his hands.

"I burnt down an entire room," I said as I grew impatient waiting for my father to gather his thoughts.

My father's eyes shot up at me.

"I feel like I'm owed an explanation before I start burning things down again."

He ran his fingers through his hair before he stood up and began walking towards me.

"You are so much more than a Commander's daughter, my little bird. You're not a Commander's daughter at all," he said as placed his hand on my cheek.

I took a step back, forcing his hand off of me. "What do you mean?" I asked.

He took a deep breath and looked at Sebastian one more time as if hoping he would leave before he began, but Sebastian stood strong at my side.

"I am not your father. You are the daughter of the Sovereign of the Sun Realm and his mate, a phoenix."

I took another step back from him and felt Sebastian's cool hand on my lower back. He knew what I wanted to do.

Run. Like I'd done with every confrontation. But I needed to hear this. Even if it changed the course of the rest of my existence.

"When you were only a few months old, your parents died trying to save the phoenixes from the massacre. I was your father's Commander—sworn to protect his life—but he chose your life over his own. He and your mother went to the phoenix village when they got word that they were being attacked. He

285

left you with me and said if I didn't hear from them before nightfall, I was to leave the Sun Realm and keep you hidden and protected.

Nightfall came and I took you and went to the Mountain Realm because it was the closest place to find safety and shelter. I found an abandoned cottage and made it our home. I never took my eyes off of you. I hunted for our food with you strapped to my back, and I slept with you in my arms every night. My only priority was keeping you alive and hidden, but it wasn't long before you grew into your powers and your tantrums, well, your tantrums would start fires." He let a small chuckle out like he was picturing an image from the past before he continued, "I couldn't find berries one day and you burnt the cottage down. I knew I had to find a way to hide your powers, or someone would come after you. We traveled to the Land of the Healers to find something to help you.

"After the massacre, the fae of the Sun Realm glamoured themselves so they could live peacefully in other realms. Sometimes, it was rare though, you come across a fae like Sebastian who can see glamours. Some of our fae were discovered and killed because others' realms feared they were planning a rebellion or would kill others for revenge of losing their homeland. When word got out, some of our fae found a healer to change their appearance in a way that no one would know.

"A few of my allies had sent word to me about the healer so I could change my appearance more effectively. They had no idea I had you. The way it was told, you were in the phoenix village and died the same day your parents did. We went to the healer, but your case was something he had never seen. The last living of your kind. You were only an infant but when you cried, you could burn down a forest. He had to work with a few others to treat you.

"Even though most assumed you died during the phoenix massacre, there were many who believed you were alive. They have spent the last eighty years preparing for the day of your return. The day you will avenge your parents and restore the Sun Realm. Those fae have spread through every realm, some even on the councils, and are waiting for you.

"Waiting for a sign from you to retaliate and take back what is ours."

I couldn't respond. I couldn't get words to come out of my mouth. All I had wanted to know was what the hell I was. I didn't expect to learn I was meant to restore an entire fucking realm and . . . and *rule it.*

Sebastian dropped his hand from my back. I looked at him to see his eyes wide and his mouth slightly opened.

I thought he had an idea of what I was, but he obviously wasn't expecting all of that.

I walked past my father to the balcony doors, pushing them open. I needed air. I needed to process everything he had just told me.

My father . . . was not my father.

That may have been the part that shocked me the least. He didn't have a parental bone in his body. He loved me and I loved him, but we never had a bond like fathers and daughters usually had.

It was always protection to him. And now I knew why.

I was . . . a phoenix? No.

Half phoenix.

Half . . . royal.

The only royal from the Sun Realm left.

Which made me Sovereign. Sovereign of a nonexistent realm that I was supposed to go to war against the other realms to reestablish.

How could I possibly do that?

"I can't be what you want me to be," I said as I turned back around to my father.

"What?" my father asked.

"Out of all the realms, you took me to the Mountain Realm where I have spent my entire life being indoctrinated that being a female makes me less than. I've been told to sit down and shut up and be nothing but a servant to the male and yet now you tell me I am meant to take back a realm and become its Sovereign.

"Not to mention you made up this 'heart condition' bullshit and treated me like a wounded bird." I stared at my father, the anger seething inside of me.

"My little bird," I said, recalling the pet name he had always called me. "Your little bird because I'm a fucking phoenix. Real clever."

I looked at Sebastian to see he was trying his hardest not to laugh.

"What?" I snarled at him.

"Your . . . your hair."

I looked at him confused before glancing over to the mirror that sat on the desk in the corner of my room.

My hair was glowing, and the ends were on fire.

"Don't you see? It doesn't matter that you were raised in the Mountain Realm. The fire, the strong-willed traits of your mother, of a phoenix, run deep in your blood.

"It didn't change your nature. You have fought since you were a faeling against every bit of submission that has been thrown at you. Don't you see that?" my father said.

I had never seen my father with such hope in his eyes.

"He's right, love," Sebastian said, drawing my attention to him. "I've been to the Sun Realm during its prime days. You embody it and its faeries and creatures with every natural instinct you have. The times I've seen you try to stay quiet and submit, it was only because that was what you thought you were supposed to do, not because it was what you wanted to do. You just have to let go of that."

"So now the two of you are ganging up on me? You two have never had a conversation but now you're on the same side?" I said, glancing between the two of them before turning my attention back to Sebastian. "And what happened to me hiding all of this? Now you want me to announce it to Alentara and put a target on my back?"

"I didn't say I wanted to go to war tomorrow. We have the rest of eternity to fight. I just want you to have everything you deserve," Sebastian said as he walked over to me.

"And you? You've been so worried about me taking my medication but now you've just changed your mind?"

"I never thought the day would come that I felt you were safe enough to be your true self. But knowing that you are mated to the shadow king, I fear more for what the two of you will do to the rest of the kingdom."

39

Chapter 39

Violet

"What's an achluo?"

Sebastian looked across the table in the library at me. It had been days since I learned what I was. My father went back to serving Calum, and I hadn't talked to him since. Even if part of me understood why he kept it from me, I was still upset with him.

I wish he had trusted me with the truth.

I was also upset with Sebastian for agreeing with my father, even agreeing with the use of the pills that he hated. But Sebastian had his ways. Ways of making me no longer upset with him.

And he was so good at his ways.

I had spent most of my time in the library since the conversation with my father, trying to learn every bit of information I could about the Sun Realm. I had very limited knowledge before because the only books in the Mountain Realm that mentioned the Sun Realm were the ones about the creation of

Alentara and the Phoenix Massacre.

Sebastian had cases of books about the Sun Realm brought in, and he had spent every day with me in the library, combing through the books for anything interesting.

Our nights were spent in my room, with minimal sleeping.

"The achluos are a very small group that take fae form most of the time but are spies that are able to hide in the shadows because, well, they become the shadows. And because they can go completely undetected, they are sent to the other realms."

"So that's how you got your gift of shadow manipulation."

He grinned as he looked back down at the book he was looking through.

He could probably tell me anything I wanted to know about the Sun Realm, but he knew how much I enjoyed books, so he seemed to be humoring me.

"I bet not knowing what an achluo was has been eating you alive," he said.

"I have looked through every book in here and nothing," I replied. Ever since he told me his mother was an achluo, I had tried to figure out what exactly she was, as I had never heard of that term before.

"They are spies. There is knowledge of them, there are rumors about them, but there is no proof that they do what they do. That would cause a little upset among the realms, don't you think?"

I let out a sigh. "I wish I had thought about that. It would've saved me a lot of time."

Sebastian laughed as he walked over to my side of the table and pushed all of the books onto the floor. He picked me up and sat me on the edge of the table before running his hand up my thigh.

"What if someone comes in?" I asked as I glanced at the open doors of the library.

"Then they'll be up for a show."

"Sebastian!" I said, pushing his hand off my thigh.

He started trailing kisses up my neck and when he got to my ear, he whispered, "I'll know long before they are close enough to hear you, let alone see you."

I let go of his hand, allowing it to return to my thigh, and tilted my head back.

He kissed his way down my neck, down my chest, and when he got to the top of my breast, he bit down. I let out a yelp, and he chuckled as he continued his way down.

He pulled up the bottom of my dress as he continued to lower himself until he was on his knees.

As he started to duck under my dress, I grabbed his hair in one hand to push him back and pushed my dress down with the other.

"What are you doing?" I asked.

"I'm . . ." he looked at me, confused, "you've never . . ." The confusion left his face and his eyes darkened. "Oh, you've been neglected, love," he said as he quickly ducked back under my dress before I could react.

He licked my inner thigh, slowly moving closer and closer to a part of me that had never felt a mouth before.

My heart began racing at the thought of what could possibly be coming.

He ripped my panties off before burying his face in me. I let out a loud moan before clasping my hand over my mouth.

As if he knew what I had done, he reached his hand up, grabbed mine, and forced it back on the table.

He pulled his mouth away from me, causing me to inch

292

farther off the table.

I needed more.

"Don't do that. I want to hear what I do to you," he said.

I tilted my head back as he pushed his tongue inside of me. He worked me, stroking me with his tongue as he gripped my thigh with a hand.

Another moan escaped me when his fingers slid inside and began pumping as his teeth nibbled down. I started panting as I felt my climax coming.

"Oh, fuck . . . S . . . Bash!" I screamed as it shattered through me. I fell back on the table, covered in sweat, while trying to catch my breath. He stood back up and leaned over me to trail kisses up my neck.

He chuckled as he said, "Bash."

"What?" I asked, confused.

"You called me Bash when you called for me the night you didn't take your pill, and you just did it again," he said, placing another kiss on my neck.

"Well, sometimes your name is too much of a mouthful to say," I said, pushing him off of me so I could sit up. The more I kissed him, the more I wanted, and I didn't think he would be able to mask both of our sounds if we went any further.

"I like you calling me Bash," he murmured as his eyes drifted lower down my body.

I grabbed his shirt, pulling him in so I could whisper in his ear. "Bash," I paused as I felt him tense beneath my hold, "you have a mess to clean up."

I jumped off the table and pushed past him as I tried to go to my room to freshen up, leaving him to pick up the books he threw across the floor.

I made it all of five seconds before he was standing in front of me and said, "Done."

I glanced back to see that not only every book was picked up, but they were also shelved.

His devilish grin left him and was replaced with a look of annoyance as he said, "Adar needs me."

I poked my lip out, toying with him because I had no doubt he was hard beneath his pants. "Too bad, I was going to return the favor," I said, tapping his length, which confirmed what I had assumed.

He let out a huff before he leaned in to kiss me goodbye.

"Bash," I said as he turned to leave me.

He brought his attention back to me, eyes wide at what I had called him. I didn't mean to, but I liked calling him that, liked having a name that only I used for him.

"I want to learn how to use my gifts."

40

Chapter 40

Violet

"Where are we?" I asked as I overlooked the land far below us. We were standing on a large, vacant cliff that must've been hundreds of meters up. The ground was a black stone with large rocks scattered around. Some seemed like they were broken, as there were scattered pieces all around. The land below looked like a forest of some sorts, but it was so far down that I couldn't tell exactly. On the other side of the forest stood an identical cliff to the one we were standing on.

Bash had woken me up long before anyone else was awake and transferred me to a secluded spot to begin my training.

I wasn't exactly sure what it entailed, especially when he started to call it *training*. Did training mean fighting? All I told him was I wanted to learn how to use my gifts, but I guess my gifts were a form of defense so in a way, it was fighting.

"Miles away from civilization. I wanted to be sure we were somewhere so no one would know what was happening."

"So this part of your realm is just . . . vacant?"

"I didn't say that," he said as he came to my side and pointed somewhere for me to look. "Do you see all of the caves scattered throughout the sides of the cliffs?" I nodded. "Some of the worst monsters in the Night Realm are tucked away in those right now."

A chill went down my spine. "Then maybe we shouldn't be here disturbing them."

"They won't come out while the sun is out. They may watch you, but they won't leave the darkness of their cave."

My eyes widened, and I took a step back. "So what you're telling me is . . . we need to make sure that you don't get mad?"

He raised an eyebrow at me before he realized what I meant. "I guess so," he mumbled.

I looked back at the caves, still nervous about what might be lurking inside.

"I like your training attire."

I looked at Bash to see him smiling down at me. A ploy to obviously take my mind off the monsters in the caves.

"I couldn't very well wear a dress to train," I said, rolling my eyes. I had put on a fitted, long-sleeved top, leather pants, and a pair of black boots. An outfit I deemed suitable to do anything Bash had planned for today.

"Well, it suits you, love." Bash reached and brushed a strand of hair off my shoulder before resting his hand there. A small tingling sensation came over my body as Bash removed the glamour that had been hiding what I looked like now.

"My god, you're beautiful," Bash said as he dragged his hand slowly down my arm. He removed the glamour any time we were alone in my room, and he always said the same thing. Even though I'd heard it so many times from him now, it still sent butterflies through my stomach every time.

"No. None of that right now," I said, taking a step back. "I want to learn."

"Oh, I have plenty of things I can teach you," he mumbled as his eyes drifted down my body.

My cheeks reddened, but I quickly turned away to try to keep his focus off of the reaction my body had given him.

"There's no need to hide what you're feeling. We are mated now. I can *sense* anything I need to know."

I knew he was right, but I couldn't help my instinct, which was to mask my emotions.

"Can we please just start? I'd like to get out of monster land before nightfall."

He chuckled. "*I'm* not training you."

"What do you mean you're not training me?" I asked.

"Well, for one, training can be difficult and I do not wish to have a phoenix pissed off at me, and two, all I can think about is ripping those clothes off of you so I don't think much training would go on."

I rolled my eyes before throwing my hands up and saying, "Who's training me?"

"I am."

I whipped my head around to see Adar walking towards us. *Oh, fuck me.*

He must've been hiding behind the pile of broken rocks behind us, waiting for Bash to break the news to me. Adar didn't hide the way he felt about me. He didn't like me. He probably had no interest in helping me and was just obeying the order of his Sovereign. Why would Bash choose him to train me?

"You're joking, right?" I said, looking back at Bash.

"No. He is the best one to help you."

"I've changed my mind. I don't want to learn how to use my gift," I said, crossing my arms.

"I'll be back to get you later."

"Bash, n—" he was gone before I could finish.

I stayed facing the other direction away from Adar. If I had known he would be the one to help me, I would've refused to come. That's probably why Bash didn't tell me.

"You can ignore me. I'll sit right here until he comes back."

"Why did you even agree to help?" I asked, keeping my back to him.

"I do as my Sovereign commands."

Of course that's his response. I expected nothing else from him. I turned around to see he had propped himself up on a rock and had his arms crossed. He had the same disinterested and annoyed look on his face that he always did.

All I wanted was to leave, but considering my only way out of here had abandoned me, I might as well take the time to figure out what exactly I could do.

I was half phoenix, half royal, meaning I could have every ability of my parents or only a few. I knew I could wield fire, but I hadn't tried to summon it since the night I burnt Bash's room. And frankly, I had no idea how to bring the fire forth again. Even if I hated to admit it, I needed help.

We stood in silence, staring at each other, waiting for the other to speak. But the way he looked at me—the way he always looked at me—just pissed me off. I knew he would have no problem wasting the day and telling Bash I wouldn't do anything, so I knew I would have to initiate this if I wanted anything to happen.

Adar could be hundreds, maybe thousands, of years older

than me, I wasn't really sure exactly, but I was going to be the more mature one today. I had no problem with him, but his attitude had always made me steer clear of him.

"I'm not sure where to start," I said, dropping my arms.

He let out a sigh before standing up and walking towards me. "Well, we know you can burn things down, so let's start with that."

I narrowed my eyes at him.

"Close your eyes and go into your mind. Since you don't have control of it yet, it will be connected to your emotions. Think of something that angers you. A moment where you felt weak and all you wanted to do was find the strength to fight back."

I thought about those weeks of torture. I thought about what happened to Astrid and about Celine and the anger she brought me. And everything I wanted to do to her. But no matter how angry I got—how hot I could feel my body becoming—I couldn't turn it into fire.

I opened my eyes to see Adar staring at me. "Your mother was a phoenix. They didn't have the ability to wield power in fae form, only when they were in bird form so maybe the same applies to you. Your incident may have been a fluke. A one time thing since you had so much energy built up inside of you and it just released."

"So what? I should close my eyes and imagine being a bird, having wings and a beak, and then I will just turn into one?"

"Pretty much," he replied.

"I don't know why I need your help then," I said under my breath as I closed my eyes.

I did precisely what I had said. I pictured myself as a bird, a phoenix, just like the drawings I had seen in the books. Golden feathers, large wings covered in flames that spanned double the size of my body. Long, majestic tail feathers and a small yellow beak.

No matter how hard I tried to concentrate on becoming the bird I was imagining, all I could think of was Adar standing there, staring at me.

This would be so much easier if I was alone.

"It's not working," I said as I opened my eyes.

"Well, I have another idea that could work," he said, taking another step closer to me.

"What is it?" I started to back away from him. I didn't like him being so close to me, but he continued to inch closer. I had a gut feeling that I wasn't going to like this other idea.

Before I could react, Adar picked me up and threw me *off the fucking cliff.* I was falling, and fast. I knew that if I didn't do something, anything, I would hit the ground soon and Bash wouldn't be here in time to save me if I tried to call out for him.

I had no other option but to bring forth whatever was inside of me. I closed my eyes and forced the thought of wings into a reality, like my life depended on it, because it did. When I opened my eyes again, instead of falling to the ground, I was rising back up, but I wasn't a bird. I had the wings of a phoenix, but I was still in my body. I didn't care how I did it or if I only did it halfway, but I did it. And now I was fucking pissed.

"What the fuck was that?" I yelled as I brought myself back to the top of the cliff.

"What?" Adar asked innocently. He was back propped up on the rock, smiling at what he had done.

"You . . . you pushed me off the cliff!"

"Technically, I *threw* you off a cliff," he said, pushing himself up off the rock and crossing his arms. "Trying to get you to shape-shift wasn't working so I couldn't think of a better way to force you to do it."

"I could've died! What if I didn't inherit that gift from my mother? What if I couldn't turn into a phoenix, and instead I was impaled by one of those trees down there?"

He shrugged his shoulders. "Then I would hope you inherited her reincarnation abilities."

I could feel the rage building at his response. He had no regard for me or my safety. He was willing to risk my death to see what I could do.

I wanted to kill him.

I could feel my temperature rising. The rage inside of me was begging for a release. I summoned the flames and instead of bursting into a ball of fire, I channeled it to my hands. My newly golden hair began flowing as if the wind was moving it, but I could see out of the corner of my eye that it was also covered in flames. I began stalking toward Adar, using my wings instead of my legs and he watched me while he ripped his sparring gloves off and threw them on the ground.

"What are you going to do? Burn me?" he said as he quickly came towards me.

I had my arms out, ready to grab him by the throat and burn him from existence, but he beat me to it. He grabbed my hands in his and said with a wide-eyed look of crazy in his eyes, "Sorry, *Tinker Bell.* I won't burn."

Oh. That's why Bash sent Adar to train with me.

He kept his hands tightly gripped on mine and I looked down to see the flames covering his hands, but not one mark of burn showed.

I ripped my hands from him and said, "I could've died." The wings I had summoned disappeared, and my feet hit the ground beneath me.

"Well, you didn't," he said as he continued to stare at me.

"What would Bash do if you killed me?" I asked.

"He'd probably kill me. But that is a better fate than having to watch his demise because he is being blinded by love."

"I wouldn't let anything happen to him. You can trust me, Adar."

"You make him weak. No matter what you do, he will always be weaker when his first thought is to ensure your safety and not his own."

I took a step back. I wasn't as angry as I was hurt by what he had just said to me. He would never trust me. We would never be able to get along even if we spent the rest of our existence together due to our ties to Bash.

I needed to leave. I never wanted to see Adar again, even though I knew that would be impossible. But for right now, I needed to get away from him. I didn't want him to see that what he said really had hurt me, because that is probably exactly what he wanted. I wanted to go back to my room and to forget what he said to me, even though I knew he was right.

My room. I just wanted to be in my room.

And a moment later, that's exactly where I was standing.

I . . . I transferred. All of the trouble I just went through to figure out my gifts but transferring . . . something so rare that only the Sovereigns can do. I could just think of where I wanted to be and it was that easy.

"Violet."

I turned around to Bash looking at me very confused. He must've known the moment I was back within the castle walls.

"I'm done training with Adar," I said as I walked past him toward the bathroom to clean myself up.

"Are you okay?" he asked as he followed closely behind me.

"Yes," I said. I pulled my shirt off over my head and threw it on the floor before taking my pants off and doing the same with them. I just wanted to forget about today.

"I-I need to go get Adar, but I'll be right back." I turned around to see him staring at my body. I knew exactly what he was thinking. He wanted to clean me himself. I walked up to him and ran my hand down his chest.

"You should leave him there," I said as I continued to lower my hand. "Maybe one of those creatures you were talking about will take pity after seeing what he did to me and finish him off since I couldn't."

He took a step back, and his eyes darkened. "What did he do?"

"He threw me off the cliff." As soon as the words left my mouth, Bash was gone. I couldn't help but smile at what he might be doing to Adar right now.

41

Chapter 41

Violet

Violent shaking woke me up. When I opened my eyes, Yara was hovering over me with fear in her eyes.

"What? What is it?" I asked, confused by her presence.

She pointed at the empty spot next to me in the bed.

Bash had come back after retrieving Adar yesterday and proceeded to profusely apologize for leaving me with him. His apologies grew better the further into the night we went. Even when we spent most of the night up doing other things, Bash always seemed to be up and out of my room before me. I didn't think he slept much at all, but I knew something was wrong this time.

"Where is he?" I asked as I sat up from the bed.

Danger.

The one word she signed had me on my feet throwing my clothes on that were scattered across the floor from where I had thrown them off yesterday.

Yara flew down the hall as I ran after her.

Bash. I said down the bond. Silence was all that returned. I could barely feel him. Something was very wrong. I knew he used a lot of his power to protect me, but he told me he was fine.

I had chosen to believe him because the truth would've been far scarier. Now I was living in that nightmare.

Yara stopped when we reached the front door and pointed for me to continue. I followed the little bit of pull that I could feel to find him.

I ran through the front gates and deep into the woods. I had never been outside of the castle walls alone before, but any creature I could possibly run into didn't scare me right now.

I'd burn anything or anyone that stood between us.

I stopped at the edge of the woods to see hundreds of armed guards standing everywhere facing the center of a field. I pushed past a few rows to see what they were surrounding.

None of the soldiers batted an eye as I pushed past them. Their attention was fully focused on something.

When I got my eyes on Bash, I froze. He was on his knees, covered in blood, with a member of his Guard holding a knife to his neck. Adar was next to him held in the same position by another soldier.

Bash's eyes rose towards me. I knew he sensed me there. His eyes widened when he met mine.

Leave, he said down the bond.

What's happening?

The soldiers around me still seemed to not realize I was there standing within them. Or they didn't care.

A small, weak female didn't bother them.

Violet. Even down our bond, it was barely a whisper. *Please find Bronwen and leave. You will be safe with her.*

Before I could say anything back, the soldiers on the far end parted to let someone through. Lilian, Nathara, Celine, and Calum. My father followed him closely behind.

Calum was in his formal attire with his crown on his head, something that rarely made an appearance unless it was a very important event. Nathara wore a formal black gown that was almost identical to the white wedding dress she had tried on and a crown to match.

It wasn't wedding day yet. No, this was something much worse.

I tucked myself behind a soldier to ensure they didn't see me.

As they moved in closer, I realized the crown Nathara wore wasn't a small crown that a consort wore to match their Sovereign.

It was Bash's crown.

My stomach dropped as I realized what this was. Nathara was claiming her birthright the only way she could.

By taking down Bash.

They stopped when they were standing in front of him.

Calum stood behind but had the same look of hatred on his face that the three females had. The look on my father's face told me he had no idea what they were walking into. He scanned the field, looking at the Guard who once swore an oath to Bash, holding their Sovereign captive.

"Sebastian Kieran," Lilian said as she looked down at Bash. "The bastard of a Sovereign. No birthright to the throne. You murdered our Sovereign and took the throne. Nathara was in line for the throne, and after this, she will be the Sovereign of the Night Realm."

They were the ones taking Bash's powers to gain control of

the Night Realm. No. They couldn't hurt him. I had to stop this.

"You committed treason, and it is time that you are punished for your crimes."

Treason.

It all came together. Celine said I committed treason. Nathara said I committed treason. And now Lilian was using the same word.

Celine had been a part of this the entire time.

I looked closer at Nathara to see she was wearing the necklace she had on during our carriage ride. She always had it on. Nathara said it was a gift Celine sent to her before Calum came to the Night Realm. It was here before anyone from the Mountain Realm arrived. That's why Sebastian didn't suspect them.

Bash, it's the necklace, I said down the bond.

Violet, no. He knew what I was thinking. Getting that necklace and stopping them. *It's not worth the risk of something happening to you.*

I'm nothing without you, I said as the fear of what they were about to do grew.

I need you to run. Run far away from here before the glamour on you drops. You need to get somewhere safe.

A knot formed in my stomach at those words. He would hold on to that glamour until his last breath. If he anticipated the glamour dropping, then that meant he had accepted that he would not make it out alive.

But I couldn't accept that.

I concentrated on the bond I had with Bash and pushed myself into his mind to find the tether that connected him to his Commander. His walls had grown weak, just like his

307

body had. I just had to find the invisible tether, wherever he held it in his mind.

Adar.

Adar's eyes shot up to look at me across the field.

What the fuck? he said.

Violet, no, Bash was trying so hard to push me out. Even when he couldn't protect himself, he was trying his damndest to protect me.

How are you in my head? Adar obviously didn't like that I could get to him, but it really wasn't the time for him to worry about that. There were far more important things.

Nathara's necklace is taking his power, I said to him.

And how do you expect me to get it? She's got an army to protect her and a knife on Sebastian's neck. I make one move, and they will take his head off.

I will cause a distraction, and you get the necklace.

Violet. Sebastian was trying his best to get between us and to stop me.

Bash, let down the glamour.

No.

I knew he wouldn't drop it without a fight. I closed my eyes and summoned the fire. He may be fighting to keep my powers hidden, but he was too weak to stop me right now. I thought of what they were doing to my mate. And what they planned to do.

I'd had everything taken from me. My parents. My power. My life. They were not taking him.

I burst into flames that expanded in every direction and burned everyone in their way. The few guards that were on either side of me were nothing but ashes now.

My power pushed through the glamour with ease, exposing

my golden eyes and flaming hair. I heard their screams, but it fed into my power because I knew that every death meant one step closer to him. All that mattered was Bash in that moment. I would kill anyone that got in my way.

I summoned my wings and rose above the fire that had made its way deeper into the Guard that surrounded us, burning through dozens.

I slowly made my way towards him, letting the flames continue to come out of my hands and burn anyone that came near me. But most had backed away. They knew their swords were no match for me. I had to keep their eyes on me so Adar could get his hands on the necklace.

They were no match for whatever I had become—something they had never seen before. I was something that enjoyed killing those who were against me. Against my mate.

I watched as Adar snapped the neck of the soldier that held a knife to Sebastian's neck and then tore through the guards that had surrounded Nathara, Calum, Lilian, and Celine with his bare hands. I had never seen Adar fight until that moment. He was quick with his kills and could sense when someone was coming from behind. He only stood back before because he knew they had the upper hand with the knife at Sebastian's neck. But now, I think he could've torn through the entire Guard by himself.

Calum got between Adar and Nathara, but Adar said something to him that caused him to back away.

My father stood back not even realizing that Calum may have been in danger. He was too busy watching me. For the first time, I didn't see fear for my safety in my father's eyes. Instead, he was looking at me with awe. Like I had become something that reminded me of a different time in his life.

A time when he was in the Sun Realm.

Adar ripped the necklace off of Nathara's neck while she stood there with fear on her face, worried what Adar would do next. But Adar wouldn't hurt her. He was saving her for Sebastian.

"Violet!" Adar yelled as he threw the necklace in my direction. It had to be broken before it took everything from Bash.

As soon as it hit my flaming hand, it exploded and threw me and everyone in the field onto the ground. The explosion had taken my breath away, and as I lay there trying to catch my breath, the ground began to shake.

I got up as fast as I could to get my eyes back on Bash, to make sure he was okay. But as soon as I saw him, the fear disappeared.

He had begun to stand up and tilted his head to the sky. He raised his arms, and the Guard got up to get their eyes on him. They knew what was coming for them.

Some fell to their knees, surrendering and begging for mercy while others tried to run from the field.

Bash's shadows began to flow from him as they covered the field and wrapped around the Guard that was once his. The betrayers. The shadows slithered towards its victims as if they were snakes going after their prey. Some made it to what they thought would be the safety of the woods, but I knew better.

The only reason they made it into the woods was because he allowed it to happen. And what was waiting for them in the woods was likely far worse than his touch of death.

Shadows formed a circle around me, but they didn't wrap around my body like they did the Guard. They formed a circle of protection to ensure that nothing could get to me. I couldn't see it, but I knew what he had done. He formed a force field around me through the touch of his shadows to keep me protected.

I stood there, keeping my eyes on him as the endless supply of shadows continued to flow. The sky turned black just as it did when we were at the pool, except this time he didn't try to stop it; he welcomed it.

An evil smile grew on his face, and as he brought his head back down to look his enemies in the eyes, the soldiers began screaming, similar to the horrid scream that came out of the paramic's mouth. It seemed however he brought death to his victims, it was full of excruciating pain. Then a second later, the shadows did what I always thought they would do. They consumed the Guard, and Bash was enjoying it.

Screeches, screams, and the whispers I had heard before came from the woods, but even as the sounds grew louder, nothing ever came out of the woods. The monsters under Bash's control were doing exactly what he had summoned them to do.

As the shadows settled, there was nothing left of the Guard.

The touch of death that not only killed, but also didn't leave a trace of what was once there.

This was the first time I had ever seen Bash fully use his power, and I had never been so turned on.

The shadow king was back.

42

Chapter 42

Violet

Bash closed the distance between him and Nathara and Lilian. The shadows hadn't consumed them with the rest of the betrayers. Instead, they held them tightly while Lilian and Nathara watched their only protection turn into mist.

I slowly began walking towards them, and the shadows that once surrounded me seemed to follow me, but didn't stop me. As Bash came to a halt in front of them, he flicked his wrist and his crown that had fallen off Nathara during the chaos flew to him and sat on his head.

"Sebastian, please," Nathara said as tears ran down her face.

"I want you to beg, he said, "Beg for mercy for what you have done."

The shadows released Nathara and Lilian and Nathara fell to her knees to beg. Lilian stood and kept her head high as she glared at Bash.

"Get up," Lillian said to her daughter through her gritted teeth.

Lilian knew her pleas would've been useless. They had attempted to kill the one person in the world that showed no remorse for what he did and no forgiveness for anyone that pissed him off.

Nathara glanced at her mother before looking back at Bash.

"I should've killed you two the same day I killed Father. But I spared you. And this is how you repay me?" he said as he looked between Nathara and Lilian.

"We were only doing as we were told," Nathara screamed as she clasped her hands together, begging to be spared.

Bash paused and cocked his head to the side at Nathara's confession before returning to his state of no emotion.

"I am the most powerful Sovereign to ever step foot in Alentara. And you are nothing," he said and then his shadows pounced on the two of them and left no trace.

Bash put his hands in his pockets, and he turned to me and said, "Those two are yours, love."

Calum looked between the two of us and his eyes widened when he saw a trail of Bash's shadows creep up me, all the way to my neck where they stayed. They caressed my neck, sending chills down my spine.

Bash chuckled when he saw the shock on Calum's face.

I saw Calum's golden crown on the ground. It must have fallen off of him when we all were thrown to the ground. I picked it up as I walked the rest of the way. My eyes were set on one person. On the one that thought she could hurt me.

Not anymore.

Sebastian did Nathara and Lilian a favor with their deaths. But death would be too easy for Celine. She deserved so much more.

"You got too greedy with this alliance, Celine. Pushing your

313

son to get as much power as he could so you could have the power. This is what you wanted for yourself, right?" I asked as I twirled the crown in my hand.

I placed the crown on her head but once it was in place, I allowed the flames to seep slightly through my hands, bringing unbearable heat with it. The heat began melting the crown, and I watched as liquid gold oozed down her head, burning every piece of her that it touched. She fell to the ground as she screamed from the pain.

Her healing had already begun, and the gold quickly hardened from the cold air, etched into her head, unable to ever be removed. For removal would undoubtedly bring death.

It was almost poetic. A constant reminder. Her beauty was gone, and she now looked how she was on the inside.

I knelt down and gripped her chin, forcing her to look at me with the one eye that hadn't been harmed by the melted gold as I said, "I will make the rest of eternity hell for you."

This feeling. The feeling of having the power and all of the control. The feeling Bash had described. I understood why everyone wanted it. But it was mine and Bash's. And I dared anyone to try to take it from us again.

I stood up and locked eyes with Calum. Sebastian had his shadows wrapped around him so he couldn't do anything to stop me from harming his mother. I knew Calum had no part in this plan when it was first formed. He wouldn't have told me about Bash's weakening power or tried to look for the object if he was in on it.

But he didn't try to stop them when he found out either.

He stood there as they prepared to kill Bash and take his throne like the coward he had always been. And for that, for my mate, I wanted him to burn.

"Let him go," I said, without looking away from Calum.

Bash dropped his shadows at my command, and Calum lunged for me.

I placed my flaming hand between us, which brought him to a halt, inches from a point of being burned alive.

He looked down at me and said, "You won't hurt me. Any pain inflicted on me will be felt by your father."

I glanced at Bash, giving a silent instruction before turning my attention back to Calum.

Calum and my father fell to the ground, screaming in pain at what likely felt like a limb was being ripped from their bodies.

Bash removed a glamour from my body. He removed a spell that had entrapped my memories. I had no doubt he could remove the invisible tether that bound my father to Calum.

Seconds later, the screaming had stopped, and even though I felt bad that my father had to endure that, I couldn't help but smile as I looked down at Calum on his knees before me.

"What's to stop me now?" I mocked, cocking my head to the side.

Every instinct in me wanted to light his ass on fire for being the coward he'd always been. For being a part of this failed attempt. For never putting me first.

But I couldn't do that. My mind wouldn't let me. He deserved so much, but his realm didn't deserve the havoc that would ensue if it were left without a Sovereign. That was all too familiar for me.

"Stand up." I watched as he stood, battling myself internally for the next words I was about to say.

"You will go back to the Mountain Realm and be the Sovereign your realm deserves. The Sovereign your father always wanted you to be. But if you ever take one step out of line, I will come and rain fire down on you."

While he looked shocked for a moment, that quickly turned into disgust as he said, "Look at what he has made you become. He turned you into a monster."

"No. He helped me become what I was always meant to be," I said, fighting harder to keep my instincts under control.

"This isn't you, Violet."

I said nothing to that. It was pointless. To him, I would always be the weak, powerless Violet. But I would never allow myself to become that again.

I thought about Bash, and the emotionless look he gave the people he didn't care about.

Starting now, I decided to adopt that practice. I turned to walk to Bash but remembered one more thing.

"You might still want to send your mother to Sartova. She might scare your Advisors and the servants with her new look."

Someone let out a quiet chuckle from behind me, but I knew it wasn't Bash's voice.

Calum stood there for a moment, probably unable to comprehend everything that had happened and everything he had learned in such a short amount of time.

But as I took my spot next to Bash, allowing him to wrap his arm around my waist, Bash said, "Leave, Calum. Never step foot in my realm again. Violet showed you mercy, but if I ever lay my eyes on you again, I won't be as kind."

Calum reached down to grab Celine off the ground before transferring away.

And just like that, an entire chapter of my life came to an end.

43

Chapter 43

Violet

"You don't have to stay. I'm safe. You've completed your duty," I said to my father as he stared at the spot that Calum once stood.

My father looked at me confused before he knelt down before me and bowed his head. "My duty will always be to you, my little bird."

I knelt down and grabbed his face in my hands. When he looked up, I realized he had tears in his eyes. "They would be so proud if they saw how strong you were," he said.

"You will always be my father. You always have been," I said as I wrapped my arms around his neck and hugged him. A hug from my father had never brought as much comfort to me as this one did. I seemed to finally understand him, and everything he did for me, always for me, on a deeper level.

"No matter what you choose to do," he said, pulling away from me, "I'll support you. You can stay here and never think about the Sun Realm again, but if you choose to fight for it, I'd like to be your Commander. If you'll have me, that is."

I nodded and smiled at what he offered, but I knew I couldn't give him an answer just yet. I needed it all to sink in first and allow the fog in my mind to clear before deciding what I wanted to do next.

I stood up, bringing my father with me. "Let's talk tonight," I said.

My father nodded.

I turned around to see Adar crouched down with his hand placed on the ground. He let out a deep breath.

"Well, now I have to find another fucking Guard," Adar grumbled as he turned around, walking back towards the castle. My father squeezed my hand before following Adar.

I was now alone in the field with the one I wanted to get my hands on since the moment I woke up this morning. I ran and jumped into his arms, wrapping my arms tightly around his neck as he held me.

"It's over, baby. It's all over," he mumbled as he nuzzled his face into my neck.

I lifted my head so I could look at him as I said, "Good, because there is something else that needs to be handled right now."

I couldn't help myself. After seeing him in his true form, the part of him that he had lost in the last few months, one thing had been on my mind.

"Your power is radiating off of you. Is this how you always are? With this much energy wanting to just explode out of you?"

"Do I scare you, love?" he asked.

I shook my head.

"I've wanted to do things. Things I couldn't do because I

was drained of my magic. And the things I've wanted to do with you, well, I don't know if you could handle it." His eyes darkened as he ran his fingers through my hair. "Now, tell me, do I scare you now?"

I shook my head again as I said, "I don't want you to hold back."

He gave me a wicked smile before throwing me towards the ground, but before my body felt the impact, his shadows were under me, making it feel like he had thrown me on a bed.

Bash stood above me, and I watched as his shadows worked in the form of hands to remove the clothing from his body. He stared down at me, cocking his head to the side as he watched me fawn over him. I couldn't help the way I looked at him. Nothing compared to the sight of my mate, naked, especially when I knew what was to come.

I felt as the shadows that once cradled me on the ground crept up me and began to remove my clothes. I looked down to see they had taken the form of hands, his hands. With every cool touch of the shadows, I was reminded that he felt whatever his shadows felt. I arched my back as the shadows removed my pants and watched Bash's body tense at what I did.

When his gaze swept over my naked body, I brought my hand to my breast, but before I could squeeze, his shadows grabbed my wrist and pinned it to the ground.

As he stood above me, he shook his head and said, "I'll be doing the touching."

I took that as a challenge and brought my other hand between my legs, but in an instant, it was pinned down to the ground also.

He chuckled as he said, "Ever so impatient."

Shadows swept over my breasts, leaving a tingling sensation everywhere they touched before reaching between my legs. I let out a gasp as what felt like a finger plunged inside of me.

"So wet," he mumbled, still standing above me, staring down as I writhed under his touch.

Shadows pumped inside of me as some came back up running over my breasts. I stared at Bash as he caressed his length and all I wanted was to do that for him, but I was pinned down.

A shadow hand wrapped around my throat, bringing even more pleasure. I could feel myself coming so close to release as his shadows pumped harder inside of me. I was trying so hard to stop myself as I didn't want it to end, but when I heard him in my mind say, Come for me, love, I couldn't stop myself. I screamed his name as the release tore through me.

Bash knelt down, bringing himself to my ear and whispered, "Good girl." He trailed kisses down my neck and every time his lips left a spot, shadows lingered, deepening the sensation. When he reached my breast, he placed the nipple in his mouth. With every movement of his tongue, his shadows mimicked the same feeling on my other nipple. He bit down, and I let out a gasp as pleasure radiated through my body.

Bash brought his lips to mine and kissed me deeply as he thrust inside of me. He released the grip on my wrists, and I wrapped my arms around him, clawing at his back.

As he pumped faster and harder inside of me, he hit his hand on the ground and vibrations ripped through the empty battlefield. Release tore through me again and Bash followed not long after.

Nothing. Nothing could ever compare to what Bash did to me.

44

Chapter 44

Violet

"This may be the worst hangover I've ever experienced." Bronwen stood at the castle doors, rubbing her head. It was midday and yet it seemed like she had just woken up. It was a relief to see her in one piece though. I had wondered where she was during everything. I knew she was alive, at least, because between Bash and Adar, they would've both died fighting before someone hurt Bronwen.

"How much did you drink last night, B?" Bash asked as we made our way up the steps.

"No more than I usually do, but I've never felt like this." I had never seen her like this: her hair a mess, makeup from the night before smeared under her eyes, and the same dress she had on at dinner last night.

Bash and Adar may have died before someone hurt her, but I knew Bronwen would have rather died than someone seeing her in the state she was in currently.

As we made it up the last step, her eyes widened when she

realized there wasn't a glamour on me.

"What the hell did I miss?" she asked.

"I found the black opal," I said nonchalantly as I walked past her.

She grabbed my wrist and pulled me back to her. "Where was it?"

I leaned in and whispered, "Around Nathara's neck."

Bronwen glanced at Bash as she said, "And where is Nathara now?"

"She and Lilian are gone. Along with my Guard that just attempted to overthrow me."

She looked between the two of us as she realized how much exactly she missed.

"Those fuckers—they drugged me!" she said, stomping her foot like a small faeling. "I missed all the fun!"

"Oh, come on, B! At least you didn't have to get your hands dirty," Bash said as he threw his arm over her shoulder and headed for the castle doors.

As we walked inside, I noticed a few servants peeking around the corner at us.

"It's okay, you can come out. It's over," Bash said. They walked around the corner but stayed in the room with us, keeping their eyes on me.

"I have been keeping something from you, love." Bash raised a hand, and I watched as the fae servants turned into something completely different. One that was once a small, frail lady with short black hair, pale skin, and deep-set black eyes was now a creature that had the same humanlike features as before, but now she was covered in black scales, had glowing red eyes, and a tail that went all the way to the floor. She gave me a small smile, showing her pointed teeth. The male that was the first servant I had met upon my arrival here was now a two-headed creature with wings. He flew above us in excitement like he had missed the feeling of being free with his wings that had been hidden all of this time.

Before I could say anything, even though I wasn't sure I had any words to express the shock I was feeling, Bash spoke.

"When Alentara was created, Queen Mother sent every faerie and creature to a specific realm that she deemed the best fit, but she didn't take into consideration the personalities of the faeries and creatures. She only looked at their appearances or their gifts to determine which realm they should go to.

"This meant that the benevolent creatures like these," he paused as he motioned to the creatures, "were placed in a realm filled with monsters that killed anything they deemed weaker. No one here is a forced servant. They are given a safe haven within the castle walls and in turn, they work."

I was in awe as my mate continued to surprise me with who he truly was. "You keep all of this hidden. You'd rather the other realms see you as someone who forces fae into servitude than them see what they really are."

"Outsiders only see monsters, not the kind souls on the inside. I'd rather them think of me as a monster than my staff be forced to endure the stares and the comments."

"But I saw Yara? I guess you told her I was the Night Realm's to keep?" I said as I rolled my eyes.

He smirked as he said, "We didn't tell her about you. She sensed it herself and wanted to see how you'd react to her. Because she can't speak, I couldn't glamour her to work in front of the guests. She wasn't supposed to show herself, only complete tasks behind closed doors. She went a little rogue and took the job of one of the glamoured staff to meet you."

"Look at you," I said, elbowing his side, "your heart isn't cold after all."

He turned to look at me. "Don't take that as me being weak. When it comes to you, I will gladly take down the world, and everyone in it."

I knew he wasn't exaggerating. After seeing what he did today, I had no doubt he would destroy anything that stood between us.

"I'm going to find Adar," Bronwen mumbled as she left the room. The servants quickly followed suit and left me and Bash alone.

"What now, love?" Bash said as he tucked a loose strand of hair behind my ear.

I stared into his eyes—a sight I could look at forever. I could spend eternity, content, here with him.

But there was something out there. Something that belonged to me. The glimmer of power I felt today, it made me realize how badly I wanted it. That I wouldn't be able to rest until it was mine. Until I got the revenge that my parents and my realm deserved.

"I want my throne."

.

Printed in Great Britain
by Amazon